KILLER SPIRIT

STELLA KNOX SERIES: BOOK FOUR

MARY STONE

STACY O'HARE

DESCRIPTION

We've got spirit
Yes, we do
Killing off victims
Next one's you!

Special Agents Stella Knox and Hagen Yates travel to Atlanta to uncover the truth about the man she trusted as a child and discover a shocking truth. When her "uncle" was killed, he took the secret of who murdered her father with him. Or did he?

Before they can investigate further, they're called to Chapel Island, Tennessee, where three teenage girls have been murdered. All popular cheerleaders. All shot at close range with a rifle. All dead, with a gruesome cheer written in blood on the gymnasium wall.

And the killer is just getting started.

When another victim is found, it's clear a stolen cheer roster listing every high school squad in the county has become a killer's hit list. Who is targeting the cheerleaders of Chapel Island? And why?

Stella and her team can't possibly protect them all. Their only hope is to catch the killer—fast.

Mystifying and mind-bending, Killer Spirit is the fourth book in the Stella Knox Series by bestselling author Mary Stone and Stacy O'Hare that will make you think twice about cheering on the home team.

1

Reese Wilder yanked down the zipper of her cheerleading bag and pushed her damp skort and canvas shoes inside. Despite the late hour and the gym's cool air, a drop of sweat slipped from her temple and landed next to her towel. She pulled out her shea butter hairspray and hit her roots before her hair frizzed too badly. Satisfied she'd done the best she could, Reese tossed it back into her bag and grabbed her water bottle.

"Crap."

After nearly six hours of solid cheer practice, only a swig of water remained in her bottle. She swallowed it greedily and resolved to fill up at the water fountain outside.

She was exhausted. Her back ached, her arms were sore, and a bruise was developing on her left shoulder. Practice had been a good two hours too long. And on a Saturday night too. Most of the team left at seven, but Taylor, Olivia, and she had stayed behind to work on a new partner stunt for the Chapel Island Crows' opening game, two and half months away.

Reese tossed the empty bottle back into her bag and dragged out her sneakers.

The office door banged open and Coach Nathania Burbank waggled her fingers over her shoulder as she crossed the floor. "Well done, girls. Awesome practice. Sorry I have to run!"

Reese lifted a thumb in reply. She was too tired to even talk, but Olivia spoke for her. Of course, she did.

"Bye, Coach Burbank. Thank you for staying. We really appreciate it." Under her breath, Olivia added, "Probably rushing off to her boyfriend's to get laid."

Burbank grinned, her perfect white teeth a stark contrast against her dark skin. "No problem. Don't forget to lock up."

The back door swung closed behind her, paused, and with the loud squeak the spring always made as it kicked in, slammed shut with a bang that could have been mistaken for a gunshot.

Coach Burbank was nice and all, but she never knew when to quit. She should have told Olivia to let them all go home at seven. They had the whole summer to prepare for the opening game. It didn't make sense to put in this much energy now.

They were wasting their time.

If Coach Burbank had made *her* the team captain instead of Olivia, the team wouldn't be practicing so hard in June. Reese was much more sensible. She knew how to balance cheer with school requirements and social life.

Junior year had just finished, but she still had summer volunteer work to keep up with National Honor Society requirements. Just because she already had a scholarship to Florida State didn't mean she could slack off now. That award depended on grades, extracurriculars, and community service.

Reasonable hours. That's what Reese would have done.

The team would have been happier, more together, more content. They were supposed to be a *cheer* team, after all.

But no. Olivia always had to have what she wanted, and she had to have it *now*.

Reese dropped to the floor and rested her back against the wall. Her thighs were stiff, her ankles sore. She jammed her feet into her sneakers.

Olivia plopped down next to her, tying her own laces.

A few feet away, Taylor pulled her sweatpants over the shapewear she didn't really need, her tight brown ponytail flipping with every move. Since they were the only ones in the school, they didn't bother heading to the locker room.

"You were okay tonight, Reese." Olivia didn't even look up from her shoes as she began her lecture. "Better than last time. I'll get you there."

Irritation ran through Reese's every cell. "You'll get me there? If you'd watched more carefully, I wouldn't have fallen twice." Reese rolled up her sleeve to show the bruise blooming on her dark skin.

Olivia took the band out of her hair and let her long, blond curls fall to her shoulders. "Not my fault. You didn't count out. If you don't communicate, accidents happen."

Reese noted, with just a little pleasure, that Olivia's sweaty hair stuck to her head, and her curls weren't as bouncy as normal.

Turning her back on Reese, their fearless captain addressed Taylor, who had finished changing and was closing her duffel bag. "You have to work harder, Taylor. You keep screwing up those splits, and you're not going to leave me any choice." The lecturing tone grew deeper, darker. "I told you, I told both of you, if you can't cut it, you're off the team. No free rides here, no second chances."

Taylor tucked the duffel bag under her arm. "You're a true leader." Sarcasm dripped from every word.

"Now, now." Reese's tone was equally bitter. "Nothing is more important than cheer, remember?"

"That's right." Olivia, not catching any of the sarcasm headed in her direction, patted Reese on the shoulder, right on her growing bruise. "That's my team mantra. Don't you forget it. What's the mantra, Taylor?"

Taylor jammed a hand on her hip and scowled.

Olivia didn't bother to look up at the brunette. "Taylor?"

Taylor sighed heavily. "Nothing is more important than cheer." Her melodic tone could have rivaled the big purple dinosaur on kid's TV.

"That's right." Olivia pushed to her feet. "If you want to stay on my team, it's cheer first, boys, and other obligations whenever."

Reese rolled her eyes. Olivia was two seconds away from growing a toothbrush mustache that would make Hitler jealous. She was such a little tyrant.

She saved her sympathy for Taylor. That girl was desperate to join her and Olivia at Florida State, but unless she improved her grades, she'd have no chance. Reese would have made sure Taylor had the time to study as well as practice. She cared because that's what a good leader did.

But no. Chapel Island had the opportunity to induct their first Black cheer captain, but they'd voted for Barbie-blond Olivia instead. It wasn't fair.

The air shifted as the gym door opened and slammed shut again with a squeak and a bang. The warm night air came in along with Coach Burbank, who'd probably forgotten something.

Prepared to offer her assistance, Reese looked up.

Her smile turned into a frown.

It wasn't Coach Burbank. This person was shorter and slimmer than Coach. The baggy, black sweatpants were too thick for the summer heat, and the hoodie was pulled up over a face hidden behind a ski mask.

Everything slowed.

Olivia and Taylor froze in place like a couple of mannequins in a department store window.

Reese stood, sliding her back up the wall. Her thighs screamed at the movement, but she barely felt it as adrenaline shot through her system.

That's when Taylor screamed.

Reese's gaze passed from Taylor to the rifle in the figure's hands.

This had to be a prank.

Boom.

Taylor flew backward as though she were struggling to perform a poorly executed cartwheel. A red cloud sprayed from her chest as she collapsed to the floor.

"Hey!" Olivia's voice, trained to lead crowds of hundreds in cheers, sounded weak against the echo of the shot.

Boom.

Gray smoke drifted from the end of the gun. It smelled like firecrackers.

Olivia crashed into the wall. Blood splattered everywhere as a red stain crept across her chest. She fell in a heap at Reese's feet.

Frozen in shock, Reese lifted her hands. Her fingers trembled. Her breath came in shaky gasps. "Wait—"

The figure advanced. The muzzle of the rifle rose.

"No...*please*—"

Reese Wilder's hopes for Florida State disappeared in a cloud of gray smoke.

2

FBI Special Agent Stella Knox didn't care that the hotel on Atlanta's Peachtree Street looked more like a building full of student dorms than a place for tourists hoping to relax in Georgia's capital city. The brown walls suggested a government institution. The white beds, beige tables, and plastic-coated parquet floors almost turned that suggestion into a homage.

But there *was* a bed. She dumped her bag on the desk and flopped backward, groaning as her spine connected with the stiff mattress.

She'd spent the past four hours sitting in a car with her colleague, Special Agent Hagen Yates. While she'd managed to nap for at least one of them, her body now wanted to crawl under the covers and sleep until the evening.

Her head, though, was telling her something entirely different. It was urging her to get up, leave her bag, and rush straight to Joel Ramirez's family's address.

The man she'd known as "Uncle Joel" had been her father's partner on the Memphis police force. They were still partners when Stella was fourteen years old, and her father was shot to death in the line of duty.

In the months that followed, Uncle Joel had helped her family cope. He'd been there when Stella's brother was diagnosed with terminal cancer, and he'd given Stella and her mother a shoulder to cry on after Jackson's death. The day Uncle Joel was also reported to have been killed at work less than a year later, Stella had felt like she'd lost almost everyone she'd ever loved.

Stella propped herself up on her elbows, anger and confusion at war. Uncle Joel wasn't all he'd appeared to be. She was going to learn the truth.

Mackenzie Drake, a cyber specialist at the Nashville FBI's Violent Crimes Unit and her newest friend, had discovered that Joel Ramirez had actually been working undercover in Memphis, and his real name was Matthew Johnson.

Matthew Johnson had left behind a family in Atlanta.

Mac had managed to locate the alias and address of Ramirez's family. His *real* family.

With their previous case over, Hagen had offered to drive Stella to Atlanta to help with her personal investigation. Somewhere in this city, perhaps no more than a few minutes away, were people who had known her Uncle Joel. And it was possible that their Matthew Johnson had told them something important about her father's death, which she was about to discover.

Stella wasn't sure which new truth amazed her more. That Joel Ramirez had a family or that she was about to see them.

She had so many fond memories of Uncle Joel. She had listened through the floorboards as he and her father talked through the night. He used to play with Jackson, her brother, in the garden during the family's weekend barbecues. The surprise on his face the first time she whipped a forehand smash past his outstretched tennis racket was a memory she's always treasured.

But the memory that haunted her was the night he'd turned up at her mother's house stinking of beer and slurring his speech.

"Psst. Hey, Stella." He leaned a shoulder against the post on the veranda and tapped on the living room window, which she'd left open for the night breeze. "Come on out here. I've got...'scuse me. I've got shomething to tell you."

Stella was lying on the sofa, reading an old Dashiell Hammett book. The hour was late. Her mom was already in bed. Uncle Joel didn't usually turn up at this time, and he never came around drunk. Something seemed very off.

She left the book facedown on the cushion and opened the door.

Uncle Joel stumbled to the two-seat cane chair that looked out over the front yard.

Stella frowned. "You okay, Uncle Joel? Maybe I should go get Mom."

He dropped his chin and waved a finger. "Uh-uh. Got a secret for you. Just for you, Stella. Shh." He tapped the space next to him.

Stella shook her head. He stank of booze. "I'm fine right here, thanks."

"Okay. You stay there. Now, shh." He lifted his finger to his lips. "What I'm about to tell you is top secret. Y'hear me?"

She nodded and folded her arms. The night was warm, but a chill had begun to sink into her bones. Uncle Joel was usually full of jokes and gentle teasing. She'd never seen him like this before, drunk and secretive. He'd certainly never confided in her. She didn't know if she wanted to hear his secrets.

"So...your dad, God bless his soul, he was...he was killed. Killed by drug dealers."

A block of concrete settled in Stella's chest. She already knew her father had been killed by drug dealers. Her mother had told her the basic details. He'd been shot in a warehouse and left to bleed out. This was no secret, and she didn't want to relive it.

"I know that. Look, Uncle Joel, maybe you should—"

"But what you don't know..." His voice drifted. His gaze stretched out over the dark lawn. Whatever he saw was invisible to her. He was looking at something, reliving something only he could see. "Is who told them about your dad? Who fixed the whole thing up? You don't know that, do you? Huh?"

Stella froze. She had always assumed that her father's death had been a kind of work accident, one of those risks that every cop takes. Wander into a drug den and get caught in a shoot-out. Die.

But if his death had been planned, if someone had organized it, that was something different. Whoever it was had gotten away with killing her dad. He was loose. He faced no justice. The concrete in her chest shattered. Its dust and debris dazed her. She couldn't quite catch her breath.

She left the doorway and sat next to him on the chair. Every one of his pores exuded the stink of beer and whiskey. She swallowed against it. "Who? Who arranged Dad's death, Uncle Joel? Who did it?"

He leaned forward until his mouth almost touched her ear. Despite the short distance, he whispered. "Dirty cops. That's who. One of his own."

Stella's breath came in short, rapid gasps. A fellow cop killing her father was impossible, unthinkable. Cops protected people. Cops took care of each other. Cops were the people she'd grown up with. Her dad's friends. People she trusted.

"Who? Who did it?"

Uncle Joel didn't answer. His head had fallen back, and his breathing turned into snoring. Stella patted him twice on the cheek, but it made no difference. She helped him to his feet, laid him out on the sofa, and went to bed. He was gone when she woke up in the morning.

He was dead before the day ended.

In the years since, throughout college and the two years she'd spent as a uniformed officer in the Nashville police force, Stella had wanted to know who those cops were. She needed to be careful, though. That's why she went to work in Nashville instead of Memphis. She was close to the city where her father died, but not close enough to trigger anyone's radar while she spent countless hours researching every officer on the Memphis force. Which ones had betrayed her father and plotted his death?

The desire to find the faceless men who murdered her father burned in her heart. She would put them in front of a judge. She would lead them to their prison cells herself. The thought was always somewhere in the back of her mind. She would bring them to justice, no matter how long it took.

Stella had joined the FBI to expand her access to information and networks that might lead her to the people responsible.

A knock on her door forced Stella's mind from the past. She pushed off the bed and opened it.

Hagen stood in the hallway, an arm resting against the jamb. He was just as neatly turned out on his day off as he was on duty. His dark blue jeans fit his long legs to perfection, and his open-necked t-shirt clung to his body, outlining his broad chest and narrow waist as though he'd just showered in his clothes. It was a small miracle to look so pulled together after driving so many hours. And especially after the week they'd had hunting down a lunatic using a family in a brutal experiment of prisoner and executioner.

He ran a hand through his wavy, brown hair and leaned on the doorframe, taking in her accommodations. "Huh. I see your room's as pretty as mine. You ready to get some lunch? I saw a Korean barbecue place as we were coming in. Love that."

Stella grabbed her day bag from the desk. "Actually, no.

Let's do that tonight. I saw a fridge in reception that had some sandwiches. Let's grab something quick and head out. I just want to get there, you know?"

Hagen pressed his hand to his stomach. "Stella, you're killing me. Vending machine sandwiches?"

He stepped aside and called the elevator. They emerged on the ground floor next to a machine that offered turkey and chicken sandwiches, burritos, and potato chips.

Hagen scowled at the fridge. "We're seriously gonna do this?"

Stella laughed. Hagen was a foodie, a guy who'd happily spend a Sunday morning buying ingredients from an East Nashville farmer's market and lose the afternoon turning out French recipes with names Stella couldn't pronounce into meals she'd never eat.

She blamed his fussiness on his upbringing. Hagen was the son of a wealthy criminal lawyer with a client list that included gang leaders, probable mobsters, and murderers. He was all set for an easy rise to adulthood until his father was gunned down on the court steps.

The murder, which occurred at the same age that Stella had lost her own father, knocked much of the spoiled brat out of Hagen. But the lifestyle that was cultivated when his dad was alive had turned him into a foodie with a love for all things gourmet. Now, even as a public employee with little time or money to indulge in fancy dishes, he still snubbed his nose at even the mention of fast food.

And vending machine food offended his sensibilities.

Too bad.

Grinning, Stella opened the fridge door and pulled out a chicken sandwich before dropping a beef burrito into his hand. "Quit bitching, get biting."

Hagen sniffed the package. "Mm, polythene. My favorite topping."

They paid at reception, nuked his burrito, and tucked into their food as they made their way toward the parking lot. Hagen was right. All she could taste was plastic wrap, and his blank expression suggested a dirt sandwich would've been more appealing than that burrito.

She took another bite and spoke through a mouthful of soft bread and flavorless chicken chunks. "It's good, huh?" She didn't even feel bad about lying because his wrinkled face was reward enough.

Hagen didn't reply. He chewed slowly as they headed toward his Corvette. Cherry red, the car was unmissable between a gray Cadillac and a silver Ford Escape. He stopped at the door, grimacing at the remaining half of his burrito. Shaking his head, he lobbed it toward a garbage can near the wall. The burrito bounced off the rim and landed on the concrete.

"Son of a…" He walked over and dropped it in the can. "You done?"

Stella took a final bite of her sandwich and tossed the remains after Hagen's burrito. Her shot landed perfectly in the trash bag, *swish*.

She already regretted the quick meal. Her stomach was a mess of nerves. Soon, she'd meet her Uncle Joel's family, the people who might be able to tell her who was responsible for her father's murder. Anticipation was always stronger than appetite.

She sank into the passenger seat next to Hagen. The car roared into life, its V8 engine screaming to be released from the parking lot and deliver its *zero to sixty in 2.8* promise.

Hagen turned to Stella. "So, where are we going?"

Stella pulled out her phone and fed the details into the GPS. The drive to the house near Piedmont Park would take less than fifteen minutes. Stella's stomach tightened further.

As they made their way past the office buildings on Ellis

Street, neither of them spoke. Stella peered out her window. The ornate brownstone of the Atlanta Legal Society building made way for a pair of concrete parking lots, but Stella barely noticed.

She'd rehearsed this meeting a million times in her head. In her imagination, she sat with Uncle Joel's widow, sharing memories and putting together a list of dirty cops Uncle Joel had suspected.

Still, Stella didn't know what she would say when she knocked on the door.

Hi, I'm Stella Knox. I was just wondering if your husband, who lived away from you for a while undercover, ever told you who might've murdered my dad? Just...over Sunday dinner or something?

She sighed.

Hagen cleared his throat, seeming to sense her mood. "You want me to put the radio on?"

Stella forced a smile. "No, I'm good. It's just...you know."

"Yeah, I know."

Stella didn't reply. Maybe he did understand. The people who killed Stella's father were also the same kind of people who killed Hagen's dad. She wasn't sure whether he was there to lend a hand and another pair of investigative eyes or if he wanted the same information she did.

She glanced at him. Hagen usually wore a serious expression, but now, his face was drawn, his jaw set. He had that same focused gaze he often wore on their way to interview a murder suspect. Stella turned her attention back to the road.

Hagen adjusted his hands on the steering wheel, his knuckles whitening from the intensity of his grip. "Hey, it'll be fine. Try not to think too much. Sometimes, you just need to trust your gut."

Stella nodded but didn't reply. She wasn't sure what her gut was telling her.

They turned up Barnett Street. The apartment buildings and restaurants turned into low-slung houses, their vinyl-sided walls painted in pleasing tones of sky blue and slate gray. Red-brick homes boasted wide double-door garages and gabled roofs. The windows sparkled in the afternoon sun.

Hagen bent over the steering wheel and looked up at the elms lining the street. "It's nice here."

"Yeah. Good to know that a cop's widow is well-looked after these days. My mom struggled for a while."

"She's okay now?"

"Yeah, I guess. She got worse after my brother died, of course, but she's got her new life now down in Florida. I think she just needed a fresh start."

"That's a good option. If you can do it." Hagen pointed to a charming, two-story, white-brick house with a well-maintained front yard. "There it is."

He slid the Corvette to a stop a few houses down. Stella took a deep breath and slowed her breathing. The house looked entirely normal. The fence surrounding the property was clean and white. The frosted glass diamond in the custom oak door, and the American flag flapping in the wind beside it, was welcoming. This was a place where families lived, where they went about their lives. And, yet, this was where she would walk back into her father's life.

She swallowed hard, trying to keep her nerves from choking her.

Hagen turned off the engine. "Take your time. We can sit here 'til you're ready."

With a stomach as tight as a taut rubber band, Stella considered her options. She was sure she'd know what to do by now. She'd just walk up to the house, and the right words would come to her automatically, as though they'd always been there, just waiting to be said. But now that she was here, she couldn't have been less certain.

She twisted the stud in her ear, the one her father had given her when she turned fourteen. Waiting until she felt ready might mean sitting there for a very long time. And a red Corvette wasn't the least conspicuous car to spy on someone's house in.

Just do it.

"Okay. Let's go."

As Stella reached for the car door handle, the front door opened. She froze as a girl ran out. She couldn't have been older than seven. Her brown hair was pulled back into a neat ponytail, and her pink top was emblazoned with a rainbow-colored unicorn.

Hagen glanced at the GPS. "You sure you got the right address?"

Stella's heart raced. A tremble passed through her. The floor seemed to fall out of the car, dropping her into a dark, cavernous pit.

A man followed the girl out of the house, about mid-sixties, with a gray comb-over that did little to hide his scalp. His belly extended a good way past the top of his chinos. His small nose turned up at the bottom, and his cheeks were loose and florid. He waved at someone inside the house, took the girl's hand, and made his way down the front yard to the street.

When Stella was growing up, his hair had just been starting to thin. His belly had been tight, with no bulge. The nose was the same. His jawline, despite his now-sagging cheeks, was the same.

Stella's gaze was fixed. When Uncle Joel died—when she thought he'd died—she'd wished she could see him one more time. She regretted not asking more questions, not taking the chance to know him better or know her father better *through* him.

Uncle Joel was part of a long line of ghosts she never expected to see again. Once you were dead, you generally stayed dead. That was it.

The rubber band in her stomach snapped, sending a sting in every direction.

Because the dead lived.

"That's Uncle Joel."

3

Hagen Yates's stomach dropped as though he had just driven over a humpback bridge too fast. But he was sure he'd heard her correctly. The old guy now fumbling with the latch on the yard gate was Joel Ramirez?

Seriously?

He tamped down on the bright flame of hope surging in his chest. Stella must be mistaken. Joel Ramirez was dead. He'd been dead for a long time and had taken the secrets of Memphis's drug trade—and the murder of Hagen's father—to his grave.

Right?

Or maybe not.

Hagen inspected Stella's face. It was pale. Her eyes were fixed on the man who had, at last, managed to open the gate and swing it closed behind him.

The expression on her face told Hagen the truth. It was really him.

If he'd known Joel Ramirez was alive earlier, Hagen wouldn't have driven down here with Stella. He would have come alone and waited. He would have taken the bastard into a lockup somewhere and extracted the information he needed about his own father's death.

No one knew more about the criminal world of Memphis fifteen years ago than Joel Ramirez.

Stella wanted justice. That was up to her. But no court could give Hagen the justice he craved.

He turned his attention to Joel. The old man walked hand in hand with the little girl, leading her to a blue Toyota mini-van. Joel opened the door and helped her into the back seat. As he bent into the car to buckle her seat belt, he laughed. His boisterous chuckle elicited a string of squeals from the little girl.

"Granddaughter?" Hagen kept his voice low, though the caution wasn't necessary.

Stella took a deep breath. "Unless he's started a new family in his old age, that's possible. My dad always said he was a bit of a ladies' man, would hit on anyone in a dress." She twisted her earring at double speed. "I think today we'd just call it harassment."

"It was a different era then."

"I guess. Dad thought it was funny. Kind of envied him, I think. Single guy, making the most of his bachelorhood. Maybe Matthew Johnson is the same."

"So, it's possible he could have met a younger woman and…" Hagen straightened. "Look, he's going."

Joel had closed the minivan door and was climbing into the driver's seat. Hagen started the engine. After the Toyota drove a couple of blocks, Hagen turned onto the road behind it. The Toyota continued slowly, as though Joel had all the time in the world. Which Hagen supposed he did.

Hagen gripped the steering wheel.

I'm following a dead man to the park or the grocery store or some everyday place.

"He was shot, right? How is he still alive?" Hagen tried not to sound accusatory. No one had known Joel Ramirez—or Matthew Johnson or whatever name he went by—had survived.

"I don't know." Stella sounded far away.

The Toyota reached the end of the road and turned onto Virginia Avenue. Hagen kept his distance, slowing long before the minivan came to a stop at the junction, not wanting to stop directly behind him. For the first time, he cursed himself for buying the flashy sports car.

Who did Joel associate with? Was he still in touch with other members of the police force?

He kept the car in sight as it turned onto North Highland Avenue. As the Toyota changed lanes, Hagen tucked into the same lane behind a white Volvo.

"Hagen, pull it back."

Hagen touched the brakes and glanced at Stella. She was looking at him like he'd lost his mind.

"Why?" Hagen frowned, confused. "You don't want to know where he's going?"

"No. Yes." She pressed her fingertips to her temples. "I mean, yes, of course, I want to know. But not like this. He's supposed to be dead, remember? He's probably been keeping a lookout for suspicious people since the day he went off the grid. If he sees a car following him, he could get suspicious and run."

"Did you skip the classes at Quantico on following suspects without being made?"

Stella blew out the longest breath in history. "No. I was there. They said something about using a team and switching cars. I'm pretty sure one suggestion was 'don't follow someone while driving a bright red Corvette.' Pull back. We could lose him forever."

Though she was right, Hagen swore quietly as he pulled into the parking lot of a hardware store. The Toyota continued down the road before turning left and disappearing from sight.

Hagen flopped back against the seat. He had been so close. Just a little longer and they could have confronted the man who had once been Joel Ramirez. They could have grilled him, pulling out every piece of knowledge he possessed about the murderers in Memphis.

Now, he was gone, and Hagen wanted to bang on the steering wheel until it looked like a pretzel.

Stella undid her seat belt and leaned her head against the rest. "We know he's alive, and we know where he lives. We can come back later, preferably when his kid or grandkid isn't around." She pressed the heels of her hands against her eyes as if trying to block what they'd seen. "Jeez. I thought I was ready for this."

Stella was right. This trip was supposed to be about her and her dad, not about him. And he knew where Joel Ramirez was now. That *was* a step in the right direction.

He touched her arm. Her cotton shirt was soft. She didn't move away. "You will be. Next time. I don't know how you can prepare to see a dead man alive and walking. But now that you know he's not dead, you can...I don't know, just let the news settle in."

Stella pulled her hands away from her face with a jerk, forcing Hagen to remove his hand. "You're right. I know you're right. I just don't understand. He was so close to my folks. Why did he fake his death? Why didn't he get in touch? How could he not have let my mom know that he was okay, even if she couldn't see him again?"

"Maybe some sort of operational security. If he's in official protection, he couldn't have told. Memphis in those days was full of people you really didn't want to piss off, and he was investigating most of them. I think we both know that."

"Maybe."

A darker thought intruded. "Or maybe he really was working for the other side, turned again, and had to go into protective custody."

Stella shook her head. "No." Her eyes were red. A tear welled in the corner. "Uncle Joel would never have done anything illegal. He was my dad's best friend. Whatever the reason he went underground, I'm sure it was a good one."

Hagen wanted to call bullshit but nodded instead. "I'm sure you're right. When we talk to him, we'll ask. Let's get back to the hotel and relax. We'll come back later."

Hagen pulled the Corvette out of the parking lot and headed back toward downtown Atlanta. He wasn't convinced Stella was right about her Uncle Joel having a good reason to disappear.

But he was going to find out.

4

The news broke as I ate lunch. There I was, just stirring my mac and cheese, when the newscaster warned her viewers of a *just horrific* discovery at the Chapel Island High School.

I giggled. Whatever could that be? Had they found a dead rat in the rafters? Was a used condom seen floating in a toilet in the girls' bathroom?

Or were three dead cheerleaders found on the gymnasium floor?

Oh, it's the third one. Whoever would have thought of that?

As I enjoyed my sarcastic musings, I noticed my little brother was fascinated. His fork stopped midair as the newscaster switched to some reporter at the scene. Or rather, a reporter outside the scene. They were such cowards. All they were prepared to show their viewers was the outside of the building, as though no one had ever seen a parking lot before.

At least they were getting the facts right.

Three girls. Check.

All shot. Check.

All cheerleaders. Check.

All very much dead.

Check.

The reporter droned on. She gave the names of the victims as a photo of each girl flashed across the screen. Their cheerleader portraits, no less. Typical. The pictures all looked the same, with the girls wearing high ponytails, identical uniforms, and big, fake, toothy smiles.

Olivia Mostrom's devil eyes glowed a bright blue. She had been such a bitch. How she wound up as captain was a mystery. She was a terrible leader. Critical, rude, with no regard for anyone's safety. Olivia always pushed too hard.

Taylor Sinn had been a useless creature. She was almost too plain looking to be a cheerleader. The name Taylor Sinn was synonymous with mediocrity. Well, not anymore.

And Reese Wilder. Her dark skin was luminous in her photo like she'd been kissed by fairy dust—if fairies delivered bitch powers. No more kissing for you.

All gone. Check, check, check.

They were special, according to the reporter. So damn special.

The scene flipped back to the studio. The anchorwoman was so serious. Her expression was intense like she was struggling with a math problem or squeezing her ass cheeks together to keep from farting.

Come on. This isn't that hard.

She kept that half-confused, half-thoughtful frown on her forehead all the way through her next question. *"Do we know anything about the assailant?"*

My spoon paused at the question, and I cursed my heart for picking up speed. I was careful, so why should I be nervous? I'd covered my face and hadn't parked in the gym parking lot. But maybe I'd missed something. It was possible. Ever since the accident, my mind had been fuzzy.

The broadcast turned back to the reporter at the scene. *"There's very little information about the assailant at the moment, Dawn. Security cameras caught a figure dressed in black approaching the building at around nine o'clock last night. The police believe they remained in the building for about twenty minutes but have been unable to make an identification at this point."*

A grainy video appeared on the television. The security camera footage showed me moving toward the gym doors, slow and steady, no hint of a limp. The doctors had been very careful about aligning my legs after the accident. This footage could be of anyone.

I shoved a spoonful of mac and cheese into my mouth and chewed. The tension in my shoulders eased. Maybe I hadn't missed anything after all.

The screen split. The anchor appeared on the left, the reporter on the right. The anchor threw another question at the reporter as though neither of them knew anything at all.

"Have the police issued anything more about the victims?"

The reporter glanced over her shoulder. Behind her, a shadow from one of the trees in the parking lot fell across the building.

"The police aren't releasing any information officially, Dawn, but a source close to the investigation has informed us that the killer arranged the victims' bodies before leaving the scene. The investigation continues."

The news cut back to the anchor, who moved on to a report about a traffic accident on Highway 70.

My brother stared open-mouthed at the TV. He was just a kid and probably found this stuff fascinating. Or frightening.

What did he know? I put my finger under his chin and flicked it up.

He moved his head away. "Ow. That hurt."

"Then eat your food. It'll get cold. You worried about the girls?"

He fed himself and nodded as he chewed. "It's scary. Are they gonna close the school?"

"Yeah, for a little while, but don't worry about it. It'll just be the high school, and it'll be opened up again by fall. Besides, the killer's going for cheerleaders. You a cheerleader?"

He wrinkled his nose. "Gross!"

"You sure? You look like you wanna wave around some pom-poms."

Disgust morphed into a scowl. "And you look like a dog's butt."

I grinned. I'd been called a lot worse than that and by people who looked even more sweet and innocent than my little brother. The things I'd heard from girls like Olivia and Taylor and Reese. The things they'd called me. There wasn't anything sweet or innocent about girls like that.

It was a shame the reporter hadn't taken the camera inside and filmed what I'd done. I was a little disappointed. The reporter should have shown everyone, let everyone see their stony little hearts on display. The world needed to see how nasty they really were.

Oh, yeah, they acted sweet and innocent on the outside, but on the inside, everything was rotten meat.

Just like me.

That was all I'd done. Shown those bitches what they did to me, what they'd turned me into.

Surely, someone'd posted what I'd done on Insta. Even now, the scene was probably whipping its way around the

Internet. Going viral. That thought gave me a warm glow inside.

I jammed a straw into my juice box and opened the Instagram app on my phone. No messages yet.

But, yeah, the world would know soon enough. I was just getting started.

5

Stella sipped her cocoa and licked the foam from her upper lip. The café two doors down from the hotel was more comfortable than she'd expected. Though most of the tables were taken, she and Hagen had grabbed a couple of plush armchairs in the corner with their backs to the kitchen. A blackboard above the counter listed daily specials that included cold cucumber soup and shrimp croquettes. Someone had drawn a pie in the corner, steam rising from the pastry.

The rumble from the coffee machine overpowered much of the café's noise, allowing Stella to focus on her own thoughts. Her head was still spinning.

For years, she's had a vague idea of what she would say when she visited Joel Ramirez's family. Now that she'd be speaking to Uncle Joel himself, she had no idea at all.

It felt like greeting a ghost. She wasn't sure of the protocol for talking to the dead.

The immediate questions revolved around Uncle Joel himself. How had he survived? Who was he hiding from? Why hadn't he told her…or her mom, at least?

A new thought occurred to her. Had her mom known and been sworn to secrecy?

Stella pushed the question away, not willing to go in that direction yet.

Another question replaced it, flaring to life for the thousandth time. Who were the dirty cops who'd been involved in her father's death?

Other questions followed. Who gave them the order? Why did they do it?

And where were they now?

If Uncle Joel...

She closed her eyes. Her fingers wrapped around her mug, clinging to the warmth.

There was another question. Should she think of him as Matthew Johnson now?

He looked different. He was older. And so was she. The relationship wasn't the same as before...and it could never be again. She certainly couldn't think of him as her "uncle" anymore.

And not just because so much time had passed.

An uncle didn't abandon the people he loved when they needed him most.

But to think of him as Matthew Johnson? That felt about as comfortable as an itchy sweater. It meant cutting all connection between him and her past, erasing Uncle Joel from the family barbecues, and removing him from the hospital ward as they'd cared for her brother.

He might not be her Uncle Joel any longer, but he had been once.

Just Joel then. Not an uncle anymore. But a man who had once been a big part of her life, half a lifetime ago.

Since Joel had remained in hiding so long, she doubted he would be pleased to see her. He might not be willing to answer her questions. The worst-case scenario was he *couldn't* answer her questions because he was still in danger. Her very presence might endanger him. And after their encounter, he'd end up somewhere far, far away, never to be found again.

Asking questions might put *her* in danger too. And Hagen.

Her mind slipped back to the black SUV that had followed them from Nashville. Or might have followed them?

Too many questions. Too few answers. Stella sipped her chocolate. The cocoa's sweetness was comforting.

Hagen drained the last sip of his double espresso and tapped on his phone. He hadn't spoken since they'd received their drinks. Stella knew he was giving her the space she needed to settle her thoughts and figure out what to do. The light coming in from the café window drifted over his face, which was serious but relaxed.

She lifted the cup to hide the smile rising on her lips. Hagen might look like he spent more time thinking about what to wear than the right thing to say, but sometimes, he did know the right thing to do and just did it. He didn't ask or make a fuss. He just got on with it.

She had been right to bring him with her to Atlanta. She could trust him.

"So, what do you think? Head back in a couple of hours and see if he's home?"

Hagen looked up from his phone. "Sorry. Just checking the Giants score. What was that?"

Stella rolled her eyes. "Baseball? Wait…why the Giants?"

"Spent enough time in San Francisco for them to rub off on me. It's not basketball, but you take what you can get in the off-season."

So, it wasn't entirely consideration for her that had prompted his silence. "I was just saying we should go back to the house in about two hours. He'll probably be back by then. And if he's not, we can just wait him out."

"Sounds like a plan." Hagen held her gaze. There was something on his mind he wasn't communicating. There was curiosity, but also something else. "Know what you're going to say?"

Stella shook her head. "No. Any ideas?"

"Not me. I still think you should trust your instincts. They're usually something you can rely on."

"Hm. I'm not sure about that. And I'm definitely not sure about it now."

"You'll be fine." Hagen tapped his phone. "You'll need to break the ice yourself, but if you get stuck, I'll be there. We'll figure it out. Maybe baseball's his thing?"

Stella gave a short nod, and that warm sensation returned as she took another sip of cocoa. Around her, people were enjoying their weekend, taking a break from shopping in town, or meeting with friends for a coffee and a chat.

Two women sat at a table by the window. They appeared to be about Stella's age, and they talked comfortably, laughing at each other's stories.

One of the women opened her eyes wide in disbelief as her friend told her something Stella couldn't hear. Had a colleague made a pass? A girlfriend sent an embarrassing text? Whatever caused the incredulity, when the woman clapped her hand over her mouth, a twinge of envy squeezed Stella's chest.

Why can't my life be that simple? Why can't I just spend a Saturday afternoon in a café with a friend shooting the breeze?

She looked away. At the next table, another woman stroked her little boy's cheek, his face almost entirely hidden behind an enormous pink milkshake. Stella smiled. Kids were so easy to please and didn't naturally worry about the future. All their fears lurked in the shadows, waiting for them to become adults before they pounced.

At the table behind the child, a man sat alone. Middle aged, heavyset. An Atlanta Braves baseball cap hung low over his forehead. No Giants fan there. His coffee was barely touched. And though his eyes were hidden by dark glasses, he appeared to be looking in Stella's direction.

As soon as Stella saw him, he bent his head and scrambled to pick up his phone.

Had he been looking at her? The thought gave her pause, but she quickly shrugged it off. She'd made herself paranoid thinking about Joel. This café guy was probably just a creep. And creeps she could handle.

Unless, of course, she *needed* to be paranoid. She was, after all, trying to contact someone who might be in witness protection. That thought sent a chill through her.

Still watching him, she leaned forward and lowered her voice. "Hey, do—"

Hagen's ringtone interrupted her. He glanced at the name of the caller. "Slade," he mouthed as he answered the line.

Stella shifted to the edge of her seat. Their supervisor calling on their day off couldn't be good news.

Hagen listened.

"Right...Jesus. Okay. We're on our way."

Stella bit her bottom lip to keep herself from screaming. She sensed the conversation with Joel slipping away, and there was nothing she could do about it. She was like a kid watching their giant pink milkshake topple over the edge of the table, spilling to the floor before even enjoying the first sip.

Hagen pushed his phone onto the table. "We've got a new case."

"I figured." Stella sighed. "So much for our time off."

"We had a day."

A day wasn't enough. It wasn't close to enough. "Where are we headed?"

"Chapel Island, Tennessee. He's texting me the address, but we need to head out right away. He said he wants all hands for this one. Lots of press attention."

"Chapel Island? That's what, a four-hour drive from here?"

Hagen nodded. "Guess we'd better get moving."

Stella took one last draught of her cocoa. They were so close. Just another day would have been enough.

Hagen stuffed his phone into his pocket and stood. "Atlanta isn't going anywhere, and neither is your Uncle Joel. And a few more days to process what you just saw might not be the worst thing in the world. We'll be back."

"Hm, yeah. Maybe you're right." Stella said the words but didn't believe them. A few more days were nowhere near enough to help her process the sight of a man she thought was long dead.

She grabbed her bag and followed Hagen toward the exit. As they made their way out of the café and back to the hotel, she passed the table where the man in the Braves baseball cap had sat.

The chair was empty.

6

Junior held the phone to his ear and pulled his hat low over his sunglasses. From behind the lamppost on the other side of the road, he watched Stella Knox and her partner leave the café.

Chapel Island, Tennessee.

That was what the guy had said. He'd thought no one could hear him, but Junior was smarter than that. He might not be a federal investigator like Stella Knox or have any kind of fancy military experience to fall back on. He might not be tall and have a square jaw or own a single snazzy shirt like that partner of hers. His own t-shirt stretched over his pot belly, leaving about an inch of exposed white flesh over the top of his shorts. But twenty-five years of tracking deer had to count for something. He knew how to watch, and he knew how to listen too.

He could hear a branch cracking out in the woods, and he could hear a whisper in a crowded café.

You just gotta listen for it, that's all. Focus. That's what track-ing's all about.

That must have been why Boss gave this job to him instead of to that bitch half-sister of his. He could be trusted.

Junior had heard where they were going even though they thought they were talking real quiet.

He'd been looking forward to following them around Atlanta and keeping track of them. That would have been real easy. Plenty of crowds in a big city. Lots of ways to blend in and stay hidden.

To follow them while they worked a case up in Tennessee was a whole different kettle of fish. He swore a little under his breath.

Chapel Island? *Where the heck's that?*

He googled it. Chapel Island was one of those big-ass Tennessee counties that took up a whole lot of space on a map, but it wasn't populated by a whole lot of people. The place was probably crawling with cops and Feds by now. He'd stand out like a sore thumb in a world of pointed fingers.

The thought made his mouth dry and set his heart beating faster, just like that time he'd gone hunting with Boss and missed a big ole buck. The look Boss had given him. His scowl was so big even the tips of the old man's ears turned red.

Junior shuddered at the memory. There had been a moment, as the Boss loaded his rifle, that Junior thought *he* was going to take the next bullet. Scared the bejesus out of him.

Would trying to follow Stella Knox in a town full of Feds be harder to manage than pleasing Boss?

Naw, who was he kidding? The Feds were nothing compared to Boss.

Knox looked over her shoulder. Junior swung a hip away from the road. He lifted his phone closer to his cheek and jammed his face into his shoulder.

She wasn't stupid, that Knox. She might've even made him in that café. He thought he was blending in, just sitting with his coffee. But she'd stared right at him. Her eyes locked onto his sunglasses like she knew exactly what he was doing there. Might as well have had a neon sign over his head declaring *Tail Right Here.*

Probably shouldn't have worn sunglasses inside.

If that phone hadn't rung, she'd have alerted her partner to him right there for sure.

And then what would have happened?

A shudder passed through him again.

Junior didn't want to find out. He stayed just long enough to hear the phone conversation, then he'd shot out of there like a cat with its tail on fire. Didn't even finish his coffee. Almost four bucks that coffee had cost him. No way Boss was going to pay him back for that.

He'd have to be real careful now. If Knox saw him again, she'd make him for sure. And if Boss found out he'd been spotted, there'd be hell to pay. Best to keep that bit of information to himself. He did need a new vehicle, though. He'd have to come up with a good reason to ask for a switch.

Junior glanced out of the corner of his eye. They were still heading back toward their hotel, making long strides like they had places to be. Naw, she hadn't seen him this time. He was sure of that. And she hadn't told the guy either.

Relief rolled down Junior's spine like a jet of cool water.

He was going to be okay. He'd follow them to Chapel Island and find out just how much they knew. The Boss would listen to his report and give him his next order. And Junior was pretty sure he knew what that next order would be.

He'd get to take Knox out like a prized twelve-pointer.

7

T he conference room at the Harris Hotel outside Gallatin, Tennessee, appeared to have been arranged at short notice and for an event that had nothing to do with the FBI. The long table running down the middle of the room was covered with a thick, white tablecloth. Little paper caps sat on top of clean, tall glasses. Leather chairs were arranged neatly around the table as though Stella and Hagen were about to join a board meeting about sales targets and share buyouts.

For a moment, Stella wondered if she was in the right place until her gaze passed from the window to the whiteboard, where she saw the names and ages of Olivia Mostrom, Taylor Sinn, and Reese Wilder in bold, black, neatly written print.

None of them were over eighteen. None of those names should have been of any interest to the FBI. And yet here they were, a sure sign that something, somewhere, had gone horribly wrong.

Hagen slipped past Stella and pulled out the chair at the

head of the table. "I've texted Slade to let him know we made it. He's on his way down."

"Right."

Stella ignored the seats. She'd spent four hours sitting on her butt that morning, another two while scoping out Joel, one hour in the café, and another four in the afternoon.

Hagen must have been exhausted after all that driving, but every time she offered to take the wheel and let him rest, he only laughed and said he was fine. She was sure he wasn't fine, but more certain he would've been much worse with Stella behind the wheel of his precious Corvette.

No wonder he looked drawn.

And no wonder all Stella wanted to do was take a long walk, then crash into bed until the start of a new day. It was barely after nine in the evening, but they'd crammed enough activity, news, and emotion into this day to fill a week.

She flicked the cap off one of the glasses and poured herself some water just as the door opened. Slade was dressed in jeans and a gray t-shirt that had seen better days. A small hole had opened in the shoulder, and too many washes had crinkled the hem. He clasped a laptop next to his ribs. After passing around the room to the whiteboard, he slid the computer onto the conference table.

"Sorry to call you back on your day off." He gripped the back of a chair and looked from Hagen to Stella. "I honestly thought we'd all get a break before we landed a new case."

Hagen stretched his back. "Killers, huh? They're just so selfish. Someone should have a quiet word with them. Tell them about our schedules."

Stella sipped the water. It was room temperature, and the temperature of the room was only a little lower than the heat outside. She put the glass back on the table and leaned against the wall. "Looks like you got called in on your day off too."

"Me?" Slade tugged at the bottom of his t-shirt. "Thought I'd get a day with the family. Watch a bit of golf. Relax, you know?"

Hagen shook his head. "Nope. No idea what you're talking about."

"Yeah...me either." Slade pulled up three photos on his laptop screen. "Okay, everyone else has been briefed. I'll catch you up now. And tomorrow morning, I'll hand out the assignments. We've got three dead kids, all cheerleaders, all shot to death in their high school gym in Chapel Island at the end of cheer practice last evening."

Hagen rested an elbow on the table. "Jesus."

"Right. That's why I've called in everyone. The victims are all high school juniors. Well, technically seniors." Slade looked up. "We've got to nail this one quick. There's already a lot of press coverage, and the local LEOs are feeling the pressure."

Stella rested her shoulders against the wall. Cheerleaders. That had never been her thing in high school. The competition, the adulation of the players, the sheer downright bitchiness that could infect any cheer team. She'd kept well away from it.

"Are we sure this isn't just another school shooting?"

Slade lowered his glasses. "*Just?*"

Stella winced. She hadn't meant to belittle the seriousness of the crime.

Slade had teenage daughters. Only a few weeks ago, they'd solved a crime where teenage boys were the targets. This one must have hit even closer to home. "Sorry. I didn't...you know what I mean. School shootings are usually troubled kids, maybe recently expelled. Someone like that should be easy to track down."

"No." Slade flipped to another photo. On the screen was a picture of the crime scene. The three girls were propped up with their backs against the gym wall—their arms strung around each other's shoulders, their legs placed in a zigzag, and their heads tilted as if they were besties posing for a photo. A deep red stain covered each of their chests. Blood had spattered over their faces and left pink smears on their thighs.

On the wall above them, written in big capital letters, were the words, *WE'VE GOT SPIRIT! HOW BOUT YOU?*

What the hell?

"The writing was done in blood?"

Slade nodded at Hagen. "We don't know whose yet. Might be all three of theirs."

Stella moved away from the wall and sat at the table. The pictures had knocked whatever energy the day still contained right out of her. "No one heard anything? Not even the gunshots?"

"The police received no reports, but the school is on the outskirts of town. There are no houses nearby, and Chapel Island is the kind of place where people are as likely to own a weapon as drive a pickup. People hear gunshots around here, they assume that either Bambi's buying it or someone's letting off steam."

Hagen fell back in his seat. "Off-season. Bambi's safe for now. What about security cameras?"

"We've got this."

Slade leaned over the top of his computer and brought up a new file. The image was low quality. A streetlight threw a white spot over the walls of the gym building that stretched and bent in the wide lens of the security camera. The yellow light from the thin line of windows below the roof looked like a set of plaque-coated teeth grinning over the parking lot.

A dark figure strode toward the building. Their back was to the camera. A hood pulled up over their head. The person shoved open the door, which swung shut behind them in two sharp movements. In under twenty seconds, three white flashes gave the old teeth below the roof a brief sparkle.

Hagen took a deep breath. "Well, that's not much use. We got them leaving?"

Slade pressed another button on the keyboard. The time in the corner of the recording raced forward until the gym door opened again. The figure that emerged walked toward the camera, but their face was entirely hidden by a ski mask. They could have been anyone. A slight of frame male or even a female. Young, old, anyone.

Stella curled the fingers of one hand into a fist, resisting the urge to reach out and fiddle with the brightness on Slade's screen. "We can't see a thing."

Slade stopped the video just as the hooded figure passed under the camera. "No, and as far as footage goes, that's all we've got. Well, so far, anyway."

"What were those kids doing there alone anyway?" Hagen's eyes were still fixed on the screen as though he could force the killer to remove their mask by staring at the image long enough.

"Practice. Their coach, Nathania Burbank, trusted them to lock up the gym." Slade shrugged. "Happens in small towns. The school belongs to everyone, even the kids."

It still didn't make sense.

Stella frowned. "Late for practice, though, wasn't it? The time on the recording showed almost nine in the evening."

"Good spot." Hagen jotted something down in his notepad. "Would have thought kids that age would have been out tearing up the town that time on a Saturday night."

"They should be. So, who would have known that there were kids in the gym at that time? It doesn't sound like something regular or scheduled. And school's not in session."

Hagen shrugged. "The killer might just have just gotten lucky. Saw the lights on, went in, and did their thing."

Stella didn't buy that for a second. "And just happened to have a ski mask and rifle with them on a June evening? Doesn't sound likely, does it? This must have been planned."

"Maybe one of the girls was followed? Even stalked in the days before the shooting?" Hagen turned back to Slade. "What do we have on the victims?"

Slade pulled the computer toward him and clicked the keyboard to pull up the individual cheerleader portraits.

The screen showed a young woman with blond hair, blue eyes, and a bright smile uninhibited by her retainer. Though posed in front of a plain, brown background, she beamed at Stella and Hagen. "Very little at the moment. This is Olivia Mostrom. Age seventeen. She was football cheer captain for the Chapel Island Crows. About to enter her senior year but already had a scholarship to Florida State."

Stella's heart squeezed. "Poor girl."

Slade touched the keyboard again. A second girl replaced the first. "Taylor Sinn, seventeen. Also entering senior year." Taylor's long, brown hair hung straight and shiny all the way past her shoulders.

She disappeared at the touch of a button and was replaced by a girl with high arched eyebrows, dimpled cheeks, and a white smile that contrasted nicely with her dark skin.

"Reese Wilder, seventeen. Same year and also heading to Florida State."

Slade lowered his head. His hands had curled into fists on the surface of the table and now appeared to support his entire weight.

Stella cleared her throat. "Why don't we think this was a targeted attack? If these three were the only targets, we wouldn't expect any more killings, and the cops could clear it up themselves. They might take a while, but they'd get there. I'm guessing the local sheriff called us because he's worried about more dead kids."

She looked to Slade for affirmation.

He nodded. "Nathania Burbank. The coach. She kept a list in her office that included the details of cheer rosters for the high schools within the county. Mostly, she was just keeping track of the competition for All State. It contained names of the girls, schools, even pictures. The list is missing. It's the *only* thing that's missing."

Stella breathed out slowly as understanding dawned, horror not far behind it. "There must be dozens of girls' names on that list."

"Over eighty-five just in the county schools. We can't protect all of them. The only thing we can do is catch the killer and do it fast."

8

S tella lay in her bed at the Harris Hotel with her arms folded behind her head. It was almost midnight, and although her body ached from eight hours scrunched in a car, her mind buzzed. She had seen too much today, and too little of it made sense. Stella pushed her head back into the pillow and stared at the ceiling.

First, Joel was alive and well and living in Atlanta.

And, now, a killer had murdered three teenage cheerleaders and may be targeting more.

High school. Heading into senior year. For Olivia, Taylor, and Reese, it should have been a year obsessed with grades and boys and cheer squad.

Stella smiled to herself. More likely, boys first with cheer squad and grades trailing far behind.

Her smile faded. That wasn't her high school story.

For Stella, the last years of school had been a period she'd passed through rather than lived in. She'd started high school numb from her brother's death, excruciatingly aware that any attachment she made could tear off at any time and leave her bleeding.

She'd distanced herself because there was no point in making friends if everyone died. Dating meant being vulnerable to loss. Vulnerability meant leaving an opening for pain to find its way in. No, thank you.

Stella *had* tried. In her senior year, she dated Will Adams. One night, lying in a field watching the moon rise, Will had taken her hand and blurted out his love for her. Her first reaction had been discomfort and embarrassment. She'd managed no more than a "thank you."

Two weeks later, she hadn't been at all surprised when he dropped her and started dating the school's bob-haired chess champion. She was barely even upset when it happened.

The children's hospice had been easier.

Just the memory of volunteering in that building, with its cartoon-covered walls and baskets of stuffed animals, gave her a warm glow. It was the only place she'd felt truly at ease in the years after her father and Jackson's deaths.

The hospice had certainty. She knew that the attachments she made there *would* be broken. She could give those kids her love for the months or weeks they had left because she knew that love wouldn't last. There was no hope, so there was no fear. She was always ready for the blow.

Girls like Olivia, Taylor, and Reese didn't live that way. They hadn't known how much the world could hurt them.

How wonderful that life must have been. While they were able to live it.

Perhaps when she had found her father's killers and brought them to justice, she could find a way to move on and be vulnerable again. But she wasn't there yet. And until she spoke to Joel, she never would be.

Stella turned onto her side.

Her room was on the fifth floor of the hotel, and she had left the blinds open so that the sun would wake her at dawn. In the distance, red and white lights passed up and down the highway. A streetlight shone a yellow ball into the branches of an elm tree, lighting the roof of the house behind it. The air conditioner hummed. Still, sleep wouldn't come.

Three girls dead.

And what about their parents?

Like Stella, they had assumed their lives would be normal. They'd send their girls off to college, miss them, and do their laundry when the girls would come home on breaks. Eventually, their daughters would marry and move away before returning with grandchildren to sit on their knees and listen to their stories.

Now, all that was gone, the future altered. A bolt from the blue had overturned a world they'd thought was safe and secure.

Ugh. Enough.

Stella threw off the bed covers and pulled on her jeans. There was a vending machine next to the elevator. Maybe a bag of strawberry flavored licorice would fill her belly and stop her brain from spinning. Maybe she'd run into Hagen or Mac or even Chloe on the way, and she could have a quick chat before heading back to her room. Getting these thoughts out of her head and into the air might just be her best chance of getting some sleep tonight.

She padded through the corridor, past closed doors, and along a dimly lit carpet decorated in squares of different shades of brown. The light from the vending machine cast a white glow into the hallway, a servant always awake and ready to dole out some sugar.

Stella pushed her quarters into the machine and waited for the licorice to drop into the tray. There was so much to choose from here, a dozen different kinds of candy for kids to demand and enjoy. Kids were so easily pleased.

And so easily hurt.

She had seen so many families ruined during her two

years in uniform. She had watched social workers take possession of too many children with parents ravaged by drugs. Those kids would finish their childhood in institutions or with foster families before eventually finding their own addictions and their own problems.

Her job was to lock away the sick minds that hurt those kids and caused so much pain.

She opened the bag and sucked on a candy. The licorice's sweet tartness slapped the thoughts of death and murder out of her head. For a minute.

The ice machine at the end of the corridor clanked out some more cubes. A neon light buzzed somewhere unseen. But none of the doors running down both sides of the corridor opened. Everyone was apparently sleeping better than her tonight.

Gripping the licorice stick between her teeth, she folded over the corner of the bag and returned to her room. She sat on the end of the bed and chewed. The candy helped. The sweetness took her out of that hotel room and back to her childhood, sitting on the porch with Jackson, fighting over the last candy in the bag.

Until she remembered it was Uncle Joel who had introduced her to the treat. He always kept a bag in the car. Stella's dad would sometimes bring some home for her and Jackson after a double shift. As though a few pieces of candy could make up for his absence.

No. Enough.

She wasn't going to think about Joel. Or her dad. Not now. She had a case to work on and needed all the focus she could find.

Stella shoved off her jeans and slipped back into bed. She took her phone from the bedside table and sent a quick text to Mac.

You awake?

The unit's cyber expert didn't write back. Instead, almost as soon as the text was gone, Stella's phone rang. She answered immediately.

"Hey, Mac. You can't sleep either?"

"Sleep? It's not even two yet. Not even close to my bedtime."

Stella grinned. Mac seemed to have even more energy at night than she did during the day. While Stella would wilt over her martini during a night out, thinking about the warm comfort of her bed, Mac would be moving her shoulders to the beat in the bar and striking up conversations left and right. Stella never understood where she found the strength.

"It's long past mine, but my head refuses to believe it."

"Ha. So, what happened today? How'd it go in Atlanta?"

Stella took a deep breath. Without Mac's help, she wouldn't have even known she needed to go to Atlanta. But Stella didn't want to talk about Joel now, and not over the phone. That was a conversation they should have quietly and in person.

"It was erm…it was something. I'll tell you about it in the morning."

"Oh, sounds good. This something is about Joel Ramirez or something about Hagen Yates?"

Stella groaned at her friend's gossipy tone. "Mac!"

Mac laughed. "Girl's gotta ask."

"Girl's gotta get her mind out of the gutter."

"Nuh-uh, best place for it. Shame Slade called you guys back. But this case…" All remnants of humor drained from her voice. "I don't know. He's put all of us on it. He even dragged Dani out of the office, and she's ready to pop that baby out any minute."

"Yeah. He's a dad of teenage girls. That case with the kidnapped boys a few weeks ago hit him pretty hard. This one must be even worse."

"Right. Can you imagine a killer targeting cheerleaders? What a creep. I mean, the odds of this being a random opportunist are pretty tiny."

Stella pushed herself up in bed. It helped to have someone to bounce ideas off. Joel Ramirez disappeared from view a little. "No. The killer spent time arranging the bodies and painting a cheer above them when they should have been running. They increased the risk of getting caught in order to send a message. The sport matters."

"Maybe all sports do? To the killer anyway."

"Maybe. Or perhaps high school does. Or gyms. Until we start speaking to people and picking up more information, we can't rule anything out."

"Right." Mac fell silent for a moment. "Maybe it's just an old-fashioned stalker with a fixation on young girls?"

"Unfortunately, there's always that. Always. Or a fellow student. Or an ex-student. Or a teacher. Or…"

Stella dropped back onto her pillow with the phone still fixed to her ear. This was one of the problems with her job. Everyone was a suspect, and no one was above suspicion.

Anyone could be the killer. Anyone at all.

Ba-bang. Bang.

The shots came one after the other. The first two from the front of the house, the third from somewhere at the back.

"Get down! Mom. Amanda, Brianna, take cover!"

Hagen's voice echoed through the hallway of his childhood home. He dived onto the floor. The carpet's thick nap burned his cheek.

Ba-bam.

Two more shots rang out. They seemed to be coming from everywhere and nowhere. He couldn't tell which way to turn. He crawled through the hall toward the living room. The front door was open, but the curtains were drawn, the room dark.

Bang.

Hagen ducked. Another shot from the other side of the house, maybe near the garage. Shooters surrounded the house. His breath came in rapid gasps.

Slow down. You're better than this. Don't panic. Take it easy.

He couldn't let them in. He had to keep them out, keep his family safe. That was his job now. An echo of a voice, a police officer telling his mother the terrible news. "Mrs. Yates, I'm sorry to tell you that your husband, Seth Yates, was shot multiple times upon exiting the courthouse this afternoon."

Hagen's hand drifted to his hip. No holster. No gun. Where the hell was his gun?

Ba-bang.

Hagen buried his cheek in the carpet and covered his head with his hands.

No! Get it together. Find the shooters. Now.

He pressed his hands flat on the carpet's woolen nap.

Three. Two. One.

In one movement, he pushed himself to his feet and sprinted to the window. Dropping into a crouch, he dragged the curtain to one side.

Nothing.

Night had fallen. The street was utterly black. The streetlights were out. Even the stars and the moon were invisible. Either someone had extinguished all the lights in the world, or they'd thrown a heavy blanket over the entire house, shutting it off completely.

Hagen grabbed the window latch and twisted. Locked.

Relief surged through him.

Bang-bang-bang.

More shots.

"Hagan!" a woman screamed. His mother.

"Hagan, help us," another scream, louder this time. Brianna. They were upstairs.

Hagen bounded up the steps, taking them two at a time.

Four doors led off the hallway. None of them looked familiar.

"Help us, Hagen!"

Where were they? Their voices came from every direction, just like the bullets.

Bam-bam.

They were all going to die, and it would be all his fault. He should have stopped them. He couldn't stop them.

Bam-bam. Bam-*beep-beep-beep...*

With a large gasp of air, Hagen opened his eyes. The hotel clock beside the bed flashed six fifteen. A sliver of light shone through a gap in the curtains. His heart raced, and his forehead was slick with sweat.

Hagen exhaled and pushed himself up onto his elbows. It had been a long time since that nightmare jolted him awake.

When he had brought justice to his father's attackers, when his family was safe, and his father avenged, the nightmare would stop. Until then, he had to stay alert. He'd keep his eyes open and seize the opportunity when it arose. Seeing Joel Ramirez had probably triggered this particular nightmare from the depths of his subconscious.

He threw off the covers, showered and dressed, and was in the conference room by half past seven, where the hotel had arranged a small buffet breakfast. The spread was much better than most hotels he'd experienced with the FBI. He helped himself to a cup of coffee and a croissant and took the chair near the top of the table to wait for the rest of the team.

Slade really had called everyone in this time. On the last couple of cases, he'd held Caleb Hudson and Martin Lin in reserve. Dani and Mac had stayed at the office in Nashville, working the phones and sifting through data. As the door opened and the room filled, Hagen quickly realized that, for this case, Slade had left no one behind at all.

The size of the team sent a jolt of anticipation through Hagen. They'd had big cases before. They'd had a gruesome case just days ago. But the murder of teenage girls was personal to the boss. And the list of possible next targets was as extensive as Hagen'd ever seen. The chief would be looking for quick returns.

Caleb and Martin nodded greetings as they descended on

the buffet. Ander helped himself to a couple of pastries and took the seat next to him.

Stella gave him a small nod by way of a greeting before making herself a hot chocolate and sitting at the far end of the table next to Mac and Chloe.

Hagen sipped his coffee and greeted the three of them with no more than a lift of the hand. Everything he and Stella had seen yesterday was now closed and locked away. Today, they had a case to solve.

With Slade aiming both barrels at the problem, Hagen would give it everything he had.

Slade was the last to arrive, his entry lowering the hubbub of the room. He stood at the end of the table and opened a folder.

"Let's get right to it, shall we?"

The room fell silent.

"The police are still checking for additional security cameras in the area, but they've had no luck yet. The school is surrounded by parking lots, woods, and athletic fields. The nearest cameras were at a gas station, and they only covered the gas pumps and the checkout counter. What we've seen is all we've got."

What they'd seen wasn't much at all.

Slade moved on. "Ballistics confirmed the bullets that killed the three girls came from a Remington .30-06 rifle."

"That's a hunting rifle." The words left Hagen's lips as soon as he thought them.

Chloe, whose father was a gun enthusiast, nodded. "Pretty standard."

"Yeah. They're as common around here as cowboy boots and Dolly Parton ringtones. But the shots were poor. They were made at close range, near enough for a headshot, but they were all aimed at the torso and landed off-center. Our unsub might be a new hunter or just someone with access to hunting weapons they don't often use."

Martin Lin kicked back in his chair. He never could sit still, always tilting or balancing on things. One day he was going to fall over. "Or maybe they're a really bad shot? Which limits our suspect list to just about anyone in rural Tennessee."

There were times when Martin's New York sass was as out of place as a yellow taxicab in a field of pickups.

Slade looked at Martin, then looked at the floor, then back to Martin—clearly telling the agent to get all the legs of the chair back on the ground.

Martin complied.

"Maybe, Agent Lin. The police have followed up with the girls' parents. They all have alibis. Olivia Mostrom's parents were at a romantic weekend getaway in Nashville."

"Nice. I wouldn't mind one of those." Dani rested one hand on her extended belly. Only a few weeks separated her from motherhood. Well, official motherhood. She had a long habit of treating the team like her own brood of chicks.

Martin grinned. "I'm sure you'll get a romantic weekend again one day." He nodded at Dani's belly bulge. "Maybe when that one turns eighteen."

Dani grinned and waved his comment away.

Caleb leaned toward Martin and spoke in a whisper loud enough to be heard in the next room. "At least she won't be taking her romantic weekends by herself."

Hagen chuckled.

Slade slammed a fist onto the table hard enough to make everyone jump. "Enough. We've got work to do."

Their leader's frustration was clear. Slade's normally pristine suit was a little rumpled. The small cowlicks in his gray hair, which he always had under control, were beginning to spiral up. "Both hotel surveillance and eyewitnesses confirmed the Mostroms' presence at the hotel. The Wilders were at home all weekend with their other three girls, as were the Sinns, together with their two sons."

Slade extracted a pile of stapled pages from the folder. He slid them to Ander, who took one for himself and passed the rest to Hagen.

"This is the cheerleader list stolen from Coach Nathania Burbank's office. For those who don't know, it's now cheer camp season. Squads are breaking in their newly elected team members. Squads will be training all summer."

Hagen picked up his packet and frowned at the long list of names. Which girl was next?

"The list focuses on four local schools," Slade continued. "Sheriff Bob Day, who's responsible for policing all these municipalities, is posting deputies at each of the high schools, but he's asked for a federal agent at each stakeout. That's why you're all here."

Hagen leafed through the pages. Each school had a list of more than two dozen names between junior varsity and varsity squads. Any one of those names could become the unsub's next target. But the team certainly couldn't find the killer if they were sitting outside some high school acting like overpaid security guards. He bit his bottom lip and swallowed his frustration.

"Ander." Slade peered past Hagen. "You've got Petra High School. It's about twenty minutes from here. Caleb, I'm sending you to Eastchester High School. That's a forty-minute drive. Chloe…"

Slade looked toward the end of the table where Chloe was making slow circles with her fingertips, relieving the pressure of her arm sling. She dropped her hand to the table when Slade called her name.

Hagen frowned. Little more than a week had passed since Chloe had been shot by a serial killer who had wanted to use her body parts in an artwork. Hagen admired Chloe's almost instant return to work, but she'd probably been too quick to jump back in. More time away would have helped her physical wound heal faster.

The nonphysical wounds would take longer. Some damage ran deep.

If Slade shared Hagen's concern, either he didn't show it, or he didn't care. He was definitely more intense about this case. "Chloe, you've got Harnsey High School. That's about forty minutes in the opposite direction. And, Martin, you've got the farthest to travel. Winter Creek High School is about an hour away. Mac, do we have everything we need tech-wise?"

Mac nodded. "Yes. I set it all up last night."

"Good. Then I want you to help out with the interviews on this one. You and Stella start at Chapel Island High School. Talk to the principal and the head coach. See what you can find out about the girls, then head over to the Sinn family and see what else you can learn."

"Right." Mac's agreement was delivered with far more confidence than she must have felt. It had been a hot minute since Mac had gone out into the field. But she was a natural when it came to talking with people, if her social life was any indication.

"What about us?" Hagen glanced at Dani before turning back to Slade.

Slade closed the folder and slammed it against his ribs. "You two can go talk to the Wilders and the Mostroms."

Hagen gave a small nod. So, Stella had Mac today, and he had Dani. That was fine. While he'd rather pair up with Stella so they could discuss Joel Ramirez, he preferred to go out and conduct interviews than babysit mostly empty high school gyms.

Slade removed his reading glasses and focused on the

team, his face stern. "Listen, all of you. I'm going to need you to keep a very watchful eye. At this point, we only know two things. One, we're looking for someone capable of the cold-blooded slaughter of teenage girls. And, two, we have a very long list of girls who meet the victim profile. Let's keep them safe. Go."

10

S tella studied Mac. The midmorning sun beamed off her sunglasses as she drove them to Chapel Island High School. She drove with the window down, letting the humid air blow through her white-blond hair. That's when she realized her friend didn't look much older than the cheerleaders.

Stella tied her own dark hair into a ponytail so the air wouldn't tangle the strands too badly.

Mac had insisted on driving because "it means I'll get to do at least one thing." Mac was the only one with a vehicle, so Stella didn't have much of a choice.

"So, I'm going to watch Special Agent Stella in action today. Don't disappoint me." Mac glanced toward the passenger seat and grinned widely.

Stella laughed. "Oh, yeah. Watch me take down the killer with one fatal blow."

"Ha. I'd buy a ticket for that. But, first, I want the preshow." Mac's expression turned serious. "What happened in Atlanta? Did you meet Matthew Johnson's family? What are they like?"

Stella took a deep breath. "No. I didn't get the chance. But

I found something even bigger than his family." She paused, still not believing what she was about to say. "He's alive, Mac. Uncle Joel. Matthew Johnson. I saw him."

Mac jerked her head toward Stella. "Holy—"

"Watch it!"

Mac slammed on the brakes as a truck cut in front of them.

Stella jabbed out her arm to catch herself. She exhaled, sure there would be a bruise from her seat belt. "Yeah, he kinda had that effect on me too."

Mac's light green eyes were like boulders. "He's *alive?*"

"He's older. Wider. Balder. But it was him, Mac. I know it was." Dammit. She should have thought to take a damn picture. "He must have faked his death when he ended his undercover work."

"Wow. Did you speak to him?"

Stella shook her head. "No. We were going to go back when Slade called us in. Frankly, though, I'm a bit relieved. I have no idea what to say to him."

Mac was silent for a moment. To Stella's relief, her friend seemed to contemplate the problem while keeping her eyes on the road this time. "You'll figure it out. I'm sure by the time this case is done, you'll have a whole list of questions ready for him."

Stella wasn't so sure. Deep down, the questions would be easy. But the potential answers twisted her stomach. Her image of Joel Ramirez, her memories of him, of her father, all of it could be overturned. Already, she felt as if her rudder had shifted again.

She didn't have long to ponder the problem, though. Ahead, a red-brick building stood at the end of the road. Old Glory waved proudly over a white-pillared entrance, and above two small windows, the name of Chapel Island High School was emblazoned in black capital letters. Below that was a navy-and-white banner proclaiming *Home of the Crows!*

Mac pulled into the mostly empty parking lot. Everyone except the administration was out for the summer. "High schools, huh? They look the same everywhere."

"Probably feel the same everywhere too." Stella stepped out of the car and took in the building. "Ten years since graduation. Feels like a century. And I can't honestly say it was a place I ever looked forward to going back to."

Mac hitched her bag onto her shoulder. "Aw, come on. Science Club. Computer Club. Beating the boys at math. I loved it."

Stella laughed. She could imagine Mac acing the science subjects and making the computer nerds feel inadequate. All Stella wanted to do in high school was finish her studies and move on. This wasn't the kind of place that produced happy memories.

The offices were just inside the entrance. A woman with dark curls sat behind a desk talking to a man in brown pressed chinos and a short-sleeved checkered shirt crumpled at the back. He turned around as Stella and Mac came in, revealing a thin face with a salt-and-pepper beard and a low brow that narrowed his eyes.

Stella pulled out her badge. "Principal Tom Bledsoe? I'm Special Agent Stella Knox. This is Special Agent Mackenzie Drake. We're with the FBI."

Principal Bledsoe extended his hand. "Sheriff Day told me you'd be coming. Let's go to my office. Mary, could you see I'm not disturbed?"

Stella and Mac nodded to Mary as Principal Bledsoe led them through a door at the end of the passage. The office was small and over furnished. The desk took up almost half the space and was covered with neat piles of paper and a small computer monitor. The window behind the desk looked out onto playing fields. A Chapel Island High pennant decorated one wall with a flash of navy blue.

As Stella and Mac took seats opposite the desk, Principal Bledsoe opened a drawer and pulled out a packet of gum. He slipped a piece into his mouth and offered the packet to Mac and Stella. "I don't let the kids chew this stuff, but what they don't know can't hurt them. And I don't stick it to the bottom of chairs."

Stella declined.

Mac shrugged and took a piece. "Can you confirm where you were on Saturday night, sir?"

Principal Bledsoe shoved the packet of gum back into the drawer. "Me? Home, like I told Sheriff Day. Had dinner with my wife, then we watched TV and went to bed. Just like most Saturdays. I got the call late that night. We've been dealing with it ever since."

Stella made a note. A night in was both entirely believable in a small town and almost impossible to verify. He wasn't setting off any alarm bells, but you never knew. "Do you have any reason to believe that anyone at the high school, whether student or faculty, would want to harm these particular girls?"

Principal Bledsoe chewed on his gum. "No. Those girls were the best of the best. They worked hard. Got good grades. Stayed out of trouble. Two of them have already been accepted to Florida State University. Bright futures, all three." He frowned, his jaw pausing mid-chew. "All three *had* bright futures. Who the hell would want to do this to them?"

Stella offered a gentle smile. "That's exactly what we're trying to figure out. Do you have school clubs that involve the use of guns? JROTC? Hunting clubs? Or shooting? Maybe trap shooting."

Principal Bledsoe rubbed his forehead as if trying to chase away a headache. "No, we don't have any clubs like that. Even if we weren't living a post-Columbine world of zero tolerance, we can barely afford the Chess Club." He offered a humorless laugh. "Honestly, we can only afford chess because someone donated an old set. Cheerleading and football are our two largest teams, and neither of those involves shooting. If kids around here want to learn to shoot, their dads teach them."

"What about troubled kids? Anyone with a violent background or someone who's used violence at school as a way to cope?"

Principal Bledsoe chewed his gum harder. "No, not really. I mean, we've sometimes had a few kids who come from rough backgrounds. Hardscrabble farms, that kind of thing. More recently, we've had a few kids whose parents have struggled with opioid addiction. But violence? We've never had anything more than the occasional fistfight. Certainly nothing like this. Chapel Island is a small, tight-knit community. Everyone knows everyone, and you can see that in the school."

Mac pointed a thumb over her shoulder. "I noticed when we came in that there were no security cameras at the entrance. None in the corridor either. Why is that?"

Trust Mac to focus on the technology. Stella hadn't tracked the absence of security cameras yet.

"We just don't have the budget for it, and crime was never an issue until now. We could either have surveillance or more teachers. We went for the teachers."

Stella poised her pen over her notebook. "Do you have Nathania Burbank's contact information?"

"Coach Burbank? She's in the teachers' lounge. We figured you people...agents...would be around today. She came in just in case you wanted to speak with her. Follow me."

Principal Bledsoe led them back past Mary, who looked

away from her computer screen. Stella could almost feel her eyes on her back all the way to the teachers' lounge.

The room was smaller than Stella expected. Three round tables took up most of the space. Two vending machines had been placed against the wall, one offering eight different kinds of soda, the other out of order. A fridge and a microwave stood by the window, and a cupboard displayed a sign urging people to please sign out any laptops they took.

Stella paused at the entrance. When she had been a kid, the teachers' room had always seemed like forbidden territory, a comfortable haven from which she would always be excluded. Now, it looked cold and institutional, less welcoming than even the FBI's breakroom in Nashville.

At the table closest to the window sat a physically fit woman with a pile of papers she clearly wasn't reading. She must have been in her late thirties, with long, black hair that fell in tight braids. Stella could picture her twenty years earlier, leading the cheer and waving her pom-poms. Or she could have if Nathania's bloodshot eyes and puffy complexion hadn't added almost a decade to her face.

"Nathania?"

The cheer coach looked up at the sound of Principal Bledsoe's voice. Her gaze jerked from the principal to Mac and Stella. "Is this them?"

"Yeah. These ladies are here from the FBI. They just want to ask you a few questions. I'll leave you all to it. If you need anything, I'll be in my office."

Nathania wiped her left eye with the heel of her hand. That's when Stella noticed that at the top of the pack of papers was a copy of the same list Slade had shared with the team.

Stella pulled out a chair opposite her. "May I?" She sat when Nathania nodded. Stella gestured to the list. "What are you looking for?"

Nathania sniffed and wiped her other eye. "Nothing. I was just...I was wondering who might be next. It will be one of the girls on this list, won't it? One of these names."

Stella covered the page with her hand and pushed the paper to one side. "We don't know that. We don't know whether this unknown suspect is looking for more victims, but I can tell you that we're here to make sure this goes no further. Okay?"

Nathania dropped her head into her hands. "It's all my fault. They were my girls. I was supposed to look after them. I should have never left them to lock up. What was I *thinking?*"

Mac placed a hand on her arm. "Hey, you were thinking they were perfectly capable of locking the door before they went home. And they were. This isn't your fault."

"That's right. You can't blame yourself for this." Stella folded her hands over the table. "Can you just talk me through what happened that night?"

Nathania swallowed and lifted her head. "Er, yeah. The girls practiced from three 'til seven as always. Olivia wanted to stay on with Reese and Taylor to work on a new routine." She took a shaky breath. "Since it was all choreography and not stunts, I left them to it while I finished the paperwork in my office. About nine o'clock, I went back to the gym. They were just packing up. I had a little bit of drive and didn't want to wait any longer, so I reminded them to lock up and headed for my car."

"On your way out, did you see anyone or anything out of place?"

Nathania shook her head slowly. "No, nothing. There was nothing at all."

"Where did you go after you left the school?"

"To my boyfriend's. He lives out in Gallatin. We'd planned to spend Sunday hiking and barbecuing. I just wanted to get out of there, you know? It was summer break. And because of cheerleading practice, I hadn't had a *day off...*" Nathania broke into a loud sob and covered her mouth with her hand. "Those girls. My girls. They were so beautiful. So talented. They didn't deserve this. And it's all my fault."

Mac scooted her chair over and rubbed Nathania's back. "You're right about the girls not deserving this, but you're wrong about it being your fault. These murders had nothing to do with you. You couldn't have prevented them. If you had been there, we might have lost you too. The only person responsible is the person who did it."

Stella nodded. "That's right. And we'll find them. Just a few more questions."

Nathania blew out a breath. "Okay."

"My understanding is that Olivia was named team captain last fall, even though she was only a junior. Can you tell me why a senior wasn't chosen?"

The coach frowned, her nostrils flaring wide. "Well, we had a problem with the seniors at the beginning of the season. All four of them were caught with marijuana on school grounds."

Interesting. Might be a lead they need.

"Can you provide me those girls' names and contact information, please."

The coach did her one better and printed off the contact information for each of the young women. She then jotted down her own contact information at Stella's request, along with her boyfriend's name and number. Nathania also agreed to provide her fingerprints and a DNA sample to rule her out as a suspect, if needed.

When Stella couldn't think of anything else to ask, she glanced at Mac. "Let's take a look at the crime scene."

Mac blanched. It'd been a while since the cyber tech had been to a murder scene. There was a difference between browsing images on a computer screen and standing at the edge of a puddle of human blood as it dried in the open air.

Nathania pulled a tissue from a box on the table and rubbed her sniffling nose. "I don't have the key. To the gym. I gave my copy to the police."

Mac almost sighed with relief. "That's okay."

But her friend wasn't going to get off that easy. Stella shook her head. "No, we need to see it, Mac. Would Principal Bledsoe have another key?"

Nathania nodded. She led them back to the principal, who pulled a key out of the drawer where he kept his gum.

"Police taped the place off, but I guess for you guys, it's okay. Just bring it back when you're done. Nathania? Can you show them the way?"

Coach Burbank seemed hesitant but nodded. She was tough, this one. Stella and Mac followed her out of the school's entrance and across the grass to the sprawling building at the end of the campus. The double doors were marked off with yellow tape. Nathania stopped a good ten feet away. More tears traced down her face.

"I'll wait here."

Stella gave the coach a small smile. "It's okay. You can go home for today."

Nathania nodded to them both, turned, and fled. Her long legs carried her hastily yet gracefully across the stretch of green lawn.

Turning back to the gym, Stella slipped under the tape and unlocked the door. "Mac? Ready?"

A slight redness had risen to Mac's cheeks.

Stella pulled on a pair of latex gloves. "You can wait here if you want. But another pair of eyes would be useful."

Mac groaned but pulled on her own gloves and stepped into the gym. She stopped almost immediately with a short gasp. Stella slipped around her before closing the door.

The air was thick in the midmorning heat and held a strong, coppery smell. A dried crimson puddle covered part of the three-point line. Another stain was smeared across the wall under the far basketball hoop. Above that smudge stretched two sentences in all caps, spelling out the message that Stella had seen on Slade's computer the previous night.

WE'VE GOT SPIRIT! HOW BOUT YOU?

Now that the words were in front of her, they looked twice as big and were three times as shocking.

Mac let out a low whistle. "They used a lot of blood to write that."

Stella stood next to Mac and stared at the message. Despite the heat in the gym, a chill passed through her. "And a lot of hate."

"Yeah."

"The blood is likely from all three girls." Stella studied the bloody script. "And they would've had to do it fast. Otherwise, it would dry too quickly. Forensics will tell us." Stella frowned, something odd occurring to her. "You whistled. What happened to your gum?"

"My gum? Oh, I left it on the bottom of the chair in the principal's office." Mac shrugged. "Old habits. Though I kinda wish I'd kept it. Minty freshness would be welcome right now."

At any other time, Stella would have smiled. With so much spilled blood in front of her, a smile felt too out of place. Though she wouldn't mind some minty freshness as well.

Stella walked across the gym floor. Her shoes squeaked against the polished hardwood, a sound that brought back memories of gym class. She pointed to a set of doors at the back of the gym. "These must be the offices."

She turned her back on the bloodstains and, for a moment, the horror of the scene melted away. This was just another gym, in another school, in another town. There was nothing strange here, nothing at all.

A name placard proclaimed *Coach Nathania Burbank*. Stella opened the door. Nathania's office was barely large enough to fit a small desk. Pictures of cheerleading squads over the years covered much of one wall. The same Chapel Island pennant that hung in the principal's office also hung in here. A corkboard contained a schedule with practices marked in different colors. A small hole topped a space in the middle of the board.

"That must be where she hung the list for the All-State cheer squad." Mac's voice behind Stella's shoulder was reassuring, an extra pillar of strength in a place where Stella needed all the strength she could find. "That's quite an effort. Kill three people. Arrange their bodies. Write on the wall, then ransack an office."

"No." Stella started to twist her ear stud but dropped her hands when she remembered the gloves. "Kill three people, ransack the office, then arrange the bodies, and write on the wall. If the killer had come in here last, there'd be bloodstains on the door and on the cabinet."

"Huh. The arrangement and the writing could have been an afterthought then?"

That was the bad news.

Stella sighed. "If so, that list is important. And the only reason it would be important is to use as a hit list."

She returned to the gym. The writing blasted its cheer again, but Stella ignored it and continued to the back door. She pulled it open and peered outside.

A parking lot stretched in front of her, extending to the woods. To her right was a set of three tennis courts with the track and football fields beyond them. There were no houses nearby or any buildings other than the school and the gym.

Mac held the door open and looked past her. "Nothing here at all, is there?"

"Total blind spot. No cameras on this side of the building, no witnesses, nothing."

Stella stared into the trees. Behind her were the gym and its bloody message. If she continued looking forward, she could pretend it wasn't there.

No time for that.

She turned and walked back into the building, breathing in its coppery air. "Let's go talk to Taylor Sinn's parents. We'll probably need to circle back around to teachers and friends too."

Why had these particular girls been targeted?

The question still swirled in her mind as she climbed into Mac's passenger seat.

11

Olivia Mostrom's house stood halfway down a long country road that ended on the shores of the Cumberland River. A narrow sidewalk and a neatly cut lawn separated the house from the road. A hedge in front of the bay window gave the grand home some humility, as though it wanted to see the world without being seen.

The high double eaves of the house's southern wing, however, overshadowed that coyness. This was a property that demanded admiration, even as it pretended to want otherwise.

Hagen drew the Corvette up next to the curb and turned off the engine. "Olivia Mostrom is the cheer team captain. Must have been pretty dedicated to land that spot."

Dani eased the seat belt past her extended belly. "Not necessarily. I was a cheer team captain once. The only thing I was dedicated to was gossiping with the other girls in the changing room."

Hagen tried to picture Dani as a cheerleader. But all he could envision was her pregnant belly threatening to bounce off her body as she jumped. Worse, the thought of her water breaking when she did a split made him squirm.

Dani laughed. "Don't look at me like that. I wasn't always this big, you know."

"I hope not. Would be the world's longest pregnancy."

Dani ran a hand over her bump. "Already feels like the world's longest pregnancy. No, I was fit once."

And not that long ago, by Hagen's recollection. Even about to burst, Dani was in good shape. Her biceps flexed as she untangled herself from the seat belt. "Not only could I see my toes, I could even touch them."

Hagen stepped out of the car and came around to Dani's side. He supported her elbow as she eased herself out of the seat. "Is touching your toes a requirement for a cheerleader?"

Dani stood and pushed her hand into the small of her back.

Hagen winced for her. He understood why Slade had brought her out from behind a desk for this case, but he still wasn't convinced it was the right move. He could have done this interview alone. Dani shouldn't be more than twenty minutes away from the nearest maternity ward.

She waddled toward the house. "Not on our cheerleader team. They made me captain because I was the only one who could do the splits."

"A true prerequisite." Hagen slowed his walk to accommodate Dani. He tried again to imagine her in high school, with ginger hair flowing past her shoulders, her freckled face beaming as she waved those pom-poms. Her belly, bigger and rounder than the basketball, made it impossible to picture.

He knocked on the door. The man who opened it was tall and slim with receding gray hair and a checkered shirt tucked neatly into his slacks. He looked past Hagen's shoulder to the Corvette parked outside his house.

"Tanner Mostrom?" At the man's nod, Hagen brought out his badge and made the introductions.

Tanner gave a small grunt by way of a reply. "That your car? Tax dollars must be paying you very well in the FBI."

When Hagen didn't reply, he held the door open.

Hagen stepped aside to let Dani in first, then followed her into a spacious living room. A gray sofa faced the television above the fireplace. But three armchairs sat below the window, suggesting that was the place where people conversed more than watched TV.

The pile of home décor magazines on the coffee table and the neatly arranged throw on the back of the sofa suggested the Mostroms cared about appearances.

"This is my wife, Susie." Tanner pointed to a woman standing in front of a display cabinet. She held a cloth in one hand and was halfway through dusting a collection of porcelain dogs. "These people are from the FBI, honey."

She turned around, a ceramic schnauzer in one hand. Hagen put Susie Mostrom's age in her mid-fifties. Her blond hair curled at the neck. She was shorter than her husband and heavier set, but the redness around her eyes was more pronounced. There was an uneasiness in her stance as if she didn't quite know where to put her limbs.

Housework struck Hagen as an unusual thing to do after hearing of your daughter's brutal murder, but everyone had their own way of coping. Susie seemed to have found hers. Maybe it was her way of controlling something in a world suddenly spinning out of control.

It was clear Hagen and Dani's arrival had forced her out of her thoughts and dragged her back to the world. Hagen inhaled deeply. He should have left her there.

Susie pointed the dog's nose at the sofa. "Oh, do please sit down."

Dani didn't wait for a second invitation. She eased herself

into the corner of the sofa. Susie wiped a corner of her dusting cloth between the dog's porcelain ears. "Can I get you anything? Water? Coffee?"

Dani smiled, her face a little red from the outdoor heat that had followed them in. "I'd love a glass of water."

"I'll get it, hun." Tanner crossed the hardwood floor toward the kitchen. "Anything for you, Agent?"

"No, I'm good. Thanks."

Hagen dropped into an armchair and pulled his notebook out of his pocket. The very act of holding pen and paper in hand was centering. Sure, they all had phones and tablets for notetaking, but nothing helped his brain to connect more than good old-fashioned writing.

"Have you caught them yet?" Susie's hand tightened on the porcelain dog so much he feared it might break. "I do hope you're here to tell me you've caught the monster who did this thing."

I wish.

"No. We're still putting together a timeline and hunting down infor—"

"Well, now." She waved a finger at him. "I don't know what's taking you so long. It's just obvious who did it."

"Really?" Tanner returned with the water, and Hagen paused long enough for Dani to take the glass. "Do you have someone in mind?"

Susie put the schnauzer back on the shelf and removed a porcelain Doberman. The statue was twice the size of the schnauzer, its upright ears ending in sharp points. The dog looked more noble than threatening.

"Well, it has to be one of the girls who wanted Olivia's position on the team. They were all jealous of her, you know. Every one of them." Her smile grew wistful. "My Olivia was so talented and so beautiful. She was known across the whole region. That was why she was elected cheer captain, even though she was only in her junior year. And she already had a scholarship to Florida State. Success like that just makes the other girls hate more. As for their parents, they're even worse. I've never known such hate."

Dani laid a hand on her belly like she wanted to guard the baby against such talk. "Enough hate to kill?"

Susie Mostrom's face flushed a bright red, making her curly blond hair seem pale. "Now, you tell me, Agent. Why else would someone do something so awful? Such nasty people. I mean, I've known mothers who put superglue in a rival's hair gel. And do you remember that Texas mother who hired a killer, an actual hitman, to rub out rivals so her daughter could make the squad?"

Hagen tapped his pen on his notepad, wondering if this mother was the type to hire a hitman. She certainly seemed intense enough. "That is a possibility, ma'am, but we must consider other motives too. The murders might not have been related to cheerleading or even to the school. Did Olivia mention anyone who was bothering her recently? Or her friends?"

Susie ran the cloth down the Doberman's back. "No, not at all. I mean, I'm sure the girls gossiped behind her back. They always do. But nothing out of the ordinary."

"No strange behavior? No unusual silences?"

Susie stroked under the Doberman's chin. "No. Olivia wasn't the sort to get stressed out like those other girls. She was made for competitive cheerleading. It gave her confidence, you know. Showed just how talented she was. She even made the All-State squad. Whoever didn't, you want to look there next."

Dani sipped her water. "At the All-State squad?"

Susie shot Dani an *are you stupid* look. "Why, yes. Investigate the alternates. One of them could have murdered my girl to take her spot. Or one of their parents could have done it." Susie's fingers curled around the dog's neck. "Cheer parents are the meanest type of people you'll ever meet. You ever seen *Dance Mommies?*"

Was she serious? Hagen shook his head. "I can't say that I have."

"Those mothers are nothing compared to cheerleading mommies."

Hagen closed his notebook, knowing he was staring one of those cheerleading mommies dead in the face. Dani watched him with half a smile. He understood, but he didn't dare to return her look, not with Olivia's parents in the room. "Right. Can you tell me where you were on Saturday? To help us with the timeline?"

"Tanner and I were in Nashville. We'd gotten an Airbnb for the weekend. We came back when Reese's mother called us trying to find Reese."

"We'll look into that. Do you mind if we just take a quick look in Olivia's bedroom?"

Susie put the Doberman back on the shelf. "Not at all. She keeps...she kept her room so tidy."

She laid the cloth duster on the shelf in front of the dogs. Hagen helped Dani out of the sofa, and they followed Susie up the stairs.

The bedroom was neater than any teenager's bedroom Hagen had ever seen. The bed was made, the desk neatly arranged. A navy-and-gold pennant hung on one wall, and even the carpet had been vacuumed so that the nap created alternating stripes across the floor.

Dani leaned in the doorway. "Is her room always this tidy, or did you arrange it?"

Susie's fingers sought the surface of the desk. Standing in her daughter's bedroom, her lip quivered. "She...she was always...she was perfect. My girl. My beautiful girl."

She dropped onto the bed and dropped her head into her

hands. Dani sat next to her and stroked the woman's back. She turned to Hagen and whispered, "I'll see you downstairs."

Hagen headed back to the living room. Dani was right. She was the better choice to cope with those emotions.

As he walked down the hallway, he studied a series of portraits of Olivia. Her bright blue eyes flashed with attitude, even in school photos. It felt like traveling through time. Olivia as a towheaded toddler. Then the pictures jumped forward a few years to her kindergarten graduation, holding a construction paper diploma.

After that, a series of middle school portraits, until finally arriving at her cheer headshot—the one the news reports flashed across the airwaves. There was space for a few more portraits. But no more portraits would be possible.

He reached the living room, with a clear view into the next space.

In the kitchen, Tanner Mostrom sat at the island, sobbing.

12

Stella hesitated on the concrete porch before knocking on the Sinn family's front door. The house was a simple but appealing single-story home in a well-maintained neighborhood just blocks from the center of town. A vase of fresh flowers stood in the bay window, the kind of white, waxy flowers friends send the recently bereaved.

She glanced at Mac. "When was the last time you did one of these?"

"An interview with a grieving family?" Mac swallowed. She always had a bounce in her step and a smile waiting to break through. But she stood straight now, her expression serious. "You know, I've never actually done one."

Stella had lost count of how many times she'd spoken to a family immediately after a tremendous loss. Gone was the fear that she would join the family's tears or stammer out her questions, afraid of sounding insensitive.

Now, she was more concerned she *could* block out the raw emotions she'd seen displayed too many times. She never wanted to lose her empathy, ever. Today, she would also need to keep an eye on Mac. These visits were never easy.

She rang the doorbell. "You'll be fine."

Mac exhaled slowly. "Machines are easier. They don't—"

The door opened, and Stella pulled out her ID. "Rick Sinn? I'm Special Agent Knox with the FBI."

Rick Sinn was in his late fifties. Most of his hair had receded, leaving a white halo above his ears. An even whiter brush mustache covered much of his upper lip. He squinted through his glasses at Stella's ID, then peered over her shoulder at Mac.

"And where are you from? Jehovah's Witnesses?"

"Oh, er no." Mac scrabbled in her bag for her ID. "Special Agent Mackenzie Drake."

Rick Sinn didn't even give the ID a glance. He stepped back to let them into the house.

Putting her badge away, Stella crossed the threshold into a small living room. A giant leather sofa sat against a half wall separating the living room from the kitchen. A pair of cupholders sat between the sofa cushions. Another slightly smaller sofa was perpendicular to this one. A framed print took up much of the space on the opposite wall, promising the Lord would fight for you if you just stood still.

Stella blinked. Standing still didn't seem like the best advice to give someone who wanted to be a cheerleader.

Or a family that had just suffered a loss.

A woman with thick lines on her cheeks sat on the love seat. Her dyed, black hair ran past her shoulders as straight as a ruler. She was younger than her spouse by about fifteen years. She bent over a photo album laid out on the coffee table.

Rick pointed at Stella as he closed the front door. "They're from the FBI, Darby. This one is, anyhow. The other one didn't sound too sure where she was from."

Mac visibly bristled. "I *am* with the FBI. We appreciate you speaking with us."

"Uh-huh." Darby Sinn nodded toward the larger sofa. "Why don't you two take a load off? Guess you're here about our poor Taylor. Not sure there's much we can say that we didn't already tell the cops."

Cheeks dotted pink, Mac took the far end of the sofa while Stella sat close to Darby. Rick leaned against the kitchen doorframe, his arms folded over his chest.

Three photo albums were open in front of the grieving mother. About a dozen pictures had been pulled out and scattered across the tabletop. Each showed an attractive, young girl with green eyes and long, brown hair. In half the pictures, she wore a cheerleader outfit, pom-poms waving.

Stella folded her hands in her lap. "She was very pretty."

"Uh-huh." Darby wiped an eye with the back of her hand. "Just looking for a picture for her funeral, you know?"

Mac audibly inhaled from the other end of the sofa. A weight settled in Stella's stomach. One of these pictures would be the last image Taylor's friends and family had of her. It wasn't fair.

Rick wiggled a fat finger over the table. "You can take out the cheerleader ones for a start. This would never have happened if she hadn't joined that stupid club."

Mac twisted to face Rick. "You didn't approve of Taylor's cheerleading?"

The man growled low in his throat. "I did not. Degrading activity. Not the sort of thing that any decent young girl should do."

Darby turned the page of the photo album, providing no visible reaction to her husband's criticisms. "Oh, honey. You're such an old…man. Girls like to dance and do gymnastics. They enjoy it."

"Yeah, that's what you told her. I know you did. And I told

you not to encourage her. Getting her thinking that she could be a professional cheerleader. Over my dead body. It's not decent. If she'd..." He gulped, his neck flushing red. "If she'd listened to *me*, she'd still be alive today."

Stella gauged Darby's reaction. Rick Sinn's comment was savage, but the barbed remark shot straight through Darby as though she were made of nothing but air.

She turned another page of the album, stopping at a photo of Taylor sitting on the bough of a large elm tree. Grinning through her retainer, the sun shone through the hem of her blue skirt.

"I did try to talk her out of cheer team, Agents. I really did. But she wouldn't listen. She loved it all too much. Her friends were in it, Olivia and Reese. It was her passion. She dreamed of becoming a professional." Darby pulled the picture out of the album and placed it on the table. "Aren't parents supposed to support their children's dreams? That's all I've ever tried to do with all three of my kids."

Stella sat back on the sofa and then immediately leaned forward again. These cushions were too thick, too comfortable for this conversation. They should have been on wooden stools with splinters to make sure they never felt too at ease.

"Taylor had two brothers, I understand. How have they taken the news?"

"Oh, Garrett's with my folks today." She swiped at her cheeks again. "He was a late baby. He's still little, only three years old. I didn't want him here for all this."

Rick shifted his weight to the kitchen's other doorpost. "Tate's pretty shaken up. He graduated at the end of May. He's moving to California now, getting ready for college over there. This whole thing's just made him more determined than ever to leave small-town Tennessee and never come back."

Darby sniffed. She closed the photo album, stacking it

neatly on the coffee table corner before pulling another one closer. Most of her physical effort seemed to be focused on the photographs. Stella decided to let her keep taking out the pictures since it seemed to bring her a measure of comfort. "Taylor wanted to go to Florida State. That was where Olivia and Reese were going. She didn't want to stay here either."

"Yeah, fat chance." Rick jutted out his chin. "With her grades? She'd have been lucky to get into community college."

Mac gasped, and Stella spoke quickly, her words dragging Rick's attention away from Mac. "Taylor was struggling at school?"

"She wouldn't have been if she'd studied instead of wasting every spare minute jumping around and waving those...*pom-poms* for a bunch of boys."

Where his wife's focus was on the memories in front of her, Rick appeared to look anywhere but at the photos. Anger was a perfectly reasonable reaction to grief, Stella understood. But Rick seemed ready to ground his daughter for dying.

"Oh, will you look at that!" Darby pulled another picture out of the album. The image showed Taylor with her brothers sitting in the bed of a pickup. They were munching the contents of a giant bucket of popcorn. "That was at that drive-in out in the fields near Bremmer Creek."

Stella smiled. "Looks like they had fun."

"Rick's right, though. Coach Burbank really is too much. Drives them far too hard. Relentless. All those weights and cardio. Even dieting." She snorted. "Like those girls need to watch their figures. Pretty sure that was why she made Olivia cheer captain. Two of a kind, those two."

This description didn't quite track with Stella's impression of the coach. "You didn't approve of the way Coach Burbank managed the cheer team?"

"Approve?" Darby flipped the page of the photo album. She hadn't raised her head to look at either Mac or Stella since they'd entered the house. "No, I did not approve. I haven't liked that woman since Taylor's freshman year. All she cares about is getting those girls to jump higher and spin faster and whatever else they do. I never minded Taylor doing cheer, but they were all supposed to be enjoying themselves. They've got enough work to do without cheer adding to it."

Mac pulled out her notebook and scribbled something down. Stella left her to it. Demanding coaches weren't unusual, and Coach Burbank had seemed authentically shocked by the girls' deaths. She didn't believe the coach had anything to do with the murders. Although, it was possible that someone was trying to get back at Coach Burbank and not the girls themselves. That was an angle they might want to investigate.

"Is Tate here right now? I'd like to have a word with him."

Rick shook his head. "Naw. He went out for a walk. Likes to be outdoors, he does. Not the sort to sit inside and mope."

"Right. We can talk to him later if we need to. Do you mind if we take a look at Taylor's room?"

Darby jerked her head away from the album. Her cheeks paled. Against her black hair, her skin looked chalky and unhealthy. "I can't go in there. I can't do it. Not now."

Rick pushed himself away from the kitchen doorway, seemingly relieved to have a directive. Stella suspected he wasn't someone who often stood still. "I'll take them." But when they arrived at the top of the stairs, he just pointed to the end of the corridor, not even looking in the empty room's direction. "It's in there."

They continued alone. In Taylor's camouflage themed bedroom, clothes laid on the bed, across the floor, and some were piled on the desk next to an open laptop, a crumb-coated plate, and two empty glasses. A six-point buck took pride of place over the bed while a packet of cookies stood open on the bedside table. However difficult entering this room would be, someone would need to do it soon or there would be an infestation of some kind.

Mac nudged Stella. "I wouldn't mind a look in that laptop. No way her parents would know the password, though. I'd have to hack my way in."

Stella nodded. "Let's add that to the warrant list."

They rifled through Taylor's clothes, checked her closet, and rummaged down the side of the bed.

After twenty minutes of fruitless searching, Stella wiped her brow and rested her hands on her hips. "I can't see anything here that's of any use. Why don't teenagers keep diaries anymore? 'I really think so-and-so hates me and wants to kill me.' That'd be a useful entry."

"Maybe it's on their Instagram stories." Mac stretched her back. "I think we're done here."

They left Taylor's room and met Rick Sinn at the top of the stairs. His head was half-bowed as though he didn't want to go to that part of his house.

Stella stopped. A bedroom door off to the side was wide open, giving her a clear view of camouflage curtains that matched his son's. A pair of antlers hung on the wall above the bed. "You hunt, Rick?"

Rick lifted his head and shrugged. "Used to. Haven't done it for years. Tate, though, he loves it. Got his hunting license now, and he's…" Rick's forehead folded into a deep scowl. "Now, wait a minute. I hope you're not thinking…my boy just lost his sister. How dare you even consider—"

Stella lifted her hands. "Hey, I didn't mean anything about Tate. We're just looking for a particular kind of gun. That's all."

Mac peered into the room. "Where do you keep your hunting gear?"

Rick took a deep breath. His chest appeared to double in size. "I keep it in the garage, where hunting gear belongs. It's in a locker. And if you want to see it, you'll have to come back here with a search warrant and one almighty bolt cutter. Now, I think you two had better be on your way."

He stepped aside. Stella led Mac down the stairs and out of the house.

The door slammed behind them.

Mac turned to Stella. "Well, that didn't go too badly, did it?"

"Like clockwork." Stella checked her phone. "Let's get over to the police station. Slade wants a debrief."

13

———

Sophie Powers bent her knees and extended her arms straight up over her head. Her thighs ached. The muscles in her calves screamed.

Back handspring. *You've got this. You can do it.*

She bent her knees farther, leaned back, and started to fall. Without giving herself time to think, she swung her arms down to create momentum. With all her power, she launched backward, flipping until her palms pressed into the mat.

Her stepmother's workout studio flipped with her. The watercooler by the back door threatened to empty its contents over the floor. Her phone, still blasting out "How Far I'll Go," appeared to be "glued" to the ceiling.

With a grunt, she pushed with her arms. Her legs went over, and the watercooler righted itself. Auli'i Cravalho asked what was beyond the line as Sophie's toes landed on the mat, and she stood straight.

"Yes!"

She shouted aloud as she held her position and gazed at the mirrored wall. There she was, her blond hair falling between her shoulder blades, her fingers reaching for the sky. She checked her posture.

That's it. Bend your back more.

She leaned back a little farther and stretched her fingers. "Perfect."

Sophie lowered her arms and reached out for her water bottle. She took a slug. The tension in her muscles eased. The cold liquid cooled her chest.

The rest of Sophie's squad were probably at home now, watching television or scrolling through social media. She was lucky. Her stepmom let her use her workout studio in the afternoon.

Her step-monster only let her use the space on rare occasions. But, today, her stepmom's offer had been perfect. Sophie could stay there as long as she wanted since she and Sophie's dad wouldn't be home until much later tonight.

Cheer camp had been canceled. Cops were posted at Petra High School because someone had murdered three girls—*three cheerleaders!*—at Chapel Island High Saturday night.

Sophie had seen the news. She'd even seen the Instagram pic of the three Chapel Island girls sitting with their backs to the wall, their feet touching, the blood smeared across the wall before it had been removed.

She hadn't recognized the girls until their cheerleading headshots flashed across the news outlets. But the Chapel Island navy-and-gold colors were distinctive. She remembered watching this team perform and remembered Reese particularly. Clearly, she'd been the most talented of the Chapel Island squad. Her gymnastics were stellar. Her smile, with her deep dimples, lit up a field.

The sight of their bodies had turned Sophie's stomach. Someone must have taken the picture through the windows at the top of the wall, so the message wasn't easy to read, but she understood. Someone had targeted a cheer team.

Envy. That was all it was. Everyone wanted to be a cheerleader, but only a few could cut it. Some couldn't cope with rejection.

Sophie shuddered before taking another slug of water and picking up her phone. One message. *The FBI are here now!!!* Plus, a gif of Joey from *Friends*, his eyes wide open in shock.

She put the phone back on the floor. No wonder Sophie's school wouldn't let them hold any camp practices. With the police and the FBI there, no one was getting back in the gym until this thing was cracked. "All the better for me."

Throwing the bottle back on the ground, she spun around and flipped her way across the mat. Again, she held the pose in front of the mirror. Nailed it.

The trials for the All-State cheer squad would take place soon. And while all the other girls were stuck in front of their screens, she would keep practicing, keep getting better.

She lowered her arms and moved to the end of the mat.

Unlike some of her overly dramatic friends, Sophie wasn't concerned that the shooter would try to hunt her down, despite killing three other cheerleaders. She rolled her shoulders and lifted her hands. Chapel Island had a lot of weirdos. It was probably just some creepy local. Might not even be someone related to cheer. Just the sight of girls in cheer uniforms could have an effect on freaks. She'd seen that often enough.

Still, those girls *were* cheerleaders. If she lived in Chapel Island instead of in Petra, she would have gone to that high school.

Sophie raised her knee and prepared for a cartwheel.

And it could have been me in that gym.

She stopped.

It would *have been me in that gym.*

She lowered her knee and dropped her arms. A chill passed through her.

This wasn't worth it. No one should die for the cheer team.

The song changed, and Demi Lovato confidently declared that it was time to take it. The bass thumped through the floor, through the mat, and into the soles of Sophie's feet. Her head rocked.

"Screw that."

She lifted her hands, raised her knee, and threw herself into one cartwheel and a second. When she reached the end of the mat, she turned, bent her knees, and backflipped her way to her starting point. "Oh, yeah!"

There she was in the mirror. Fierce. Confident. Her fist on her chest. "No one's going to stop me. I'm gonna live. I'm gonna live big. I'm gonna be a Wolverine!"

"No, you're not."

The voice came from the doorway. It was rough and husky. Not her stepmom.

Sophie slid her gaze across the mirror. A figure stood right behind her, like an unnatural shadow.

Anger struck Sophie like a hard slap with a hot, wet towel. Who the hell was this? And what gave them the right to burst her dream?

She spun around, her hands on her waist. "Can I *help* you?" The anger faded. In its place came a cold fear that froze Sophie's feet to the floor. The figure was dressed in black, their face hidden by a ski mask. Their hands gripped a rifle.

The person stepped forward. One step, two. Their gait was a little off, like they had a limp they were trying to disguise. At first, Sophie thought the intruder was tall, but as they inched closer, the masked figure became smaller. Within seconds, Sophie was looking directly into furious, bright blue eyes.

The rifle rose.

No.

Sophie's guts twisted as she opened her mouth to scream.
Boom.

Sophie ducked just before the mirror shattered. Instinct, fueled by adrenaline, drove her to the back door. She had to get out. She had to find help. She sprinted. Broken glass bit into her thin sneaker soles.

Boom.

The watercooler exploded. Water sprayed up the wall and into Sophie's chest, gushing over the floor.

The door was right there. She just had to reach it, and she'd be outside. She could run. She could scream. Someone would help her.

She slipped on the wet floor. It felt like an ice rink all of a sudden.

Grab the door handle. That was all she needed to do. This wasn't a handstand or a backflip or a cartwheel. All she had to do was reach, grab, and twist.

Her hand touched the cool metal.

Boom.

The pain was instant. Searing, burning, overpowering. The bones in her forearm shattered.

Sophie's scream faded until it only bubbled in her throat. She lay on the floor. Her arm was bent and twisted, but she tried to crawl away. Every time she tried to move, a sickening wave of pain burst down her side and knocked her back down.

The figure stepped closer. The hem of the dark pants slid up their leg, revealing a stretch of metal instead of skin and bone.

Sophie looked up and met those angry blue eyes again. She knew who stood over her now, though they'd never met.

Click-clack.

The rifle bolt drew back and pushed another round into the chamber.

Sophie lifted her left arm, the one not shattered by a bullet. "Please, no. I know you. I know what happened. It shouldn't have happened. Please."

Again, the muzzle rose.

Boom.

14

L aughter bubbled over the front lawn and landed on the sidewalk outside the Wilder family home, the sound as loud and vibrant as the jet stream from the water sprinkler. At first, Hagen found the cheery sound incongruous with a mourning family.

Three girls ran in and out of the spray, their bare feet slipping over wet grass. None of them could be more than ten years old. The tallest one, and Hagen assumed the oldest, wore a bright yellow bathing suit. The other two wore blue.

A woman sat on a lounger near the front door, a safe distance from the water. Her phone lay untouched on the armrest. Her sunglasses faced toward some point beyond the girls, somewhere far away.

But even with half her face covered, Hagen knew this was Reese Wilder's mother. The jawline was the same. The hint of dimples in the cheeks was the same. In fact, all the girls on the lawn shared the dimples.

Renee Wilder turned her head in their direction, tracking Hagen and Dani as they headed down the walkway. Then, without looking away from the two agents, she called out,

"Hey, girls. Can you drag the sprinkler away from the path? Looks like we got some visitors."

One of the girls grabbed the hose and pulled the spray deeper into the grass. Water stopped landing on the path, but it was too late for Hagen's shoes and the hem of his trousers. The sprinkler flipped onto its side, sending a jet straight into the ribs of one of the smaller girls. She screamed and giggled before running to the edge of the front yard.

The woman rose from the lounger and met Hagen and Dani on the front walkway. She pushed her sunglasses into the springy coils of her Afro, revealing eyes that were red and raw.

"You two must be from the FBI. Susie texted me, told me you might be coming. I'm Renee Wilder."

"Yes, ma'am." Dani pulled out her badge. "I'm Special Agent Danielle Jameson, and this is Special Agent Hagen Yates."

Renee glanced at Dani's belly and looked away. "You two go on inside and sit down. My husband, Pete, will take care of you. We're trying to keep things as normal as possible for Reese's sisters. I need to stay here and keep an eye on them."

"Yes, ma'am," Dani repeated herself but didn't immediately follow Renee's suggestion. "I'm sorry, but I understand you were the one who found the girls?"

Renee grunted. "If by *found the girls* you mean *saw my baby dead on a gym floor*, then, yes, I found the girls." There were no tears in her eyes. Renee Wilder was rebuilding herself from stone from the inside out, but Hagen sensed she was a moment from cracking. "Reese was late. I called around. Olivia's parents were out of town and Taylor's parents hadn't even noticed the time. Finally, I went to the school."

"And the door was unlocked?" Hagen tried to keep his voice gentle. He didn't want to be the reason this woman broke down in front of her girls.

"Since the girls were supposed to lock up, I figured they'd just forgotten. Please…" Her voice cracked. "I can't talk now. My girls…"

She pushed open the front door just as Pete Wilder reached it. He waved them into the house, a phone held to his ear. Renee drifted back to her chair and let the sprinkler spray her bare legs.

Hagen swallowed and followed the larger man through the living room and into the kitchen. *Renee Wilder saw her daughter on display like that, blood everywhere?* The woman was even stronger than he'd thought. Pete Wilder was broad and fit, with close-cropped black hair and square features. All the women in the family looked alike, with dimples and an RNF, "resting nice face," but their man seemed more rugged. Pete pointed at the chairs by the kitchen table and turned away to finish his conversation.

"Thank you…yep…I appreciate that…me too. Bye."

He lowered the phone and slid it onto the table as he took his place opposite Hagen and Dani. "I'm sorry about that. The phone's been ringing nonstop." He sighed, sorrow casting shadows across his face. "People are being very kind, but I just don't know what to tell them."

Dani's expression was the very definition of sympathy. "Your wife said you were trying to keep things normal for the other girls."

"Yeah." Pete leaned back and ran a hand over the top of his head. He had a prominent widow's peak, emphasized by the fact that his hair was shaved almost to the scalp. "Those girls worshipped their big sister. They all want to be cheerleaders, just like…" The words caught in his throat. He stifled a sob.

Dani passed him a tissue. "Take your time."

"I…" Pete blew his nose. "I'm sorry. They know the funeral is less than a week away and that she won't be coming back, but we just don't know how to tell them *how* she died. I don't want my girls going through life scared. Children need to know they're safe."

He looked toward the kitchen doorway. Through the window at the end of the living room, the girls were still running across the wet grass, their bathing suits clinging to their skin. Their laughter rang all the way through the house. The sound of children comfortable and confident in their surroundings.

Hagen could already hear that laughter turning to tears when Pete and his wife sat them down and told them that Reese would never come home because someone had shot her. His stomach tightened.

That's so wrong. Kids' lives should be filled with laughter and more laughter. No one should make a kid feel threatened.

He needed to find the person who'd brought such misery to this house, and he needed to do it fast. "Do you know if anyone in the town ever had a problem with Reese? Or with your family?"

Pete shook his head. "No. Chapel Island has been great. I mean, there aren't a lot of Black families in this town, but we've never felt anything but welcome here. It really is a perfect place to raise a..." His words caught again. Dani reached a hand across the table, a gesture of reassurance. "It's okay."

"No." Pete swallowed. "We didn't have a problem with anyone, and Reese was a popular kid. Everyone loved her. She was a go-getter, you know? Fearless. Upbeat. Always full of energy. She was hoping to land that cheer captain spot last fall, and she broke up with her boyfriend a few months back, she was almost never down."

Hagen pulled out his notebook. "Who was her boyfriend?"

"Tate Sinn. Nice kid, but Reese didn't want anything serious. She was too focused on her future for that kind of thing. She called it off."

A child's scream pierced the kitchen. Pete and Hagen shot to their feet, Hagen's knee banging the table. Just as they were both prepared to barrel to the door, Renee Wilder yelled, "Put down that hose!"

Dani shifted in her seat, redistributing her weight while Pete and Hagen sat back down, exchanging sheepish grins. "How'd Tate take it?"

"He was kinda cut up for a while. Reese felt pretty bad about the whole thing. But she got through it okay."

Hagen made a note about Reese and Tate's relationship. Stella and Mac were talking to the Sinns that morning. If Tate was there, comparing notes might turn up something. Teenage heartbreak usually just meant more moping than usual, but the broken heart of a teenage psychopath could produce something else entirely.

He tapped his pen on the notebook. "What can you tell me about Tate?"

Pete shrugged. "Like I said, he's a good kid. We even went hunting together a few times. He's heading off to college in California soon. I think that's why Reese broke it off. She knew they were on borrowed time." He frowned and held up a hand. "Look, if you're thinking of him as a suspect, you're barking up the wrong tree. They were young, and he's smart enough to know the relationship wasn't going anywhere."

Hagen noted that Pete and Tate went hunting. He underlined the note.

A jazz trumpet blasted from the kitchen table, and Pete lifted his phone. "Listen, I need to take this. The cops have already searched the house, but you're welcome to look around. Anything that can tell me why my baby is never coming home again."

He took the call and strode toward the living room. Hagen glanced at Dani. Both hands were on her belly, and her face was pale.

Hagen leaned close. "You okay?"

"Yeah, I'm fine. Just...when he mentioned his baby never coming home, I—"

"Right."

Hagen tightened his jaw. Doing this job was hard enough. Doing this job when you were ready to squeeze another human being into a world filled with killers and kidnappers and psychopaths had to be a hundred times harder.

Warmth filled his chest. He admired Dani's strength. "You want to sit there while I look around?"

She shook her head. "No. I'll come with you. Just help me up. These seats weren't made for two."

Hagen took Dani's elbow and helped her to her feet.

Reese's bedroom was similar to Olivia's. Both rooms were neat and organized. But there were two beds in this room, both reachable by a ladder, leaving space for the desks underneath them. It reminded him of a dorm room.

Dani leaned against the doorway. "Whichever of those three girls shared this room with Reese is really going to feel it."

Hagen stood in the middle of the room and rocked on his heels. He could feel it already. That absence wasn't going anywhere. "There's nothing here, is there?"

"No. And I don't think we're going to get any more out of her dad. Not today, anyway. I don't think the news has fully sunk in yet."

Hagen knew she was right. "No, I don't think so. We'll check on the status of her phone and other electronics, see if we can find something that might give us a lead." They'd find nothing helpful here. "Let's go."

Pete was still in the living room when they reached the

bottom of the stairs. He pulled his phone away from his ear. "You guys need any more help?"

Hagen shook his head. "If we need anything, we'll get in touch. And, sir?" He paused, then decided to make a promise he didn't know if he could keep. "We will find whoever did this."

Pete looked confused for a moment, like he wasn't entirely sure what someone had done. He blinked as the realization of his daughter's death struck him again and responded with a short nod.

Hagen opened the front door. Outside, the three little girls were still laughing, still running through the sprinkler.

He hated that, soon, their hearts would be broken.

15

The Chapel Island Sheriff's Department looked more like the entrance to a mall than a center of law and order. The long portico, with its thick eaves and arched windows, seemed to promise hot coffee, cinnamon buns, and a wide selection of household goods at affordable prices, instead of long interrogations and hard cell beds. Apparently, the Chapel Island tax base wanted to treat its small police force right.

Stella's stomach had always clenched when she entered the doors of the Nashville police station when she'd worked there. This station seemed to invite her inside to report the loss of her cat and offer to console her with a cup of hot cocoa.

Mac held the door open for her. "Guess we're not in Nashville anymore."

"No." Stella stepped through the doorway. She was met by a deputy who smiled from the reception desk and pointed to the first room in the corridor. "It's worse. Small-town police, big-ass crimes."

Mac grinned. "That's what we're here for. Wouldn't come for the small-ass ones."

Slade was already in the briefing room when they entered. He stood at the end of the table, in front of Hagen and Dani, who filled the first two seats. Hagen looked as fresh as he had that morning, like he'd just stepped away from the breakfast table and was ready to start his day.

Dani's cheeks were red, and her shoulders rested heavily against the chair. Fanning her small notebook in front of her face, she smiled as Stella and Mac took their seats. "Hey, guys. How did you get on? Any cooler for you?"

Stella poured herself a glass of water from the jug on the table. "About as well as you could expect. Want some?"

"Please." Dani slid her empty glass toward Stella as if she were the smoothest bartender in Tennessee. "It was good to get out from behind my desk, but I've got to tell you, this shoe leather stuff used to be a lot easier."

Slade batted his phone across the table, from one hand to the other, absently admiring the gleaming surface. "We do appreciate it, though, Dani. You know I wouldn't have called you in if it wasn't necessary."

Dani gave a small nod and sipped her water. Stella cupped her hands around her own glass. She had never felt a need to question Slade's decision-making before, but she really wasn't certain that calling in Dani *was* necessary. Maybe he was too close to this case, too desperate to see it cracked.

Dani smiled. "Happy to help."

Slade pushed a button on his phone. "I've got the others on a conference call, so now that everyone's here, let's get started. Chloe, what's happening at your end?"

Chloe's voice echoed from the device's speakers. "Very little. We've had a steady stream of parents going into the school to see the principal. The gym's closed, but no sign of any hooded, masked killers."

"Ander?"

"Same here in Petra. There's been a lot of media attention. There are at least three different television stations with cameras pointing at the front of an empty school. It must make for some pretty dull TV, though, because there's been nothing to see here all day."

"Martin?"

"Same. I've staked out cemeteries that were livelier than this."

Stella snorted.

Slade scowled at her. "Caleb?"

Caleb's voice sounded farther away than the others. "Visiting cemeteries in your free time, huh, Martin? That where you get your dates?"

"When I need a date, I just call your mom."

Stella smiled. The day had been difficult and tiring. Listening to Martin and Caleb tease each other helped to push away some of the tension.

Slade brought them all back to the case. "Have you seen anything at Eastchester, Caleb?"

Caleb's deep voice suddenly boomed across the table, much louder than before. "Negative. Just a bunch of worried parents and some pretty shaken summer school kids."

Slade nodded. "Okay. Stella, Mac. What did you learn at Chapel Island?"

Stella took the lead. "Very little that we didn't already know. Neither the principal nor Nathania Burbank, the cheer coach, had any idea why those girls were targeted. Both their alibis seem solid, though we'll check it out more completely. And there's no additional video footage. The school couldn't afford to put in any more cameras."

Slade lifted a hand to his forehead and rubbed his temples. "That's what I figured. The sheriff here is trying to find all the security camera footage he can, but Chapel Island isn't big on surveillance, and you saw where the high school is."

"Right. On the edge of town with nothing around it but trees and sports fields." She pulled a piece of paper from her bag. "We did learn that the four senior cheerleaders were tossed from the team for using marijuana. We're going to check each of them out."

Slade nodded. "Hagen, Dani. Fill us in."

Hagen shrugged. "We spoke to the Mostroms and the Wilders. Nothing stood out. Pete Wilder mentioned Reese had recently broken up with Tate Sinn, Taylor's brother. Apparently, he was pretty cut up about the whole thing, but Pete Wilder thinks Tate's a good kid and knew they were heading to Splitsville at some point anyway. He did say that they used to go hunting together."

Stella tapped her notebook. "Yes. We saw his room. He's got a camouflage curtain and bits of dead deer hanging on his wall. He wasn't there, but I asked his dad if we could see his hunting gear."

Slade fixed his gaze on Stella. "And?"

"And he said no. He got pretty angry when I asked. If we want to check that rifle, we'll need a search warrant."

Slade pushed his glasses back onto his nose. "Dammit. We're going to need more than camouflage to get a search warrant for a kid who hunts in rural Tennessee." He straightened his back. "Look, he's over eighteen. You don't need his parents' permission to ask him for his rifle. And if he refuses, you can grill him."

Stella frowned. On one hand, an ex-boyfriend targeting an ex-girlfriend would be no surprise. But, on the other hand, it also meant Tate killed his own sister, which didn't sit right. "Is that what you want me to do?"

Slade lowered his head to his hand, looking thoughtful. "I

don't know." He paused. "No, not yet. We need to be careful. If he's just a grieving brother, then we're going to make things worse. Let's call it a night. I'll set tomorrow's assignments in the morning."

16

M y mom barely moved from the sofa. She'd sat in the living room all day, just staring at the TV, waiting for the next local news bulletin. She was still there tonight, her legs curled up beneath her, her chamomile tea long cold on the table.

I sat next to her and opened my phone. My group chats were going wild. The FBI was hanging around the school. The place was full of cops. Someone had heard of an active shooter. Someone else was sure the killing was a gang initiation ceremony, and now a different gang would look for revenge.

Snort.

My mom rubbed my knee, careful to keep her hand on my thigh. She didn't like to think about my injury or the accident that caused it. "You okay, hun?"

I didn't move. I also didn't like to think about my injury or the accident. I wanted to rip her fingers away. But I stayed still and gave her a, "Yeah, fine."

My mom tried to smile but it wobbled at the corners as she pointed at the screen. "News is coming on."

I watched the anchor shuffle her pages as the music faded. She announced we would now be going straight to the scene of the shooting at Chapel Island.

The broadcast cut to the same reporter standing outside the same gym building and the same sets of worried parents frightened for their darling daughters' lives. This had been going on all day.

Nothing had changed. There were no breakthroughs. And no suspects.

And, apparently, no new murders.

The news was slow on the uptick.

I opened the games folder on my phone and slashed a flying watermelon with my finger. The juice splattered over the screen.

My mom just kept staring at the television. "Those poor girls."

Ugh. There's nothing poor about those girls.

Those girls were monsters. They were all pretty on the outside, sure. They'd arrange their hair and spend hours doing their makeup. They could jump and split and do all the things they were supposed to do to cheer on their team.

But, inside, there was nothing but darkness. They were all bullies to the core.

My mom didn't know them like I did. She just saw kids like her own getting killed. Mom didn't understand.

She didn't get it, and that was why she suffered. And she did suffer. She even kept a little plastic bag full of tear-soaked tissues on the floor by the sofa. It wasn't fair.

A pineapple arced across my screen. I let it go.

It wasn't right. After all they'd been through, my folks shouldn't have to suffer like that.

Those girls, even dead, just spread their evil wherever they went.

And, soon, Mom would hear about Sophie. That would just make her cry more.

The thought made my tummy ache. A papaya and a kiwi passed across my screen safely. My blade glinted but remained still.

I did kinda wish I hadn't done it. Maybe I'd gone too far. Maybe the gym was enough. The message had been sent.

But was it received?

Sophie f'ing Powers. I'd remembered her from a football game a couple of years ago. She must've been JV captain at that point. Her drab blond hair was in a tight ponytail that pulled her eyebrows up and made her look insane. She was *screaming* at one of her squad members, her face all purple and cruel.

And she'd been listed for the All-State competition, as if she deserved such a privilege.

I split an apple with the swipe of a finger. A banana flew in pieces to the edges of the screen.

Once I'd seen Sophie's name, I saw the big picture. It was right there in front of me, and that's when I knew…

Those first three were just a drop in the ocean.

I was making the world a better place. Making my world a more tolerable place. Someday, even my mom would understand this. She had to.

A kiwi. *Splat!*

Sophie the Slut was just like the others. I'd followed her from her house and watched her go into that studio. She didn't suspect a thing. I knew she was alone. And what did she say as I came in? How she was going to lead some great life, become some great cheerleader?

"I'm gonna live big. I'm gonna be a Wolverine!"

Ugh, please.

A mango. *Splat!*

And what did she say before I ended her cruel-bitch life?

"Please, no. I know you."

Bitch, you don't know me.

A watermelon again. *Giant splat!*

They were all the same, all disgusting. Spoiled brats who thought the world and everyone in it revolved around them. Well, it didn't. We were all a lot better off without the Sophies and Reeses of the world making everything worse.

Yeah, Sophie deserved it, just like the others. *High score!*

I'd felt so much better after leaving the studio, like waking up after a bad cold with your fever gone and your sinuses cleared. Shooting Sophie was like a double dose of acetaminophen and a hot bubble bath.

And, now, I was fine again. No more fever. No more misery.

When I'd gotten back home about an hour ago, I put away that rifle and vowed to never touch it again. I was done.

Then I went into my room and looked at that list again… There were still more girls. There had to be. So happy and so beautiful. And so clueless. And with such mean spirits.

I closed the app, set my phone on the table, uncurled my good leg, and leaned closer to my mom.

It was enough now. I didn't want to see my mom suffer anymore. Let her put all this stuff behind her. She'd soon forget about it, and we'd all move on.

As I put my arm around her shoulders, she gripped my hand and held it tight. There was a tear on her cheek, and she held a wet tissue in her other hand. She pulled me in for a hug and whispered in my ear. "I'm so glad my babies are safe. I'm so lucky."

I hugged her back and nestled my cheek in her shoulder. That's when my stomach started to hurt again. I didn't want to upset her. I really didn't. But she was still looking at them and not me.

I'd stop. I would. I promised myself that I'd throw away that list.

Maybe.

17

Junior stretched his arms and arched his back and wished Special Agent Stella Knox would do something more interesting than hang out in a hotel room. The pain at the bottom of his spine shifted up a couple of vertebrae but didn't disappear. He slid forward in the driver's seat until the discomfort settled into a dull ache.

His eyelids drifted lower. The hotel grew fuzzy. The window of Stella Knox's room dimmed.

A loud snore jerked him awake.

"I wasn't asleep. I wasn't." He snapped his head around, searching every corner of the car. He was still alone.

His tension eased. "Boss catches me sleeping on the job, there'll be hell to pay."

He took a deep breath, brushed the empty cookie packet from his lap, and lifted the soda cup from the holder next to the driver's seat. The cup was empty, but a long slurp of melted ice sent a refreshing chill into his stomach.

"Not gonna fall asleep again. No, sir. Just a little tired is all. That's what spending all day in the car by yourself will do for you."

He took another slurp of sugary iced water and stuffed the cup back in the holder.

The hotel window directly in front of the car was dark, but he knew he was parked opposite the right room. He'd seen Stella Knox lower the blinds almost as soon as she got in.

He'd been a little disappointed when those curtains had been pulled shut. Hoped he might get a thrill for a moment. He sniggered at the thought.

"Gotta get your perks where you can in this job."

That Stella Knox was real pretty. That tanned skin, long, brown hair, and that slim figure of hers. Not too tall. He didn't like tall ladies. Oh, yeah, she was real nice, all right. Shame he'd probably have to take her out, but that was the way of the world. Too cruel for pretty little things like Stella Knox. He'd be doing her a favor.

He checked the analog clock on the dashboard. Almost ten o'clock. He tapped it twice.

Analog. Stupid things.

There were no numbers on this clock, just those confusing little lines. Digital clocks were much easier to read. "Should be lucky I didn't get a car with a sundial, I guess."

He chuckled at his own joke, but irritation at the quality of the car Boss had given him still pinched his guts. First generation Camry. "Damn Toyota's probably older than me. Probably older than damn Boss."

He rubbed an eye and pushed the thought out of his head. He confessed to Boss about possibly being made earlier and had been told to drive this antique "out of an abundance of caution." Junior missed the air-conditioning, the roomy seats, and the digital clock. But he'd just show Boss that he could be trusted, and he could have the SUV back, that was all.

He glanced at the clock again and counted the lines from the top down and around to the left. "Near ten o'clock, huh?"

The hour was getting late. Did that mean Knox wouldn't be going out again?

Junior scratched his cheek. His two-day bristle rasped in the quiet of the car. His mouth was parched despite the melted ice he'd just slurped up.

If she didn't leave her room, how was he gonna get the bug in there? He had to get in somehow.

He opened the glove compartment and pulled out the device. Real clever. Looked like one of those little power strips. Even had a couple of spots to charge a phone but hidden away inside was a little microphone. He just needed to plug it in the wall, and Knox would be none the wiser.

Whatever she said, he could just sit here in the car and pick it up. If she talked about her Uncle Joel, he'd get to tell Boss all about it. If Boss found out that she was digging too deep, getting too close...well, Junior knew what he'd be asked to do.

The thought warmed his insides.

He reached into the glove compartment and took out his Glock, checking to make sure the magazine was loaded. It was. The weapon felt even better in his hand than the bug. He placed it back inside, tossed the bug in on top, and grinned. "And if she talks dirty with that other feller...well, I'd hear all about that too."

He chuckled again and stretched his back.

But what if she didn't come out? What would he do then? Was he supposed to wait out here all night? He didn't like the sound of that. He was struggling enough to stay awake, but if he slept in this seat, he'd barely be able to walk in the morning.

"My back will just be one solid rod of pain. No way I'm doing that."

He frowned. A thought struck him. If Stella Knox was holed up in her hotel room, then she wasn't in her apartment in Nashville.

"Heck, I could drive over there right now, plant as many bugs as I wanted, and she wouldn't know a damn thing." He tapped the side of his head. "Smart thinking, dude. Got some good gray matter in there, after all. Wait 'til Boss hears you figured that one out."

He closed the glove compartment, turned on the engine, and flicked on the headlights. "Now, it's going to be quite a drive to Nashville. Let's see if we can find ourselves a little mu-uu-sic."

He twisted the dial. The radio crackled from a Christian station to something in Spanish to something else in Spanish and on to a station that seemed to only play "Hotel California." He moved the dial until he found Walter Hayes complaining that his girlfriend had broken up with him.

Junior gave a deep nod. "That'll do me."

He released the brake and lifted his eyes from the radio. He froze. In the window directly opposite him with the curtains half drawn stood Stella Knox. The light was behind her, but she seemed to stare straight into the parking lot, directly at him, though the reflection of his headlights glared right at face level.

"Shee-eeet."

Panicked, he slammed his foot on the gas and turned the wheel.

The tires squealed against the tarmac as Junior burst onto the road. His heart raced. He sat straight in the seat. His hands fixed on the steering wheel. He was fully awake now.

"Aw crap, I'm in trouble. She made me for sure. Stupid. Stupid. Stupid."

He bit his lip, and when that didn't ease his fear, he beat the side of his head with his knuckles.

"You eejit. And the way you came out of that parking lot. If she wasn't suspicious before, she sure is now. Must have seen what kind of car you're driving."

Junior gripped the steering wheel again and shook it hard. It wobbled. No way he could follow around a federal agent in a car that had been made. She'd be onto him in a flash. Next time he pulled up near a house where she was talking to people, she'd have him out of the car and in a cell before he could say, "Jack Robinson."

No two ways about it. If he was going to get this job done, he was going to need a different car. Again. That conversation was not going to be fun.

"Shee-eet."

Throwing the empty soda cup onto the floor in front of the passenger seat, he pulled his phone out of the side of the cup holder. He glanced away from the road, dialed, and jammed the phone between his ear and his shoulder.

Boss's voice sounded right next to him, gruff and mean. "What the hell's the matter now?"

Junior swallowed hard. "Been tracking that federal agent like you said."

"If you're doing what I said, then what the hell you telling me about it for?"

"Well, I got a...y'see, the thing is...I...now, how can I say this?"

"Boy, either you spit it out, or next time I see you, I'll stick my hand down your throat and drag your intestines out."

Junior gave a nervous laugh. Boss could be so funny with his threats, but he didn't mean them. Right?

Then why am I sweating?

"You see, the thing is, I need...I probably need to switch vehicles again. An SUV would be good. Or a truck. A truck would be fine."

The phone was silent for a moment before Boss's voice

returned, slow and deep. "What the hell did you do? Did you crash that car?"

"No, no. Nothing like that."

"Did it break down? No reason a car like that should break down. Quality manufacturing."

"No, it's erm…" Junior licked his lips. "I think she might have seen me, is all. Can't be sure now. But she was kinda looking out the window, and I'm pretty sure, I mean, I think she might have, that is, I'm not—"

"You damn fool!" Boss's voice was loud enough to make Junior's ear buzz. "I give you one damn job. All you had to do was follow that woman around and find out what she knows. Dammit, I could have sent a trained monkey to do that, and it would have complained less. How the hell do you get made doing a job like this?"

Junior trembled. He remembered that time when that new kid had come into the office and admitted that he'd lost the guy he was tailing. Boss had gotten so mad. His cheeks had turned white, his hands shaking. He'd picked up the fire extinguisher from the corner and brought it down so hard on the new kid's head that Junior heard the crack of his skull.

Boss hadn't stopped there, though. He'd slammed the bottom of the fire extinguisher down again and again on the kid's face. And when he was done, when the side of his face was shaped like a cereal bowl, he'd pulled out the pin, squeezed the handle, and covered the kid's face with foam.

When he was done, Boss laughed like he'd just done the funniest thing in the world.

Junior swallowed again. His stomach twisted.

Thank the lord I'm doing this over the phone. The thought of doing it in person made his bowels threaten to loosen.

Boss's voice sounded again, slower this time. Calmer. "All right, you'll get a new car. Keep your head down and keep your distance. And don't screw up again."

18

The following morning, Stella received the same text as the rest of the team. *Report to Chapel Island SO ASAP.* After a very quick shower and stealing an orange from the hotel buffet for breakfast, Stella arrived at the station. The first person she ran into was Mac.

The expression on Mac's face shifted from relaxed to concerned as Stella climbed the stairs to the Chapel Island Sheriff's Department oversized portico. When Stella reached the first landing, Mac pushed herself away from the pillar and stood with her hands in her pockets, her head tilted to one side. Her white-blond hair flashed in the early morning sunlight. "You okay? Something's up."

Stella gave her an uneasy smile. She hoped her thoughts weren't so easy to read for everyone.

"No, I'm good." She looked into Mac's eyes, trying to keep her expression neutral. "Just something...I don't know. Silly, maybe."

The worry was still on Mac's face, creasing her brow. Mac jerked her head toward a large elm tree in front of the police station. She took Stella's elbow and led her behind the trunk, away from the gaze of anyone entering or leaving the station. "What's on your mind? Tell me."

Stella rested a shoulder against the tree. The sun had barely risen, but already, the morning heat was prickling the skin on her cheek.

She didn't want to be outside for long, but Mac was right. This wasn't something she wanted to talk about where others could hear. "I think someone's following me."

The words sounded too strange, too absurd when said out loud. She wasn't a drug lord on the watch for law enforcement. She had never been involved in the kinds of years-long investigations her father once led in Memphis, investigations that attracted attention and made enemies. If she had stayed in the police force, that might have happened. But she didn't. She'd joined the FBI, and she hadn't been here long enough to make enemies.

But Mac didn't laugh and tell her to stop talking nonsense. She nodded slowly, her face serious. "You think it's something to do with this case?"

"No. It started when we were leaving for Atlanta. A black SUV seemed to be following us. Then there was a guy in a coffee shop. I thought he was looking at me."

She glanced at Mac, who lifted her eyebrows in a "but was he cute?" fashion.

"No, not like that. This was...different. More intense. He disappeared when I caught his eye. I thought I saw him again on the other side of the road as we were leaving. And last night, there was a car in the parking lot. Opposite my window."

"He was in it?"

Stella shook her head. "I don't know. It was dark, and the headlights were on. I couldn't see the driver or the plates, but I was sure the driver was staring straight at me."

"That's creepy."

"Yeah. I don't know. Maybe it's nothing, but I don't think so. I suspect it's got something to do with Joel, but I really don't know who they are or what they want from me."

Mac squeezed Stella's arm. "Just do me a favor. Be careful, eh? If you see him again, call someone. We'll figure it out."

Stella smiled and covered Mac's hand. She still wasn't sure whether she was right to be worried, but that worry was already starting to ease. "Thanks, Mac. We'd better get inside. I see Slade."

As if to confirm her statement, a car door slammed in the distance.

Mac frowned. "Maybe you should tell him. He'd want to know one if one of his agents might be in danger."

The tension came roaring back. Danger? Until then, Stella hadn't considered herself at risk. The guy in the café had been worrisome. But she was confident enough to know that had there been a confrontation, she would have come out on top.

But she didn't know if this was someone working on his own or if she had somehow caught the attention of a larger organization. Maybe someone had seen her and Hagen staking out Joel. A dark thought crossed her mind. She might have led the bad guys—whoever they were—straight to him.

The two agents came out from behind the tree in time to see Slade marching up the sheriff department's steps. His head was down, his thoughts no doubt buried in the case.

Could she speak to Slade about this? About her father? She'd been in the FBI for less than a month. She didn't want to drop a personal problem this heavy onto her superior's lap this early in her career. Especially while they were hunting for the killer of teenage girls. The thought tightened her stomach.

Slade was open and approachable, but even he had limits.

"It's okay. I'm not there yet. Just keep it between us, okay?"

Mac didn't look convinced but nodded. "Sure."

She peeled away from the tree, and Mac followed. Together, they reached the entrance at the same time as Slade. He nodded a brief hello before the deputy at the reception desk pointed to her right and sent Slade striding at double his usual pace in the opposite direction of the meeting room.

Mac glanced at Stella. "What do you think that's all about?"

Stella shook her head. She didn't want to worry Mac unnecessarily, but her intuition was in overdrive, fearing the worst. "Guess we'll find out in a minute. Let's go."

The rest of the team had already assembled. Caleb and Martin hung out by the front. Dani had pushed out a chair and lifted her feet. The day hadn't even started, and Dani's ankles were already swollen. Mac and Stella took seats near the back, with Hagen and Ander.

When Slade came in a moment later, his jaw was set, his shoulders hunched. He marched straight to the end of the table and addressed the room.

"I've just spoken to Sheriff Day. They've found another body."

Stella lifted her face to the ceiling. She knew it. They'd been on the case for a day, and, already, the killer had struck again.

A flutter passed through her guts. She wanted to charge out of that room, run through the streets, and search every house until she found the killer and dragged them to the cells.

Dani spoke first, "Who's the victim?"

Slade's voice was flat and even. Professional. "Sophie

Powers. Seventeen. From Petra. Cheer captain for the Petra Wolverines football team. She was on the All-State list stolen from Coach Burbank's office."

Ander leaned across the table. His eyes were wide, his face pale. "Wait. I was at Petra all day yesterday. Nothing happened."

Slade gave a small nod, acknowledging Ander's concern. "It didn't happen at the high school. Sophie was found this morning in her stepmother's fitness studio."

The color returned to Ander's face. Stella exhaled slowly in sympathy. In the space of one minute, Ander had mentally lived their collective worst nightmare. To have sat outside the school, sipping coffee and joking with the cops, while the killer snuck in and murdered a girl would have been soul crushing. Stella might be tempted to hand in her badge and gun if it had been her. She was glad Ander didn't have to go through that.

She almost lifted her hand but managed to keep it in her lap. "When did the murder take place? Any witnesses? Anyone in pursuit?"

Slade shook his head. "No. Based on the initial impression from the county coroner, the murder could have taken place as early as six or seven in the evening through about midnight. Her stepmother said Sophie could use the space to practice. From what I'm told, the stepmother and father had an event that lasted late into the evening, and they assumed Sophie was in bed by the time they returned. This morning, the stepmother went to her studio and found the body."

The room was silent until Hagen spoke. "And we're sure it was the same killer?"

"Not officially. Ballistics still have to do their work, but—"

"Could be a copycat." Chloe lifted up her phone. "Images

of the murder scene are floating around on Instagram. Cops didn't secure the scene properly. Looks like some kids took photos through the high windows."

A muscle in Slade's jaw twitched. Stella wasn't sure if his reaction was anger, frustration, or regret. It could have been all three. "These days, nothing's secured properly." He looked up. "Martin, Caleb, Chloe. Head back to your schools and keep an eye out. We have to assume the killer *will* strike again. Don't let it happen on your watch. The rest of you can join me in Petra."

Stella rode with Mac and Hagen on the twenty-minute drive to Petra. For the first ten minutes, no one spoke. Mac drove, her eyes fixed on the road. But Stella, riding shotgun, couldn't tell where the cyber agent's thoughts were. She could be thinking about failing Sophie Powers. Or, perhaps, Mac wondered what she'd find on the girl's phone or computer.

Stella knew, for herself, the tragedy and the job had to be kept separate.

"There aren't enough of us." Hagen's voice behind her in the back seat broke Stella's thoughts.

She twisted around. "Enough for what?"

"To protect everyone. Schools are out, and no one's going to be there now that we've canceled camps. An agent and a squad of cops outside every school in the area won't stop the shootings if the killer hits the girls at their addresses or places of work or where their stepmothers work. We'd need every deputy in Tennessee posted outside homes and businesses."

Mac adjusted her hands on the steering wheel. "Do you think the killer will really try to take out four entire cheer teams? One by one?"

Stella closed her eyes to do the math again. Four teams.

Over eighty-five kids. They'd catch the killer before they finished, but how many would die before then? The thought sent a chill up her spine.

Then she opened her eyes, a realization hitting her. "No. Not all of them. Just the cheer captains. There's only one on each team. The killer has already murdered two. They're first in line."

Hagen patted the back of Stella's seat. "Smart thinking."

Mac kept her eyes on the road. "I hope you're right. But you're basing your conclusion on a sample size of four victims, two being captains."

"But it gives us a starting point." Stella didn't want to sound defensive because, of course, Mac was right. Maybe the killer had a personal connection to Sophie and the Chapel Island cheerleaders that led to their deaths. But they had to find a logical way to track potential victims. The cheer captain angle was as good as any at this point.

Ahead of them, a row of police cars lined up between the fitness studio and the deli opposite it, which told Stella they'd reached the murder scene. Slade was already there, standing on the sidewalk next to a short man in a police uniform. His hat was pushed back on his head, and his thumbs were jammed into his waistband.

Mac pulled up behind the coroner's van.

Slade turned as they climbed out of the car. "Stella, Mac, Hagen. This is Sheriff Bob Day. We've been occupying his conference room."

Sheriff Day rocked on his heels. "Grateful for your help."

His voice was firm and confident. Stella found herself wishing the sheriff's confidence was well-placed. Judging by the results so far, it didn't seem to be.

Hagen addressed him. "Have you got any spare deputies, Sheriff?"

Sheriff Day lifted his hat. "Sure do. I just keep them under here and bring them out whenever the going gets tough. How many do you need?"

Mac stifled a laugh, not entirely successfully.

Hagen's expression didn't change. His poker face was legendary. "At least two, please."

He turned to Slade. "Stella had an idea. We've lost two cheer captains so far. The killer might be targeting them first. We can't protect all the girls on that list simultaneously, but we should be able to guard the remaining two captains."

Stella jumped in. "An Ava Breckin in Winter Creek and Britney Smith in Cotton Grove."

Slade nodded. "Sounds like an actionable strategy. Sheriff?"

"I'll get on it." Sheriff Day turned and walked away. His shoulder twisted toward his chin as he spoke into his radio. After a few minutes, he came back. "I've sent some deputies to patrol around the girls' houses. Best I can do. Now, you folks will want to see the crime scene."

He led them under the police tape and through the entrance of the fitness studio.

The first thing that stood out to Stella was the broken mirror. It was everywhere. Silver shards were scattered across the wooden floor, decorating the practice mat. The busted water cooler, toppled on its side, created a wet mess that embellished the imagery, making the glass fragments glitter like beach stones in the sun. Larger pieces of the mirror, still clinging to the wall, reflected the puddle of murky pink water that covered half the floor. A young lady, not quite a woman, was on her side, one shoulder resting against the bottom of the water cooler.

The girl's eyes were open, as was her lower jaw and the front right quarter of her skull above her temple. The shattered glass behind her was stained as deep a red as the bloody mass of her head. She'd died surprised and terrified. Stella read both emotions on her bluish face.

Above her, where a stretch of the back mirror still clung to the wall, *TOUCHDOWN* had been finger painted in crimson letters.

Stella's heart twisted with both sadness for the victims and anger at what had happened to them. Knowing she could still feel these conflicting emotions simultaneously was a relief. The horror of a room like this still had an effect on her. Years in law enforcement hadn't made her immune.

"Watch your step." Sheriff Day pointed at the floor. "Glass everywhere. Don't want you folks crunching up the evidence."

Two figures stood by the window. One was a middle-aged man. His face was long, and his cheeks were gray and sagged at his jawline. He wore the white overalls of a coroner.

The other man had a round belly, broad shoulders, and a thick, black beard that almost hid his double chin. He wore a Chapel Island deputy uniform.

They approached as Stella, Hagen, Mac, and Slade stood by the door and took in the scene.

Slade waited for the coroner to draw close. "Any idea when the medical examiner will be here?"

The coroner glanced at his watch. "Called Nashville a half hour ago, but they couldn't give me an ETA."

Slade grimaced. "Any idea if the same rifle was used?"

The coroner pulled off his gloves. The latex snapped as it left his fingers. "That's for forensics, I'm sorry to say. I'm here to declare death and help with notification of the next of kin. The rest is left to the boys at the forensic center."

"Any guesses?"

Based on the small frown at Slade's question, he didn't seem inclined to speculate. "Could be the kind of wound a hunting rifle would make at close range—the width of a room. Or the kind of wound a large handgun would make. Again, to be sure, you'll have to wait for the ballistics report."

He fixed Slade with a look and left the studio. Slade watched him go, irritation clear on his face. Once again, Stella was struck by how personally Slade was taking this investigation.

The deputy approached. He touched the tip of his hat. "Sheriff."

"Steve. How'd it go with the girl's parents?"

The deputy scratched his beard. "Not too great, if I'm honest. Her stepmom found the body, but she was fine. Kinda shaken but holding up. Kid's dad passed out cold when he heard the news. Had to call an ambulance for him. We sent a car to notify the girl's mom. That didn't go so well. She had already downed half a bottle of bourbon by the time we got there and threw the other half at our squad car when we turned up."

The sheriff sighed. "Where is she now?"

"She's in a holding cell at the jail."

"Dammit, Steve. You should have taken her to the hospital. She's upset, not a criminal."

The deputy sheriff gave a low, ironic laugh. "Now, I'm not so sure about that. After she threw the bottle at the squad car, she threw a fist at Sergeant Williams. Broke his nose. Our victim's mother now has an assault charge to ponder as she goes cold turkey in a jail cell."

Sheriff Day rubbed the back of his neck, looking like he wished he could rub away the weight of this case. "Jesus."

Slade dropped a hand on Hagen's shoulder. "Take Dani and head to the hospital. See what you can find out from the kid's dad and stepmom. Stella, Mac. You two go to the jail and talk to the mother. We know all the victims are cheerleaders, but there must be another thread that connects them. We need to find it before the killer finds their next target."

19

When Hagen and Dani stepped into Kurt Powers's room at the Petra Medical Center, they found Sophie's father on a gurney with a rough hospital blanket tucked up to his chin. His head was turned to one side, his brown eyes, the same shade as his now-deceased daughter's, staring unseeing at the window and its drawn curtains.

A woman sat in the corner of the room. She wore leggings and a leopard skin top. As she flicked through her phone, a lock of burgundy-dyed hair fell over the back of her hand. Hagen assumed this was the stepmother.

She looked up without lowering her phone as Hagen and Dani entered the room. "Can I help you?"

Kurt didn't move. They must have given him some kind of sedative. Hagen couldn't imagine anyone lying so peacefully after receiving the kind of news this man had just heard.

He pulled out his ID. "We're with the FBI. You're Jenifer Powers? Sophie's stepmom?"

Jenifer turned her phone over and rested it in her lap. The

phone's glitter-coated case shone even in the room's dim light. "That's right."

Dani dragged a chair into the room from the corridor and settled into it. The seat was too small for her.

A short wave of dread passed through Hagen as he saw himself trying to drag Dani out of the chair, her belly stuck between the armrests.

He shook the thought out of his head and turned back to Jenifer. "We need to ask you a few quick questions. I understand you were the one who found Sophie this morning?"

Jenifer swallowed hard. She hugged her phone close to her chest, as though it were her greatest source of comfort. "Yeah. I sometimes let Sophie use my studio when there's nothing scheduled. When they shut down the camps, I thought she could use it to practice. She was always practicing, that girl."

"And you didn't think anything was wrong when she didn't come home earlier in the evening?"

"We got home late and assumed Sophie had already gone to bed."

"You didn't check?" Dani stretched out her legs and then pulled them back again. Nothing about that chair was going to make her comfortable.

Jenifer shrugged. "Kurt was, well, he was more than a little tipsy and went straight to bed. I didn't check because she's a big girl. What a girl does at that age is her business."

Hagen leaned on the end of Kurt Powers's bed. He wondered whether Kurt would agree. Fathers often saw their daughters as little girls forever, and everything they did was always their business. Hell, he still felt that way about his sisters sometimes. "You didn't notice anything was wrong until you walked into the studio this morning?"

"I noticed something was wrong *before* I walked into the studio. Door was unlocked, see. At first, I thought the kid had gone out and left the door open. Oh, I was all set to kill her…" She stopped herself, realizing how that sounded. "That is, I thought she'd…y'know. And then I went in, and I saw the mess, and I saw her. Lying there like that. That was when I called the police."

"Right." Hagen took a deep breath. "And—"

Dani interrupted him. She threw a question directly at Jenifer. "Do you have an alibi for the last twenty-four hours?"

Hagen lifted an eyebrow. *Where the heck had that come from?* He'd never seen Dani get aggressive. She was showing a whole new side, more mother bear than mother hen. He couldn't say he didn't like it.

Jenifer's eyes opened wide. She leaned forward in her seat until her head was almost over her toes. "Do I have a what?"

"An alibi. Where were you for the last twenty-four hours?"

"Yeah, I got an alibi, lady. He's right there." Jenifer pointed at the bed. Kurt exhaled gently in his sedation. "He's my alibi, and I'm his. Or was. My poor Kurt almost having a heart attack and dying the minute he heard the news not good enough for you?"

She dropped back into her seat. But she wasn't done. She scowled and jabbed a finger in Dani's direction. "I'll tell you what you should be doing. You should be talking to Sophie's mother. Ask *her* what her alibi is. See if you can get her to admit that this…this nightmare is all her fault."

Hagen stepped away from the bed, putting his full focus on Jenifer. "You think Marisa Powers had something to do with her own daughter's murder?"

Jenifer lifted a shoulder. A look of disgust came over her face. "That woman's capable of anything. She'd sell her own soul for a bottle of bourbon. Probably sell her daughter's for something harder."

That was a hell of a thing to say. Clearly, there was no

love lost between the two women. "She's got a drug problem?"

"Drugs. Booze. Gambling. There's not a problem you can name that she ain't got. That's why Kurt up and left. And why he got custody of the kid. Woman's seven different kinds of screwed up." Jenifer tapped the arm of her chair. She glanced at Kurt and lowered her voice. "I'm telling you that woman's trouble. Here, look."

Jenifer turned on her phone. She tapped the screen twice and turned it around to show first Dani, then Hagen. The phone displayed a text conversation. At the top was a message from Marisa.

You've turned her against me, and I won't allow it. She's better off dead than believing the bullshit that comes out of your mouth, you sadistic bitch.

Hagen raised his eyebrows. A chill settled on the back of his neck. Sophie's own mother had wished her kid dead right before she was murdered.

Jenifer pointed lower on the page. "Here, look at this one. You can see how desperate she was."

Hagen followed Jenifer's finger to Marisa's next message.

Kurt won't answer his damn phone! Tell him I need my alimony now or there's going to be trouble! I need that money!

Dani glanced at Hagen. "She seems nice."

Hagen smiled, casting a glance at Jenifer. Both of Kurt Powers's spouses seemed cut from a similar cloth. They were only getting one side of this conversation. Jenifer, from his brief interaction, seemed like someone who would say something to provoke Marisa. He could imagine the woman in front of him typing something that pulled a trigger.

He stretched out his hand to take the phone. "Do you mind if I just take a look at the rest of that exchange?"

Jenifer whipped the phone back to her chest. "Damn right I do. My messages are private. You want to read my stuff, you get yourself a search warrant or something. I know my rights."

Hagen withdrew his hand and sighed. "I'll do that."

As he took Dani's elbow to help her squeeze out of the seat, Jenifer lifted her phone again and tapped out a message.

Hagen's eyes met Dani's. Every conversation had two sides, and Jenifer's refusal to show hers told him they'd be talking to her again real soon.

20

S tella walked half a pace ahead of Mac as they made their way down the corridor to the holding cells at the Petra Police Station. She was ready to confront Sophie's mother, but Mac seemed hesitant.

"Shouldn't we have a police officer protect us or something? Marisa Powers has already busted the nose of one cop."

Stella stopped and faced the cyber agent. "You scared?"

Mac didn't look scared, but she did look small between the police station's gray walls. The fluorescent tubes in the ceiling only made her white-blond hair lighter. She seemed to fade into the building until all that was left were her pale pink lips and green eyes. She should have been back in Nashville, safe behind her keyboard and monitor.

But then Mac jabbed a finger between Stella's ribs…hard.

Stella twitched from the pain. "Ow."

"No. I was thinking about you. I just figured you might like a big, burly police officer to protect you. The one who met us at the entrance looked nice." Mac wiggled her eyebrows. "I know you like those big, square chins."

Whirling on her heels, Stella ignored her friend's attempt at matchmaking and continued marching down the hallway. She tried to stop a smile from growing in response to Mac's mischievous laugh but was only half successful.

"Be good," she hissed as they approached a corrections officer waiting outside Marisa Powers's cell. "And, see, we're not alone."

The CO greeted them with a nod, reached into her pocket, and pulled out a key. Her chin wasn't square enough to tempt Stella, but she seemed competent, nonetheless.

The sound of a cell door opening always made Stella straighten her back. It was such a *serious* noise, a reminder that locking people up was serious business.

She braced herself. Stella didn't need a corrections officer —even one with a big, square jaw—to protect her. But the account of Marisa Powers attacking cops did suggest she might be a raving lunatic and could pounce at any time. She positioned her feet at right angles and balanced her center of gravity.

The door swung open. In the corner, on the edge of the cell's cot, sat a small woman with limp blond hair and dark roots. Her knees were pulled into her chest. Her eyes stared at the entrance to the cell.

Stella relaxed a little.

Marisa Powers reminded her of the young woman from her last case, a meth addict who had assisted their killer. The young woman, once caught, had collapsed in on herself. Marisa had the same pinched cheeks, the same pallid, scab-marked skin. But she appeared much more defeated than the mad scientist's accomplice ever had.

Stella turned to the woman holding the door open. "Thank you, Officer. We'll be fine from here."

She walked into the cell. The air-conditioning barely

reached this end of the station, and the air stank of sweat and damp concrete. Mac leaned against the wall as the door clanged shut behind them.

Stella sat on the end of the cot, giving Marisa plenty of room while remaining nonthreatening. Marisa Powers didn't move, but her black eyes remained fixed on Stella as though they were too scared to look away.

"Hello, Marisa. We're from the FBI. I'm sorry for your loss."

Marisa pulled her knees deeper into her chest. Her legs were as thin and wiry as dry spaghetti. If Marisa stood up, Stella was sure that the woman's knees would buckle under her. She pushed a lock of hair away from her eye. "You here to take me to prison? 'Cause of what I did to that cop?"

Stella shook her head. "No. We just want to ask you a few questions. About your daughter."

Marisa gave a small nod and swallowed. From the sticky sound it made, the woman appeared to be dehydrated. "Uh-huh. Well, if you're gonna ask me if I have an alibi, I don't. I was alone all day yesterday, and I was high for most of it. That's the god's honest truth. I never meant to hurt that cop. But when they came, I was already three sheets to the wind, and I…I thought they were just lying to me. I couldn't believe it. I still…I can't…my Sophie. My poor Sophie."

A tear ran down Marisa's cheek and stuck a lock of hair to her face. She sniffed and pushed it away.

Mac lifted a foot and rested the sole of her shoe against the wall of the cell. "Do you know of anyone who might wish to harm Sophie? Was there anyone she had problems with?"

Marisa snapped her head up. She glared at Mac.

Stella braced herself. Mac had touched a live wire of a nerve.

"Damn right I do." Marisa scowled. "My ex's bitch of a

wife, that's who. That she-wolf hated Sophie. She was jealous of her. That's what it was. Kurt, he's got ten thousand issues, but one thing I will say for him is that he loved our little girl. Loved her to bits. That whore of a wife of his couldn't stand it. If anyone was gonna kill Sophie, it would be Jenifer."

Stella took a deep breath. That was one hell of an accusation. "What makes you say that?"

Marisa lowered her legs from the cot and leaned into the corner of the cell. Accusing her ex's new wife seemed to make her comfortable. "She told me so. It's all there in black and white. The number of times she's sent me a text message threatening my little girl. Should be enough for you to lock her up right now and throw away the key."

Mac frowned. "What did she say exactly?"

"Why, you name it. Just the other day, she called my baby a 'stuck up little bitch' who had 'some karma coming.' That's what she said. She wished she could put Sophie six feet under and just call it a day. You take a look at my phone if you don't believe me. It's all there."

They certainly would. "The cops took your phone when they brought you in?"

"Damn right they did. You take a look. I don't care. You read my messages. You'll see just what a bitch Jenifer is, what she's capable of."

Stella pushed herself off the cot, thinking about Marisa's accusation. It wasn't a stretch to think that jealousy led to murder, but they had three other cheerleaders' deaths to explain. Jenifer might have been jealous enough of her step-daughter to kill, but Stella doubted she had a connection to the other victims.

Unless she was copycatting off the other murders in order to get rid of the girl?

The thread seemed to break there, but if Marisa was

willing to let them read her phone—a phone that had to be packed with evidence of drug purchases and maybe some dealing—she had to be pretty sure. Or pretty desperate. Or pretty full of hate toward Jenifer.

Still, it was worth a look.

21

Coach Burbank's list sat on the bed next to me. The sheets were kinda crumpled after I'd stuffed the papers under my mattress, but there it was, one long list of girls' names.

All those little brats so keen to jump and cheer and just be adored? It caused the fire in my belly to grow hotter.

You're only there because I had to give up my spot. You stole my life. I was better than all of you! You keep stealing my life!

I reached for my phone and opened Insta. One by one, I searched the names on the list. There was Kathy Davies, all retainer smile and pinchable cheeks. Camila Morales, hair in bunches, hands on hips. Miranda Pelham beaming at the camera, pointing at the sky.

Putting on a little weight there around the middle. Better lay off those cheeseburgers. Otherwise, they'll be laying you off the team.

I could probably discard Miranda. Life would take care of her soon enough.

Not one of those girls was anything special. They were all going to end up packing shelves in a grocery store or marrying some dense forklift driver and spend their lives pushing out kids and worrying about the mortgage. None of them were going to make it out of their small Tennessee towns.

They, like me, were stuck now. No futures.

No. Kathy, Camila, and Miranda weren't worth my time or bullets. I needn't worry about them. I moved on.

After twenty more minutes of cyberstalking a bunch of nobodies, I got bored and flipped to the last page.

Ava Williamson of the Harnsey Hornets.

She was pretty with that long, red hair, so thick and wavy. Brown eyes. I thought they'd be green with hair like that, but no. Deep brown and wide as an anime character. Made the whites pop. Or maybe that was just the filter.

I flicked through her pictures. There weren't too many selfies. Fewer than most of the other girls. She liked nature, I could see that. There were some roses and some beach flowers. Florida, the post said.

Everyone loves Florida. Just sucks them all right in. Free tans and cocktails.

Not that I could ever walk on a beach again.

The reminder stoked the fire burning deep in my belly. What else could Ava do that I now couldn't?

Cheer. Jump. Run. Swim.

So many, many things.

Ava liked animals, it seemed. There was a goat and a horse. And lots of pictures of dogs and cats. Little Miss Perfect even volunteered at an animal shelter. In one picture, she was hugging a puppy and scratching a cat's head, that sweet smile spreading right across her cheeks.

She wasn't even posing. No, she really was happy.

Her Insta smile was much different than the one she'd given me when I'd gone to the gym one last time to watch last season's championship game. That one had been full of sugary sympathy. Not like she meant it, though. She hadn't sent me so much as a *feel better* text after the accident. She cared more about puppies than she did about me, a fellow human being.

I scanned some more of her stupid story, and that's when I knew the rifle was coming back out of storage.

My stomach turned. Her puppy shots turned to selfies, posey and pretty. Who was she trying to impress?

I hated her.

I know what you're doing, Ava Williamson. You're no angel. Enough is enough!

She was happy. She was truly happy. Those smiles *were* real. She was enjoying her life, sucking up all the good things it had to offer her. She was enjoying the things I should be enjoying.

Right into my marrow, I hated her.

"I was you once."

I whispered those words to myself. They sounded right. I had been that happy, that *involved*, that successful. Before everything stopped. Before everything changed.

It was like there was nothing inside me, just a giant sucking gap swallowing all my joy. And all around the edges of that gap was a fire burning and smoking and raging out of control.

"Those poor girls. Those poor, poor girls."

My mom's words were like gas on the flame. She was downstairs, crying again. Every time the news came on with some reporter banging on about this tragic—*oh, so tragic!*—event, she'd reach for the tissues and ruin her mascara.

It drove me crazy.

I wanted to tell her to stop her bawling. She didn't know those girls, not like I did. They were trash, all of them. Posing and preening, demanding attention, taking whatever and whoever they wanted, leaving nothing for the rest of us.

The fire around that hole surged. Flames roared. I could feel them. They burned so hot.

Mom was wrong. She shouldn't have been crying. She should have been dancing around the room. Letting off firecrackers. Waving banners.

Heck, the news should be declaring today International Dead Bitches Day. *Just grab a rifle and wipe out your local cheerbitch.*

Like this Ava.

Harnsey was only about forty minutes away. I could sit with Mom and Dad for dinner, take a drive, deal with this princess, and be back in time for Netflix and a goodnight kiss.

I grinned at the thought.

So, I would do Ava Williamson next.

Right?

But I'd said I was done. And Ava Williamson, she looked happy. And like she cared. Well, cared about animals anyway.

Was I going to kill a "good" person?

My guts twisted. The fire burned.

Do it. Make the world a better place.

No regrets. No doubts. I didn't care. The fire didn't go out. It didn't cool down or disappear. The flames still raged, still wanted to burn up everything around it.

In fact, the thought that I was going to kill someone who might be good gave me a little thrill of anticipation. The fire was going to be fed something sweet and juicy.

I recognized something inside me had broken along with my leg. I didn't know if I would ever feel anything except this heat.

All I really knew was that my plan felt good.

22

The officer at the reception desk at the Petra Police Station hooked a thumb to the left. "They're in the evidence room."

Hagen pulled the door closed and observed the woman. She didn't look up from her paperwork. She was young, and her black hair was pulled back into an efficient bun. What he could see of her face, though plain, was attractive.

He and Dani had just arrived, and this cop already seemed to know where they needed to go.

"Who's in the evidence room?"

Her pen moved as she spoke. "Your colleagues. Knox and Drake."

Hagen glanced at Dani, who shrugged. Efficiency.

That Stella and Mac were still at the police station was a good thing. The four of them could swap notes and see if anything clicked. Hagen was curious to see what evidence they'd unearthed.

"Where's the evidence room?"

Still, the deputy didn't look up. She pointed to her left

again. "Over there. Behind the door marked..." she rolled her eyes, "*Evidence Room.*"

Hagen offered a smile, which she didn't see because she still didn't look up. He wondered how long she'd refuse to meet his gaze. "You guys know what you're doing round here, huh?"

"Yes, sir." She filled in another blank on her paperwork.

He strode in the direction of the officer's finger, pausing only to knock on the reception desk twice with his knuckle as he passed. Still no face-to-face contact.

The evidence room was the first on the right. The door was unlocked. Inside, behind thick glass, rows of metal shelves stretched deep into oblivion, each packed with gray, cardboard boxes that took up most of the space. Between the high walls and claustrophobic, narrow corridors between shelves, plus all the unanswered questions looming in the air, the place was cramped.

Stella and Mac stood at a narrow counter. In front of them, behind the glass, an officer sat with his index fingers extended, poking at a keyboard. A generally lost expression covered his face. He seemed a little less efficient than his front desk coworker.

Stella held a phone, and Mac was peering over her shoulder, reading a screen that had cracked in about three different places.

Dani closed the door behind her. "If you're looking at cat videos and not sharing, Mac, I'm going to be very annoyed."

Mac looked up and grinned. "Hey, Dani. No cats. Just a big cat fight. Sophie Powers's mom and her stepmom texting each other like a couple of beauty queens fighting for the crown."

"Oh, yeah?" Hagen stood behind Stella and gazed at the screen. Beneath the cracks and around Stella's finger, he could just make out Marisa stating that her daughter was better off dead than...something. He couldn't see the rest.

"We saw some of that talk on Jenifer's phone. Nasty stuff. Looks like Sophie's mom is more generous than her step-mom, though. Jenifer wouldn't let us see her phone without a search warrant. Made me wonder what she was hiding."

Stella lifted the device. "Well, you can see her replies here. It's not worse than Marisa. They're both terrible to each other."

Mac nodded, her white-blond hair filling with static. "Bitches, both of them. Though there's other stuff in here. We've got Marisa begging for more time from someone who sounds a lot like a dealer. Could be fun tracing those messages back."

The officer looked up and rapped a finger on the glass. "Hey, can you guys take it out of here? There's an interrogation room on the other side of the corridor. Some of us have got work to do. Sign for that phone, and you can take it to the other room."

Hagen peered through the glass at the officer's computer screen as he signed the chain of evidence sheet. A web page displayed a recipe for barbequed chicken. He rolled his eyes and led the way out of the evidence room.

They crossed into the closest interview room. A square table stood in the middle of the sterile space with two chairs on either side. A camera peered down from the corner of the ceiling, and a wide mirror took up most of one wall. Hagen entered slowly. It was one thing to be watched and recorded while grilling a suspect. It was quite another to feel that he was being watched while talking about a case.

While he had been taking in the room, Dani had already eased herself into one of the chairs with a deep sigh. After Mac and Stella took the seats next to each other, Hagen joined the group.

Stella slid the phone onto the table. "It's a shame we're leaving the drugs to the cops because, in one message here, Marisa agrees to store something for the dealer in exchange for some of the debt. It was only a couple of days ago too. That stuff's probably still sitting in her house somewhere. Easy catch."

Dani sighed and stretched her back. "Strange. That means Marisa was so eager for us to arrest Jenifer that she was willing to go down for possession. She must really think that Jenifer murdered her daughter."

Hagen spun the phone toward him. He flipped absently through the texts without really reading. Every now and then, a curse word caught his eye. "Or she must really hate her ex's wife."

Stella split the difference. "Could be both. But I don't—"

The strings of Vivaldi's "Summer" rang from Dani's bag. She pulled out her phone. "Hold that thought. Hey, Boss. I'm with Mac, Stella, and Hagen. Putting you on speaker."

"What have you got?" Slade's voice echoed through the room. Its deep tones suited the place with its all-seeing camera and black metal table screwed to the floor.

Dani answered for the group. "Between the four of us, we gained access to text conversations between Jenifer Powers, Kurt's current wife, and Marisa Powers, the ex. The two women have a pretty toxic relationship."

"An ex and the new wife? Would be more surprised if they were best buddies."

Dani pulled Marisa's phone away from Hagen. "Jenifer claimed Marisa said her daughter was better off dead than close to her stepmom. Marisa's phone confirms that. And there's more. Looks like Marisa owes money to some shady drug characters. These texts show Marisa is hiding drugs in her house."

"And Marisa let you see her phone?" Slade seemed surprised by this revelation. "Woman must still be high."

Stella leaned closer to Dani's phone. "I think Marisa's willing to go down if she can take Jenifer with her for killing her daughter. She blames Jenifer for Sophie's death. There are a ton of messages from Jenifer to Marisa threatening to kill Sophie."

Hagen leaned back in the chair. The plastic dug into his back. "A stepmom killing her stepdaughter? Domestics like that are a dime a dozen. But a stepmom killing her stepdaughter *and* three other girls? That's a very different kind of killer. What's the connection between Sophie Powers and the murders at Chapel Island?"

"Maybe there isn't one." Stella twisted her ear stud.

Hagen braced himself. Stella often played with her earring when she was lost in thought, as though her ear was attached to her brain and just needed a little fine-tuning to drag out a new idea.

She twisted her stud harder. "Maybe we're talking about separate individuals using the same type of gun. That hunting rifle is pretty common. Maybe Jenifer saw the cheerleader shootings as a perfect opportunity to take out her stepdaughter. Or hire someone to do it for her."

Hagen glanced at her. "Or maybe Marisa did the same thing. Or someone she owed money to took the opportunity to send a message."

Mac nudged Stella with an elbow. "This goes against the cheer captain angle you came up with earlier."

"Well, that's still on the table too."

"It's actually tighter than these theories in my humble opinion." Hagen shrugged.

"Since when are you humble?" Mac teased.

Slade broke the backchat. "There are still too many possibilities. We need to narrow them down. I'll work on a search warrant for Marisa's house and the stepmom's phone. Stella, Mac. Head over to the hospital and interview Jenifer more officially. Hagen, Dani. Have a crack at Marisa. See what else you can get."

When the screen went black, Hagen turned to Stella. "Feels like a tag team."

23

Stella and Mac strode down the corridor of the Petra Medical Center and found Kurt and Jenifer Powers walking toward them. Kurt's face was pale and drawn. His shoulders sagged. Jenifer gripped his arm. She seemed to be the only thing holding him up.

Stella reached for her ID. "Jenifer Powers? My name's Stella Knox. I'm with the FBI."

Jenifer rolled her eyes so hard her head rolled with them. She kept walking. "I already spoke to your friends. I got nothing more to say. Now, if you don't mind, I'd like to take my husband home."

Stella stopped in front of her, blocking her path. "Ma'am, I need you to come with me."

Jenifer glared at her. Kurt Powers was a tall man with biceps that bulged under the sleeves of his t-shirt. His jawline looked like it could take a punch from a sledgehammer and not even bruise. Yet, he blinked and swayed slightly. Jenifer pulled her hand from the crook of her husband's arm and pointed a finger under Stella's nose.

"You listen to me, you bitch. You don't know who you're

dealing with. You get in my way, and I'll make sure the next thing you block is a hospital bed. Now, move!"

Jenifer Powers was slim and fit. Her leggings outlined taut thigh muscles and strong calves. But there was little weight behind them and nothing to absorb a blow. If things escalated, one good swing and Jenifer Powers would be sliding half-conscious down the hospital wall.

How the currently fragile Kurt Powers would react to the sight of his wife taking a beating wasn't something Stella wanted to consider. Stella bent her knees to lower her center of gravity in case it came to that.

Mac stepped in front of Stella, the top of her white-blond head reaching little higher than Jenifer's chin. A pair of handcuffs dangled from her fingers. "Now, you listen to me, *b—*" Mac managed to bite off the word, but barely. "You can either come with us willingly, or in handcuffs for threatening a federal officer." She tilted her head back and glared up at the other woman. "And if I do arrest you, you can bet the next thing I'll be blocking will be your bail request. Now, choose!"

Stella blinked. She leaned close to Mac's ear. "Mac? That's not how—"

Jenifer Powers stepped forward. She stared down at Mac. She was a good eight inches taller than the agent. Stella tensed her muscles. She'd never seen sweet little Mac get in someone's face before, but her colleague held her position. Mac didn't move. Stella pushed down a smile. There was more to Mac than strong database skills.

Jenifer held her gaze. After a moment, she leaned toward her husband. "Honey, I'm gonna call you a cab to take you home. I guess I'm going with these agents."

Well...this wasn't the way she would have gone about it, but she'd take what she could get.

Stella took out her phone. "Actually, I'll call for an officer to drive Mr. Powers home. The officer can stay with him until our interview is complete."

❄

TWENTY MINUTES LATER, the three women sat in one of the interrogation rooms at the Petra Police Station. Jenifer's arms were folded in front of her, her legs crossed.

Stella had both her hands on the table, her fingers intertwined. She was ready.

"Jenifer, we've seen the texts you sent to Sophie's mother."

Jenifer shrugged. "What of them?"

"They're hateful. Threatening. Nasty."

Jenifer scowled, making her well-maintained face seem twenty years older and a thousand times meaner. "That cokehead deserved it. I could have said a lot worse. I should have said a lot worse."

"Oh, I think you said more than enough." Stella opened her notebook and scanned a page. "I've printed some of your messages. How about this from three weeks ago? *'Your daughter's a bitch, just like you. She's gonna get what's coming to her.'* Or how about this one? *'You keep bothering Kurt, and I'll cut your kid into tiny pieces.'* That was written…three days ago."

Jenifer squirmed in her seat. She adjusted her shoulders. "I didn't mean anything by it. Just wanted to get under that bitch's skin, that's all. She knew it was just words."

"Did she?"

"Course she did. She's a strung-out moron with no more brains than a squashed cockroach, but even she ain't that stupid."

Mac leaned over the table and fixed Jenifer with a serious stare. She spoke slowly, calmly, and her tone gave her words a singsong cadence. "But the courts won't see it that way,

Jenifer. They'll just see you threatened the life of a teenage girl days before she was murdered. All those text messages are a goldmine of evidence. You're in serious trouble unless you can explain a few things."

Stella looked at Mac from the corner of her eye. Mac sat back and folded her arms, mirroring Jenifer's body language.

Jenifer swallowed hard and shrugged too deliberately to pretend she didn't care. Her face seemed to grow paler by the second. The scowl faded away, leaving nothing but sadness and desperation.

Stella turned to a clean page in her notebook, taking advantage of the moment of civility. "We need to know where you were all day yesterday. If your alibi is clean, you'll be in the clear. If there's a gap or you don't want to cooperate, well…we and the courts will just assume the worst. After all, you were the last person to see Sophie alive."

Jenifer uncrossed her arms and dropped both her hands flat onto the table. The moment of civility had fled. "Now, look, I told you people where I was yesterday. I was with my husband. You ask him, okay? You want to bother a guy about the day his daughter was murdered, you go right ahead. I'll have the press, the mayor, the whole damn town on top of you people like a ton of bricks."

Stella didn't flinch. "You were together all day?"

The woman's nostrils flared. "No, we weren't together *all* day. Some of us have to work for a living. Not like you people with your government wages and your fully paid health insurance. I finished my last lesson at one thirty and went home. I told Sophie that she could use the studio for the rest of the day."

"Did you lock the doors?" Mac leaned forward again, her forearms resting on the table.

"The front studio doors. Sophie was in the back. She

has…had…her own keys. I don't know if she locked the back."

Stella noted Jenifer's statement in her notebook. "And Kurt was at home when you returned?"

"No, he was at work. He does landscape gardening for the city. He got home about four, and we were together after that. We had an engagement to attend, and we didn't get back until late."

Stella noted the hours. A small, angry fire burned in her chest. This woman was complaining about *her* government job. Stella had never finished a day at four in the afternoon, let alone at one thirty. She'd had one day off in the last three weeks. And Jenifer's husband worked for the city.

She was starting to hope that Jenifer *had* done it. Arresting her would be a pleasure.

"What did you do between one thirty and four, when your husband came home?"

"I cleaned the house. Read a magazine out in the yard. Took a bath and started preparing for the evening." Jenifer rubbed her eyes, as if she could pull the memory from her sockets. "I just enjoyed my afternoon. Enjoyed my life. You should try it sometime. You might like it if you weren't so uptight."

Mac frowned at Jenifer, looking like a stern parent. "You realize you just told us that, for about three-and-a-half hours, the window of time of death, you have no real alibi. And you have acknowledged you'd threatened Sophie. You know how this all sounds?"

"I'm telling you what I did. And I don't give two hoots whether you believe me or not." Jenifer's voice rose, as did her waving hands. Where her cheeks had been pale, they were now turning red.

Stella bit her lip. Jenifer fit the mold as a *potential*

murderer for Sophie—but only Sophie. She didn't feel like a good candidate for the other three cheerleaders.

Doubt nagged at her about Jenifer being responsible for Sophie's death, too, though. Every domestic murder she'd investigated as a cop had followed a flaming row. A reach for a gun too close at hand. A decision made in an instant and regretted for a lifetime.

Jenifer was angry, yes. But her emotion felt like habitual anger and jealousy, more like an unflattering but benign feature of her personality. Sound and fury signifying nothing.

Still, she wasn't finished with this evil stepmother yet. "Do you or your husband own any firearms?"

"Firearms?" Jenifer frowned. "Do we have guns, you mean? No, not really."

"Not really?" Mac raised her eyebrows. "Either you have guns, or you don't."

"Well, we don't have any handguns. Never saw the need out here. And I can take care of myself anyway."

No handgun, so no sudden fall of the red curtain or fatal flash of anger at the end of an argument. The chances of a family fight dimmed but didn't extinguish completely. Stella pushed a little further. "What other weapons *do* you own?"

"Kurt's got some sort of rifle. He likes to go hunting with the guys in the season."

Stella took a deep breath and made a note. "You've got access to a hunting rifle."

So, Jenifer Powers had no alibi for the time her stepdaughter was murdered. She had threatened the girl's life just days earlier. She had access to a firearm that could match the gun type used to kill both Sophie and the other three girls. That firearm wouldn't be something generally kept at a dance studio. She would have needed to go home, retrieve the weapon, and go back for the murder.

Means and opportunity existed. Stella could even see a motive for killing her stepdaughter, but not the Chapel Island victims.

The door of the interrogation room opened. Slade waved Stella outside and closed the door behind her.

"Got a search warrant for Marisa Powers."

24

"You can save your good cop, bad cop routine for the newbs, Agent. I've seen it all before."

Hagen found Marisa Powers curled in the corner of her cell just as Stella had described. Despite the heat, she had wrapped her blanket around her shoulders as though her bone-thin arms could hold no heat.

Hagen leaned against the barred cell door and almost felt sorry for her. Almost.

Drugs did terrible things. They ravaged bodies and destroyed minds. But Marisa's problems most likely started with herself. If she and others like her didn't say "yes" that first time, drug dealers would have no customers. Gangs would have none of the power they'd accumulated, and they wouldn't be able to terrorize entire neighborhoods. The murder rate would be a fraction of its current level.

If she'd only said "no" that very first time, Marisa might have kept custody of her daughter instead of seeing her raised by a stepmother who hated both their guts.

And men like his father would still be alive.

Whatever shit Marisa Powers was in now, she had only herself to blame.

It wasn't that simple, Hagen knew, but dammit, it should have been.

"That's fine because all we've got is bad cop, bad cop."

"She don't look too bad." Marisa lifted her chin toward Dani, who sat on the opposite end of the jail's cot, one hand resting on the top of her belly. "She's a mom. You can't be a bad cop and a mom. Not the way she's touching that baby."

Hagen shifted his gaze from one woman to the other. There was Marisa Powers, a failed, bereaved mom, wasting away and probably going away too. And there was Dani, an expectant mom, fit, healthy, and with no reason to believe her family's future would be anything but happy and successful.

Two opposite paths. They were so close and yet moving in such different directions.

Hagen snapped his fingers hard to pull Marisa's attention. "She's not the one talking to you. I am. And I can play bad cop enough for all of us."

Marisa rested her shoulder against the wall of the cell. Her dirty-blond hair fell in such a way as to accentuate its dark roots. "You think I care? You've got my phone. I've got nothing else to tell you."

"You do know if the cops find those drugs you agreed to hide, you're going to big girl prison, right?"

Marisa pulled the blanket tighter around her. "I don't care. My daughter's dead. My little girl's gone. There's nothing you can do to me now worse than that."

Dani removed her hand from her belly and placed it behind her on the cot. She arched her spine. The move didn't seem to help. She still winced and kept her other hand in the small of her back. Marisa watched her try to make herself comfortable. She shifted to make room for the expectant mother.

"Marisa, do you know if Sophie took drugs?"

It looked like they *were* doing some good cop, bad cop.

For a moment, Marisa's chalk-white face seemed to pale even more. Her eyes widened, and her mouth drooped open, as though Dani had found the one horror that could trump the misery into which she had fallen.

Almost as fast as it had come, Hagen watched the realization come back to her face—it didn't matter anymore. Her child was gone, and even if Sophie had been hurting in the past, nothing could hurt her now.

She swiped at a lone tear crawling down her cheek. "I don't know. How should I know? And even if I did, I wouldn't tell you. She's gone now. Let her rest. You've got my phone. You know everything about me. Now, please just leave me alone."

Hagen glanced at Dani. Her eyes were fixed on Marisa, an image of all that could go wrong in motherhood. Marisa was right. They weren't going to get more out of her than they would her phone or from searching her house. Certainly not while she was in this state.

The cell door pushed into Hagen's back. He stepped aside, giving space for Slade to slip his head into the room.

"How's it going in here?"

Hagen shrugged. "Gangbusters."

Slade inspected Marisa with narrowed eyes. She'd turned her attention to the newcomer but lowered her head under the weight of the SSA's scrutiny. No one entering that space could do anything to make her life better.

Slade watched her for a moment, his face unreadable. "The police are going to move her out to Chapel Island. Stella and Mac are taking the stepmom there now. We need to meet them. This new murder has given the case a whole new look. We could be searching for two murderers instead of one."

Dani staggered to her feet. "Is that what you think?"

Slade shrugged. "It's a possibility we can't discount. I'm not sure yet."

Marisa chuckled. It was low and throaty, as though it had bubbled up from the bottom of a well, lifted by a sudden release of noxious fumes. Her eyes were open, though the side of her head still rested against the cell wall.

"You're all so cute. Two murderers. You don't think Jenifer couldn't kill all those girls? She murdered my daughter. I know she did. Bumping off three other girls wouldn't bother that psycho any more than squishing a bug."

Hagen turned his attention back to her, curious. "But why? Why would she kill all those girls?"

"Because she's a lunatic, that's why!"

Hagen winced at her shrill pitch. Slade took half a step back, and Dani blinked in the force of the blast. None of their reactions had any effect on the woman on the cot.

"She murdered my little girl! She killed her. She killed them all!" Whatever calm Marisa had managed to muster broke. She ripped her blanket away, throwing it to the floor. Then she screamed at it, as if the blanket had taken her child.

Slade gestured for Hagen and Dani to follow him into the corridor.

Through the walls came screams of "murderer" and "bitch" and, finally, quieter and accompanied by deep sobs, "Sophie, my Sophie."

Slade nodded to an officer, who locked the door. "Let's give her a few minutes to calm down, then we'll take her out. Hagen, what do you think? One unsub or two separate cases?"

Hagen rubbed his right temple. Marisa's screaming still echoed through his skull. "I don't know. Marisa's not entirely wrong. Someone who can murder one teenager can just as easily kill three others. But I don't know what links them or why Jenifer would kill any of them. I just know we need to find out soon because, if we're wrong about either of these cases, we've still got a killer out there."

Slade nodded. "Let's not waste time then. I just gave Stella the search warrant for Marisa Powers's house. Go with her."

25

The evening breeze blew hot air over the back of Ava Williamson's neck, but the grass was cool on her bare feet. Occasionally, the wind took some of the drops from the watering can, lifting them away from the magnolias and sprinkling them over the bottom of her legs. Each droplet gave Ava a refreshing chill that didn't last long enough.

Her mother had always loved this corner of the garden, and never more than at this time of year. The cherry parfait roses were in bloom. Creamy white with a subtle red edging made her think they'd added the color in a desperate attempt to attract bees. The zinnias were bunched together, their yellow petals intent on copying the sun. And there was the purslane next to them, their clusters of orange-red blooms showing off their beauty against the green grass.

Ava breathed in the blooming garden bouquet. As the evening heat dropped, the air filled with their sweet aroma, too thick for a perfume but just perfect for sitting in a lounger and relaxing with a good book. The scent made her smile.

That was how Ava's mother would have spent an evening

like this, with her lounger positioned so her head was almost among the flowers. The parasol would have covered all but her feet, and she would have held a romance novel in her hands to take her away from the everyday world entirely.

"I wish you were here, Mom," Ava whispered. "I wish you were with me now, telling me that everything's going to be okay."

Two years had passed since Ava's mom died, but it felt like two decades, maybe more. Life had gone on. With no other choice, Ava had kept up her grades. She worked hard at cheerleading. She was thinking more and more about college, preparing for the day when she would leave this place and start building her own life. But throughout that time, there had always been something missing. Would it always be like that, she'd often wonder?

She watered these flowers every day by hand, to feel the warm memory of her mother. Just being here in the early evening brought her closer to her mother and made the loss a little smaller.

Ava lifted the can and doused the blooms.

She shivered. It wasn't the breeze. These flowers, which had once made her think only of her mom, now reminded her of the bouquets she had seen on the news. There had been piles of them outside the gym in Chapel Island.

Three girls murdered while practicing their cheers. And another girl, another cheerleader, murdered in Petra.

She'd even met one of the girls who'd been killed.

Olivia Mostrom had been the rising star of the Chapel Island High School cheer team. She'd watched her warmup routine before one of their competitions last year, seen the way she tumbled and jumped. She'd landed so confidently, arms outstretched as though ready to receive the accolades of the world.

But during the event itself, she'd slipped. It was probably

just a drop of sweat left on the gym floor by the previous team, but Olivia's right foot had slid forward as she came out of a cartwheel, causing her to land awkwardly. The team had lost points, and Olivia had limped off, holding her ankle, tears streaming down her face.

Ava had felt so sorry for her. She was happy when she learned about Olivia making team captain.

"It's so awful, Mom."

She carried the watering can to the rose bush. On the nearest bloom, a bee rustled through the stamen, searching for nectar and collecting pollen. Ava took a step back. Her EpiPen was in the house. Better let the bee finish its business before she watered that section. She'd have an hour or two before her allergy kicked in if she were stung, but she was alone and didn't want to go through the reaction by herself.

The headache. The dizziness. The shortness of breath. It had only happened once when she was about six years old, but it had been terrifying enough.

She put the watering can down and took two more steps back.

Her phone buzzed, causing her to jump. She glanced at the bee. The little critter continued to rummage between the petals, still looking for something sweet. She pulled her phone out, looked at the screen, and laughed.

Her sister had sent her a picture with two of their cousins. They were all pulling faces at the lens, tongues sticking out, noses pushed up.

"You clown." She responded with a laughing gif.

The phone buzzed again. This time it was a message in the team's group chat. A few of the squad members had taken to hovering in the field just behind the parking lot, watching the cops watch the high school. The JV captain sent her a picture of the cop car.

The cops are still outside the school. No news, though. Wish they'd catch him already!!!

Ava hesitated, not sure how to respond. The cops were doing the best they could. She picked the smiley face blowing a kiss emoji, which felt neutral and supportive and sent it out.

Just as she went to repocket her phone, it buzzed again with a Snapchat notification. She opened it. A tingle swirled in her stomach. She had a new friend in her life, maybe more than a friend. It wasn't going to lead to anything. She didn't think so, at least. But it was the first connection she'd felt since her mom died, and she was going to enjoy it for as long as it lasted.

She turned so the roses were behind her. She lifted the phone and smiled softly into the camera, making sure the blooms framed her just right. With a push of the button, the image was sent off to her crush.

Hope he likes it. Hope I don't look too desperate.

The bee buzzed off. Ava slipped the phone back into her pocket and picked up the watering can. Her life was on track.

Snap!

Ava whirled, then chuckled to herself for being jumpy as she caught sight of a squirrel leaping from branch to branch, causing a second broken stick to fall to the ground. She lifted a hand to cover her hammering heart.

She should have gone with her sister and dad.

They'd traveled north for her uncle's birthday, a rare chance to bring the family together. But Ava had so much to do. She was assisting the new captain with the choreography for the fall season. And her mom's garden, well, it wasn't going to water itself.

But she wished she wasn't here or that her sister and dad were back. She didn't want to be by herself. Not with all this going on.

She poured the water over the bottom of the roses. The soil darkened but the plant drank greedily, soaking it in as quickly as it left the can.

They'd be home before she knew it, her dad reassured her on the phone last night. "Stick close to home and avoid the school."

With all the plants tended to, she decided to carry the can back to the faucet. She'd leave it by the wall, and she'd stay in the house all night. With the doors and windows locked.

"Just a couple more days...until they're back." She spoke in a happy voice, both to comfort herself and the plants. It was something her mom always told her to do. "I can make it 'til then."

Boom.

She jumped at the sound just seconds before realizing something had stung her leg. "Ow!" She reached down to slap the bee. Her hand came away bright red. "What the—?"

Boom.

The watering can dropped from Ava's hand. Drops of blood landed on the bottom of the roses.

The ground soaked it up too.

26

Marisa Powers's house stood, barely, on the outskirts of Petra. The single-story building had pale blue walls that had recently received a fresh coat of paint. The color shone in the late evening sun. The renovation must have been a rare moment of indulgence for Marisa, a chance to make the place feel like a home using some cast-off paint on a Sunday afternoon.

But the effect was limited. The tin roof was streaked with rust. The table standing on the porch was nothing more than a giant cable spool. One of the windows had broken, the space filled with a sheet of creased cardboard.

Stella pulled Marisa's key out of the plastic bag from the Chapel Island Sheriff's Department and strode to the door. Despite the late afternoon hour, she was glad to be there. She didn't want to go back to the hotel, not yet, not when there was still so much to do, and not when at least one killer—and possibly even two—were still on the loose.

Hagen stopped at the foot of the steps. "Nice catch for a new real estate investor. Could probably buy this place for a song, fix it up, make a good twenty, thirty grand on the resale."

Stella jammed the key in the door. The lock was rusty, so she had to jiggle it. She peered over her shoulder. "You got plans for a second career, Hagen?"

He rubbed his temples, which he'd been doing ever since they'd escorted a freaking-out Marisa into her new cell. "Maybe one day. I heard there's life outside the Bureau. Never actually seen it, but I'm guessing it hands out fewer headaches."

Stella pushed open the door. "I don't believe a word of it. And if there is life outside the Bureau, and if it does have fewer headaches, I don't think it's for the likes of you and me."

She stepped inside. The room was dark. Faded gray curtains covered the windows. They were thin and ripped in places, thick from dust in others. An old mirror hung on one wall in the living room, its silver frame soiled by brown spots. The sofa was stained, the kitchen cabinets had long lost their doors, and the floor was so worn that a good half-inch stood between the top of the old linoleum and the bottom of the skirting boards.

Stella pulled on her latex gloves as Hagen followed her inside. "Fixer-upper, huh? More like a knock-'er-downer. Preferably in a great big hole."

Hagen nodded. "Yeah. Maybe I should just stick with the day job." He pulled gloves out of his pocket. "I'll take the bedroom."

He headed past the kitchen, leaving Stella alone in the living room. She took a deep breath. The air smelled of mold, unwashed laundry, and a faint odor of old cat urine.

Drugs and alcohol. Someone, in a moment of weakness, said "yes," opened the door, and all hell came in.

She'd drawn her weapon countless times when stepping

into drug dens like this. Her father had been killed because of the drug trade. Without drugs, without the people addicted to the high, she would still have her father.

Stella closed her eyes. Enough. People made mistakes. She and her colleagues helped them and tried to make it harder for others to make the same mistakes. That was the job.

She opened her eyes and went to work. She lifted the sofa cushions and peered behind a low bookcase packed with paperbacks and piled with old newspapers.

An empty bourbon bottle sat on the top shelf next to three framed photos of Sophie. Two showed the girl in her cheerleader uniform. Her smile took up most of her face in the close-up. She struck a pose, pom-poms outstretched, in another. The third picture must have been taken when she was about ten years old. Sophie sat on a swing, her legs outstretched, her white tights wrinkled below the knees.

Sophie might not have lived with her mother, but her mother certainly seemed to live with Sophie. The more Stella saw, the less she thought Marisa had anything to do with her daughter's death. This was a house of sadness. She doubted even the most heartless drug lords would go after such a pathetic target as Marisa Powers.

Stella called to Hagen. "There's nothing here. I'll check the other bedroom."

It was clear that no one had slept in the spare room in a very long time. The cheap parquet floor had flaked in the middle, leaving a long, dark scar. The ceiling was water stained and bulged ominously in the middle. Old clothes were strewn along one side of the room. A mattress covered with a grimy, faded blue sheet rested under the window. Another empty bourbon bottle stood next to it.

Stella lifted some of the clothes. A t-shirt had a large vomit stain over the front. A pair of socks had turned from white to dark gray. A sheet of paper rolled into a tight tube was propped on a piece of cardboard under a pair of shorts. Stella sighed. Jenifer had been right to call Marisa a coke-head. She just hoped that Marisa hadn't lied, and they weren't currently walking through a meth lab.

Under a pair of torn jeans, a line of small, black pellets led to a hole in the wall. Stella recoiled. "Hagen. You find a rat in there, you keep it in there, okay?"

"I find a rat in here, I'll keep it for you." His voice was muffled through the wall. "It'll do you good to have a friend. Scoot too!"

Stella chuckled at his comment and that he remembered the name of her fish. Hopefully, their banter would scare off any mice or rats.

She placed both hands under the mattress and lifted. Near the bottom right corner, just past the fold of the sheet, was a horizontal slit about six inches in length and about three inches from the edge.

Stella hesitated.

Something alive could be in that hole. A rat might leap out and run up her arm and onto her face. Or maybe a rattlesnake found a good spot to get out of the sun. She took a deep breath in and prayed for the nerve to do what must be done.

Maybe she should call Hagen and get him to do it.

Screw that.

She held the mattress up with her left hand and placed the fingers of her right hand around the slit. Gently, with a dry mouth and with the muscles in her arm starting to trem-ble, she pushed the bottom of the mattress.

Nothing jumped. A slight *crinkling* sound came from between the springs.

The mattress wasn't a king, but it was an older model double and heavy enough. Stella wouldn't be able to hold it up much longer. She held her breath and slipped her hand into the hole.

Something sharp scratched against the side of Stella's gloved finger. She froze. Slowly, she twisted her wrist. Her fingertip landed on something cold. A spring had fallen out of place, the bottom sticking up at an angle. She breathed out in relief.

Her fingers caught on something soft and plasticky. She held on to it, withdrew her hand, and let the mattress drop to the floor with a loud thud. A cloud of dust rose from the edges of the mattress to settle over the dirty clothes.

The ordeal had been worth it. In Stella's palm was a tightly wrapped block of white powder.

"Dammit." Stella's voice was quiet before she raised it to get her partner's attention. "Hagen."

She'd hoped they wouldn't find anything. It was bad enough Marisa had lost her daughter. Now there was a good chance she was about to lose her freedom as well.

Hagen came into the room. He lifted the package from Stella's hand and examined the contents. There was no triumph on his face either. "Damn. Guess the chemists will tell us whether it's heroin or cocaine, but I'm betting it's not talcum powder."

"Not unless she's trying to freshen up this mattress."

Hagen took in the grimy room, his expression grim. "Some room. Her bedroom's better. It's a mess but not as bad as this. And together with three empty bourbon bottles, there must be at least five pictures of Sophie in there. None in here."

"Yeah. I'm guessing this is where she comes to get high. There's a tube on the floor. It's like she's doing it where her daughter can't see her. Or where she can't see her daughter."

"I'm not surprised." Hagen weighed the package in his hand. "There must be more than half a kilo here. That's a

Class A felony. Quite a risk to take when you've also got a kid to raise."

"She wasn't raising her Sophie. Dad and Jenifer were."

"Right. Still, don't know how you can do that and look your child in the face."

"And yet she led us right to it." Stella shook her head. Marisa had given up. "She knew that once we had access to her phone, we'd find the drugs. That's a hell of a sacrifice. She must have been absolutely sure the texts would bring Jenifer down with her."

Hagen looked at the block of white powder, thoughtful. "Marisa Powers is a junkie. An alcoholic. You ever tried to have a conversation with someone like that? Jenifer was probably just frustrated. Junkies live in their own worlds."

"Not all of them. And it doesn't mean she's wrong."

Hagen tossed the package on the mattress. It bounced and rolled into the middle. The block wasn't big, but it dominated the room.

"But it doesn't mean she's right. Or do you think Marisa's self-sacrifice makes Jenifer a bigger suspect?"

Stella peeled off her gloves and pulled out her phone. They'd found enough for now. The locals could do the rest of the search. She brought up Slade's number, but before she dialed, she turned to Hagen.

"Jenifer's got no alibi. She's got access to her husband's gun, and we know she's made threats to her stepdaughter's life. Sophie's mom certainly believes she did it. But you're right. It's not enough. I don't like either of them for the murders. Let's get forensics in here and get back to base. Square one."

❄

Half an hour later, Slade met them in the Chapel Island Sheriff's Department's meeting room.

"Good work, you two. Sheriff Day is with his team at Marisa Powers's house. They'll tear the place apart and see what else they can find. If they can get Marisa to name her supplier, they might be able to roll up a drug network." Slade dropped into a seat at the head of the table. "I don't think that needs to concern us, though."

Hagen scrubbed his face with his hands. "No, it doesn't."

"Martin, Caleb, Chloe, and Ander have all had quiet days. There's been no movement at any of the other schools. Or at the two cheer captains' houses."

"And no progress with the Chapel Island murders either." Hagen pressed his thumbs into the sides of his temple and rubbed hard. "I mean, that's why we came here, right? And we've got nothing. We've made no progress since we've started."

Stella kicked out her legs, the stretch relieving her tense muscles.

The thought that Sheriff Day was about to catch a local dealer gave her a warm sense of satisfaction. One more supplier off the street meant one less creep tempting people to ruin their lives. It was small, but it was a win.

"We certainly seem to be in a bigger mess than when we started. We've got one more victim, two *maybe* suspects, no evidence, and no connection at all between our *maybe* suspects and the first victims."

Slade drummed his fingers on the table with no rhythm.

To Stella, it seemed like new gray hairs were sprouting among his light brown ones before her very eyes. She wondered, again, if he was too close to this case, given his relationship to teenagers.

He looked first at Stella, sensing her gaze and maybe her

thoughts, then at Hagen. When he spoke again, there was more optimism.

"We *will* get there. Jenifer and Marisa will both spend the night in jail here. We'll have one more go at them in the morning. If we can show that either woman killed Sophie, we'll see if we can draw a connection to Chapel Island. And if there isn't one…well, we'll have cracked a copycat case."

Hagen stretched his neck. "And if we can't show that one of them killed Sophie?"

Slade sighed. "Then Jenifer will go free. Marisa might be held for the drug charges, though they'll probably let her go based on the circumstances."

They sat in silence for a moment, letting the day and their efforts settle down around them. It was a companionable quiet. Finally, Slade stood.

"In the meantime, we need to bring the focus back to Chapel Island. Stella, I want you and Hagen to talk to Tate Sinn, Taylor Sinn's brother, first thing in the morning. We've had trouble nailing him down, and from what I hear, he's driving to California tomorrow, so get there early. See if he has any suspicions about who might have killed his sister and his ex-girlfriend. See if he'll let you take a look at his weapons. Look for anything that might seem off. We need more reason for a warrant."

Stella nodded and pushed to her feet. Today had been a mess. Tomorrow, they'd straighten things out.

She hoped.

27

Stella left the faucet open until her glass was almost full. The sound of running water washed through her brain. Her muscles eased. Her thoughts slowed.

For more than two hours, she'd been trying to sleep. For most of that time, she'd done little more than move the scratchy hotel sheets from one side of the bed to the other, beat the pillow repeatedly, and check the clock incessantly.

Her body ached with exhaustion. Her brain demanded rest. But nothing could convince her eyes to stay closed so she could drift away.

She wanted to dream of her studio apartment, of the bay window above the sofa where she liked to perch, or of the sunset turning the windows of the stores opposite her perch a deep crimson. Instead, her thoughts threw up images of Marisa Powers's skeletal arms, a hollowed-out mattress, and the two pink eyes of a giant rat living between the springs.

Sleep was far, far away.

She turned off the faucet and carried the glass to the hotel window. For the third time that night, she pulled the curtain just enough to see outside. The parking lot was empty.

Stella still wasn't certain whether she'd seen something there the night before. Someone *could* be watching her. Or she could be too much on edge, her radar too sensitive after her shock in Atlanta.

Stella sipped her water and let the curtain fall back in place. She'd always trusted her gut. That tingling she'd get when something was off was usually on the money. Sometimes, her instincts could figure things out and make connections long before her brain could see the links.

No. She was sure someone had been watching her in Atlanta. And she was sure that that same someone had been sitting in the parking lot the previous night.

The thought made her shudder. The water sloshed over the edges of her glass, wetting her bare feet.

"Shoot."

Stella rested the glass on the bedside table next to her phone and wiped her legs with the bottom of the curtain. She climbed back into bed, her brain now distracted by who could be following her and why.

She closed her eyes.

The road to Atlanta appeared in front of her. Atlanta held the answers. She had to go back.

Next thing she knew, she was running, not driving...

The night was black. Her bare feet slapping against the tarmac. No matter how hard she ran, no matter how fast she tried to move, her destination felt as far away as ever.

Two blindingly white beams appeared in the distance. Their intensity burned her eyes and forced her to blink. They grew brighter with the deep roar of an engine. A car was coming fast. Right at her. But she couldn't move. Refused to move.

The car's horn rang. Urgently. Repeatedly.

She was paralyzed by fear.

The honking morphed into a bell.

Beep. Beeeep.

Stella's eyes jerked open, and she took a sharp gasp of breath. If this was sleep, she could leave it.

Her phone was ringing.

"Dammit."

She reached for it on the bedside table. The glass fell to the floor, landing on the carpet with a thump and a splash.

An explosion of anger burst in Stella's chest. "Dammit!"

Ring. Riing.

Stella pushed up in bed and grabbed her phone.

Mom.

What the hell?

It was almost two o'clock in the morning and even later in Florida. There was no good reason to call anyone this early. She tried to brace herself.

"Mom. What's going on?"

"Stella?" Her mother's voice was soft, shaky. "That you?"

Annoyance flared, but Stella tamped it down. "Mom. Of course, it's me. What's wrong?"

"I'm at the hospital."

Stella sat straight up. Her heart raced and hands shook as a shot of adrenaline bolted through her system.

Barbara Knox Rotenburg's voice had the same hushed tone and meticulous transparency as when she'd told Stella about her father's death, about her brother's diagnosis.

Mom.

Stella's breath came faster. She hadn't felt fear this strong when she'd burst into a shack to face a psychopath or when she'd been disarmed by a mass murderer in a hidden basement. Her mom was all Stella had left. She was her last living relative, her only connection to the world outside law enforcement.

Somewhere at the back of Stella's mind, that dark road to Atlanta crumbled into blackness. She blinked twice and forced herself to calm down. Her senses sharpened. The room came into focus.

"Mom, what happened? Are you okay?"

"Yes, I'm…I'm fine. It's Jonathan. He's had a heart attack."

Relief surged through Stella. It was quickly followed by guilt. Stella had never thought much of Jonathan, her mother's second husband. On the rare occasion they saw each other, conversation never flowed much beyond a summary of life in Nashville and a roundup of the Florida real estate market before descending into silence. But he did make her mother happy and content. And that was all that mattered.

"Is he okay?" Stella shook her head. She was too tired. *Of course*, he wasn't okay. He'd just had a heart attack.

"The doctors are looking at him now. We came straight in. As soon he started complaining of pain in his chest, I called for an ambulance. I always say to him, 'You feel bad, don't wait. Better safe than sorry.' The doctors say it probably saved his life."

Stella eased back under the sheets. "How's he feeling?"

The other side of the phone was silent for a moment. "He's…a bit shaky. It was terrifying." She paused. When she spoke again, her voice shook. "The nurse said the doctors will probably want to keep him in for a few days, run some tests."

At the other end of the line, her mother sniffed away a tear. Stella took a deep breath. "Doctors always want to run tests, Mom. It doesn't mean anything."

"Uh-huh. I know. I'm just going to wait here for a bit. Make sure he's okay. Then I'll…I'll take a taxi home by myself and wait." Another pause, this one longer than the first. "Is there any way you can come down? Just for a day or two?"

Stella closed her eyes, not wanting to have this conversation now. "Mom, I—"

"I know, I know. I can't expect you to drop everything and come. You're very busy. Just like your father was."

The comment struck her like a whip.

She and her brother had usually been in bed when their father came home from work, and he seemed to have spent more weekends on duty than off. For Stella, that just made time with him more precious, and she understood now what could pull a law enforcement officer away from his family. That was something her mother could never understand.

"I'm sorry, but I'm in the middle of a case. I can't just... you said he's going to be okay."

Another long silence. "Yeah. He'll be okay. I've got to go. The doctor's coming."

"Mom, I'll call you tomorrow. Let me know if—"

The phone went dead. Stella turned off the screen and slid it back onto the bedside table. She took a deep breath. It would be okay. Her mother had friends in Florida. She had plenty of them. She wasn't alone, not completely, not like she'd said.

She sat up and punched her pillow. She moved the blankets, tossing this way and that.

Finally, she lifted her phone again, and played some soothing rain sounds on her sleep app.

As the clock ticked over to four, she drifted off to sleep.

28

H agen rested a hand against a pillar in the breakfast room at the Harris Hotel and waited. The coffee machine gurgled twice before spitting out a broken stream of thick, black espresso. The liquid settled in the bottom of the cup—the scent of Arabica beans almost strong enough to strip the paint from the walls.

Hagen pushed the button again.

As the machine belched its complaint, Hagen glanced around the room. The morning had barely begun. Only Stella was up, sitting in the corner by herself, rolling her neck, her hands wrapped around her mug.

Hot chocolate. It had to be.

Hagen chuckled. Stella had one of the sharpest minds and strongest instincts he'd ever come across. And more courage than most.

It took some steel to track down her father's former partner. He'd seen her face down mass murderers. He hadn't seen her in a fistfight, but he had no doubt if push came to shove, she'd be right in there, shoving back.

And, yet, she needed her comforts. Hot chocolate being one of them.

One day, when all this was over, when they'd found the people responsible for their fathers' murders and given them the justice they deserved, Hagen could see them relaxing in some quiet cabin in the snow somewhere. The fire in the grate would crackle. The plush rug under their feet would be soft and warm. Stella would hold a giant mug of hot chocolate topped with the lightest froth of hot milk, and he would—

Pttth.

The coffee machine spat into his cup.

Hagen collected his questionable double espresso and crossed the breakfast room and slid his drink onto the table next to Stella.

"This will wake you up more than that." Hagen took the seat across from her. "That stuff will just send you back to sleep."

Stella lifted her spoon and let the froth drip back into the cup. "That would be fine by me."

She did seem to crawl into the morning. They sure differed in that regard. He'd been up since six and had already run five miles. As soon as he'd finished his coffee, he'd be ready to grab the day by the horns and wrestle it to the ground. Stella looked like she wanted to nap 'til it was time to go back to bed.

"You okay? Didn't sleep well?"

"No, my..." She swirled her cocoa. "I don't sleep well in hotels."

Hagen tore open a sachet of sugar and dropped half into the cup. He folded the top of the rest of the small packet for later. There was something Stella wasn't telling him, something bothering her. Well, she was entitled to her secrets. There was plenty he wasn't telling her either.

He stirred the cup. "I'm sure we'll get another briefing at some point in the day. Maybe even two. You can catch up on your sleep then."

Stella laughed, seeming to come to life as though whatever coldness had settled in throughout the night just melted away. "Maybe. But I've got an early start. I'm supposed to talk to Tate Sinn this morning. He's going to be on the road for days. Have to catch him before he goes."

Hagen made a face. "I'm just going to say it. He's leaving before the funerals."

Stella lifted a shoulder. "Right. Odd, isn't it?"

"Very. Let's get going. I'd like to find out what he knows."

Stella spooned some of the cream from her cup into her mouth. She licked a thin line of froth from her top lip. "You think he'll know something?"

"I'm not sure. If we were just talking about the death of his ex, I'd have him at the top of my list of suspects. But his sister too? Plus, another girl? And then *another* girl at a different time and location? That's harder. I think we'll have a better idea when we speak to him."

Stella nodded. "Right. In any case, he just graduated. Four years at Chapel Island High. Plus, with a sister and an ex-girlfriend there, both cheerleaders, he must know what was going on between those walls." She took a long drink of her hot chocolate and put the cup back on the table. "And I'd like to see that hunting rifle of his. Let's go."

They set off in Hagen's Corvette, heading past the Chapel Island Sheriff's Department and continuing along the main road toward the Sinn family residence. In about half a mile, the downtown area would magically give way to rows upon rows of quaint, single-family homes with manicured yards and charming front porches. They were almost there.

When they were just a few blocks out, traffic slowed, then crawled to a halt.

Hagen rapped his fingers on the steering wheel. "What the hell's going on up there?"

Stella opened the window and poked her head out. "Looks like a truck is on its side, and…what is that, tomatoes? They're all over the road. Must have just happened. The blue-and-whites haven't even turned up yet."

Hagen inched the car forward before touching the brakes again. "Great. Now we might miss him." He slammed the top of the steering wheel with the heel of his hand and leaned on the horn.

Stella side-eyed him and dropped a hand onto his arm. "Easy there, big fella. If we're stuck, he can't go anywhere either."

Hagen glanced at the back of her hand. Stella's touch alone relaxed him. Shame from his anger heated his cheeks.

Cool it.

Hagen placed his hands at nine and three on the steering wheel, demonstrating that he had himself collected and would proceed responsibly. "I just don't want to interview this guy by phone. I want to see him when he talks."

"Me too." She removed her hand. "He's probably still in bed. He's a teen and it's nowhere near noon."

Hagen agreed with a small smile and relaxed further, but then a gap emerged between the Ford in front of them, creating a small lane on the right. He jerked the wheel and jammed the gas, bringing the Corvette onto the sidewalk so he could cut the corner. He pulled into the parking lot of a small convenience store. "Let's walk from here. It'll be faster."

His assessment proved correct. They strode past the line of traffic that had now ground to a complete halt. Someone up ahead, who shared his frustration, shouted out of his SUV window. Behind them, a siren suggested police were heading to the scene and struggled to get through.

Stella ignored the noise and focused on the Sinn house up ahead. "Here we are."

The garage on the side of the house was open. An old Ford pickup stood in front of it, its bed half full of cardboard boxes. More boxes were piled next to the back wheel, where a young man in a camouflage tank top and cargo shorts was ripping off a piece of duct tape.

Stella leaned into Hagen. "Guess this teen is an early riser."

"Hope this isn't a case of early bird gets the cheerleader."

Despite her best efforts not to, Stella chuckled.

Tate Sinn was a good-looking youth, almost six feet tall with broad shoulders, skin kissed golden from the summer sun, and muscular arms. Two curtains of wavy, brown hair fell over the sides of his forehead. His face was unshaved, a good three days of light bristles accentuating his dimpled chin. He looked more like a surfer dude than a hunter from rural Tennessee. It was hard to see him as the son of the conservative Rick Sinn.

Hagen had seen guys like this too many times—jocks who thought they walked on water. Hell, Hagen could have been this guy if not for the untimely death of his father, shifting everything. Tate moved with a cocky swagger. College would soon teach him that he wasn't that special.

Hagen pulled out his ID. "Tate Sinn? We're with the FBI."

Tate stared at the badge. Hagen stepped forward, holding it out in front of him. Let him see those big blue letters and that shield. Let that official stuff work its way in.

Tate licked his lips but didn't appear nervous. They were just a little chapped from the sun. "Uh-huh. You want me to call my dad? I think he just got up."

Stella rested an arm on the side of the truck. "Actually, no. We wanted to talk to you, Tate."

"Uh-huh." Tate eyed Stella up and down. He kept his gaze on Stella's face just half a second longer than he should have.

That delay, and the smile that followed, were enough to make Hagen narrow his eyes.

The guy's a creep.

"We're sorry for your loss." Stella held Tate's stare.

"Thank you." Tate lost his smile, letting his guard down at the mention of his sister's death.

At least he had the brains to look a little sheepish.

Hagen pulled out his notebook. "It seems you were close with a lot of the squad. Your sister, for one. I understand you dated Reese Wilder. Is that right?"

Tate bent so that Hagen couldn't see his face. "That's right."

"And how long did you two go out before she dumped you?"

Tate was in the middle of picking up a box. He stopped, straightened, and stared at Hagen. "She didn't *dump* me. We broke up. It just didn't work, is all."

"Right. How long?"

He shrugged. "Dunno. About eight months."

"And did she ever mention anyone who was bothering her? Or her friends?"

Tate dropped the box into the back of the truck. "No. I mean, her friends had guys hitting on them. They were cheerleaders, you know. Kinda goes with the territory. But no one weird."

He reached for a fishing rod next to the wheel. Stella pointed at the box next to it. "That all your hunting and fishing gear?"

Tate unscrewed the rod handle. "Uh-huh. My dad told me you wanted to look through my hunting gear. Something about ruling me out as a suspect. You think I could kill my own sister? Or Reese? Jesus. You really think I'd do something like that?"

He gripped the bottom of the fishing rod in his fist. It sat in his hand like a club.

Hagen adjusted his balance. If Tate got physical, Stella would have to be fast. And so would he. She didn't move, though. She just tapped the side of the truck and tilted her head.

"No, I doubt a brother would kill his sister *and* his ex-girlfriend." She looked directly into his eyes. "Maybe one or the other, but both seem kind of unlikely. We'd like to check your rifle anyway, though. Maybe someone stole it or borrowed it. Maybe you left it somewhere. If there's someone else's prints on it, that might help us catch the person who did this."

Tate weighed the end of the fishing rod in his hand before tossing it over Stella's arm into the back of the pickup. "You must think I'm some kind of idiot. That I'm stupid enough to leave my hunting rifle unlocked where any gangbanger can get their hands on it."

Hagen scoffed. "You get a lot of gangbangers around here?"

"You tell me. You're the cops, aren't you?"

"Agents. We're federal agents."

"Whatever. All I know is I checked my gear last night when my dad told me you wanted to see it. Everything was locked away exactly as I left it. See that gun safe over there? The steel one?" He pointed to the back of the garage, where a tall, slim, metal cabinet stood against the far wall. A brass padlock the size of a man's fist hung from the door.

Hagen nodded. "Yeah."

Tate picked up a closed cardboard box that was bursting at a corner. His biceps flexed, but the weight didn't slow him down. He heaved the box over the top of the pickup and shoved it in place in the bed. "That's where I keep my gun. Lock hasn't been touched. And this is as close as you're going to get to it."

Hagen straightened his back. The kid didn't know everything. He might not know whether his lock had been picked. Someone may have broken into the cabinet some other way.

But Tate was probably right. That was a good gun locker.

Tate stepped back and rested his hand on the side of the truck, as if he suddenly didn't have the strength to hold himself up. "Listen to me. I'm not a freaking murderer. My sister's death is…it's tearing my family apart. My mom, she's…she's falling to pieces, man. I don't know who did this or why anyone would. All those girls were popular. Everyone loved them. Including me. Me more than most, actually. Taylor and me, we were only a year and a half apart. Hung with the same crowd."

His words were powerful, but they would've hit Hagen harder had Tate been talking to more than just Stella.

Stella lifted an eyebrow. "Is that why you're leaving before they're even put in the ground? Is that why you've been "out walking" every time we've tried to speak with you?"

He pushed himself away from the truck, regaining some spirit. "My dad's lawyer said I don't have to talk to anyone if I don't want to. So, if you're not going to arrest me, then I'm going to ask you to get out of my way because I'm out of here."

Hagen hooked a thumb over his shoulder toward the traffic. "In that? I wish you luck."

Tate looked past Hagen toward the road. The young man's mouth formed a grim line, then his jaw dropped.

Hagen turned around, following Tate's gaze. In the traffic immediately outside the house, a taxi had stopped. One of the vehicle's windows was down, and, in the back seat, sat Marisa Powers.

Stella crossed her arms over her chest and spoke quietly to Hagen. "Think she made bail?"

Hagen shrugged. "Her dealer probably covered it to ensure she won't take him down with her later in court."

Marisa waved. She lowered the window and removed her sunglasses. She ignored the federal agents and looked straight at Tate. "Hey, handsome. Didn't think I'd see you again so fast."

Tate locked eyes with her. A hand raised in the smallest of greetings before his brain put a stop to it.

As the traffic cleared, the car in front of the taxi lurched forward. Her driver sped fast behind it. Marisa Powers pushed her sunglasses back onto her face, covering her tear-filled, bloodshot eyes as they pulled away.

Hagen turned back to Tate. "You want to explain that? Handsome?"

29

Tate's cheeks flushed a deep red, his embarrassment obvious. His mouth curled into a line, and Stella could practically see his mind whir as he debated what to say. He exhaled audibly instead of speaking.

Stella smiled to herself. A flustered teenager. Fun. Especially one who had just been so cocky and full of himself.

Deciding Hagen wasn't being too hard on him after all, Stella knocked twice on the side of the truck. "Hey, my partner asked you a question, Tate."

The young man kicked at a rock. "Wh…what?"

"How do you know Marisa Powers? Because she seems to be pretty friendly with you."

Instead of meeting her gaze, Tate bent and lifted another box. Sweat collected on the front of his tank top, turning the camouflage pattern dark brown. "I used to mow people's yards for money. This county is small, so I'd sometimes drive out to Petra or even Winter Creek. Mari…Mrs. Powers. She was one of my customers."

Hagen shoved his hands in his pockets and rocked on his heels, seeming to be as entertained by this turn of events as

Stella. "One of your customers, huh? So, you're saying you, ahem, mowed her lawn?"

"I…" Tate blushed even deeper. His cheeks were nearing crimson.

Stella strained to keep her face neutral and professional. She was enjoying this way too much. "She mentioned something about seeing you again so soon. Have you…mowed her lawn recently?"

Tate slammed a box into the back of his truck and reached for the tarpaulin folded behind the cab. "Look, I turn nineteen next week. I can do whatever the hell I want…and *whoever* the hell I want. I haven't broken any laws, and there's nothing you can do about it."

Stella nodded, acknowledging his point. Tate was right. They might be able to use Marisa Powers's relationship with the boy as leverage if they needed to, but Tate hadn't broken any laws. Even in Tennessee, it wasn't illegal to sleep with an older woman. Not for eighteen-year-olds.

However, he was now a potential link between two crime scenes.

"What about Sophie?"

Tate sighed. No recognition showed on his face. "Sophie?"

"Sophie Powers. Marisa Powers's daughter."

"I never met her. Marisa mentioned her sometimes. But she was never around when I was there."

Hagen chuckled. "That was a stroke of luck."

"Yeah, I feel *so* lucky."

Stella moved her arm out of the way as Tate slid the tarp over his boxes. Once Tate tied down his stuff, he'd be gone. "Did Taylor know Sophie? They were both cheerleaders."

Tate wrapped the rope around the tie down anchors on the edge of his old truck. "Damned if I know. I didn't have much to do with Taylor's friends…after Reese." He wiped sweat away from his eyes. He seemed weary. "Look, there's like a million cheerleaders around here. They don't even have to know each other to bitch, and that's all they do. Bitch about each other. So, yeah, they were probably rivals."

Hagen tossed Tate another length of rope. "You should double that up. You've got a long drive." Hagen's expression was serious now, with no hint of the teasing from earlier. It made him appear more distinguished, someone you could trust and open up to. It was an expression Stella had seen several times in quieter moments. "That breakup with Reese. It must have hurt."

Tate looped out the rope and stretched it over the back of the bed. He tightened the knots on the anchors with long, hard tugs. "Yeah, I thought we were good. But like I said, all those bitches care about is making the next cheer squad. I'll get over it."

"Bitches, huh?" Stella was growing angrier by the second. "That sounds mighty close to a motive to me."

Tate applied the last tie and pulled the rope tight with a grunt. "Then arrest me." He held out his hands.

Stella would give a month's salary to cuff those wrists together and get this case over with, but they didn't have nearly enough on him. Even the judge had refused to sign a warrant, stating that more direct evidence was needed to access his gun. Unlike what people saw on TV, cops couldn't tell a suspect to "not leave town" in the real world.

Dammit.

Tate dropped his arms. "If you'll excuse me, I've got almost a week of driving ahead of me, and I'm already starting late. So, I'll say goodbye to my folks, and I'll say good riddance to this town and to the both of you."

He stormed into the house and slammed the door behind him.

Stella set off ahead of Hagen in the direction of the car, a short walk away. "He's still sore about getting dumped by Reese Wilder, isn't he?"

Hagen pulled out the car's remote as he followed a patch of green grass back to the parking lot. "Yeah, but sore enough to kill? I'm not sure. And to kill his sister too? Hard to see him doing that to his family."

They walked in silence, both pondering family struggles. When they reached the car, Hagen pressed the remote to unlock the Corvette.

Stella opened her door and climbed in. "Prisons are full of people who murdered family members. And from murders of passion. It's hard to imagine someone doing both." She buckled in. "It's odd he knew two of the girls and was pretty darn close to the mother of a third victim, though."

Hagen started the engine. "True. But those connections aren't enough. We can't arrest him for being a *Rico Suave*. We start to map how those girls interacted, and we could throw up a whole new suspect just as big as Tate Sinn."

Maybe there was one person who tied all these girls together, someone with a motive to kill as well as the means and opportunity. "We should probably draw that map. Who do you think would be the best mapmaker for us? Who knew who these girls were friends with and what they did together?"

Hagen raised an eyebrow. "You mean who's the biggest gossip in the county? Susie Mostrom seemed to have a strong opinion about the other girls. And their parents."

"Then I think we should revisit Susie Mostrom."

30

My brain was about to explode. I couldn't believe what I was seeing.

Or, rather, *not* seeing.

I wanted to scream at the TV.

Mom was in the kitchen making lunch. And the news still played in the living room, but it was reporting on a truckload of spilled tomatoes near a residential community in downtown Chapel Island.

No one cared about damn tomatoes or traffic jams! Why weren't they talking about another dead cheerleader?

Ava's story should have been leading the news. Another cheerleader taken care of. Another one of those bitches blasted out of the way, just like she deserved.

The news anchor should have been waving little flags and dancing on her desk. The city should have been declaring a national holiday and announcing open season on anything with a pom-pom.

But, no. Instead, we got a wink and a bad joke about promising to "ketchup" with the reporter at the scene of the tomato debacle later. Even my mom groaned at that, and she laughed at my dad's jokes.

Someone should have found Ava by now. Her body should have been on the way to the morgue. Cheerleaders across the state should have been crying into their megaphones and hiding in their closets, terrified to leave their rooms in case someone gunned them down.

What the hell was going on?

I dropped onto the sofa and turned up the volume. Maybe I just couldn't *hear* what the lead story was.

"Anything more about those girls?" Mom called from the kitchen.

"No." I kept my voice calm, trying not to show any signs of irritation. "Just a big traffic jam. Now weather. It's going to be hot and sunny. Big surprise."

"Oh." Mom punctuated her words over the sound of chopping vegetables. "Lucky we don't have to go anywhere today."

I didn't answer. The weather had given way to the business news. There was nothing about a murder. Maybe the police had silenced the story. Maybe they'd told the reporters not to talk about Ava Williamson's death so they wouldn't scare the other cheerleaders. Maybe they'd done it just to spite me.

I grabbed my phone and flicked through my messages. There was nothing there either. Nothing in my group chats. And nothing on social media. The police might be able to keep the reporters away, at least for a while, but nothing could stop online gossip.

Nope. It was like nothing had happened at all.

I'd driven to Ava's house last evening, casing the place out carefully before finding a gravel lane in which to park. Once I was sure my car was hidden from the road, I'd tramped back through the woods behind her garden. Wasn't easy to walk there, not with my...not in my condition. But I wasn't going to let that stop me. It had stopped too much already.

Ava had this real nice yard with plenty of grass and these flowerbeds that were all in bloom. They must have paid a lot of money to a landscape gardener to own a yard like that. It was so pretty.

I wasn't going to do anything. Not at first. I'd just wanted to watch, to see what Ava's perfect life was like.

And she'd always been perfect. Always had a friendly smile, always surrounded by friends. A kind word for everyone.

But not for me.

Perfect, my ass. Not anymore...

As I watched, she came out of the house, a big metal watering can in her hand. She was wearing a frilly halter top that bared her shoulders, looking like a princess from a Disney movie. I almost expected a bluebird to land on her wrist, gaze up at that long, red hair of hers, and sing her a little song.

Ugh. I wanted to puke.

A police car drove around the cul-de-sac in front of her house, but she was so immersed in her phone, she didn't see it. I ducked low between the trees and watched it closely.

There was only one reason for the cops to be near Ava's house. She lived out in the middle of nowhere. Their sirens weren't on. The police must have been on patrol, watching out for all the cheerleaders.

Because nothing was as important as cheerleaders. They even got their own police protection.

The thought stoked my fury. It just wasn't fair. Who was protecting me?

I crouched lower, though it made my quadriceps ache. I had to be careful. Lucky I was only doing reconnaissance because, if I had taken a shot as soon as Ava had come out of the house, I'd have been in a dozen different kinds of trouble with those cops around.

Because I had brought my rifle with me. Just in case.

The police car stopped for a few seconds before it drove away. I watched it go. Then I rose a little from the undergrowth and turned my attention back to Ava.

She was on her phone, probably texting with her fan club. Now, taking a selfie with the damn roses.

I recognized that smile.

She put the phone away and sprinkled that water over the flowers so delicately. Little iridescent rainbows were created as the sunlight hit the streams. At one point, she stopped to...to what? Admire her handiwork? Her skill with a watering can?

Yes, Ava. You're so talented. Only you can make the ground wet.

That was when she spoke to herself.

But I could only hear "...until they're back" and "I can make it 'til then."

Those words were enough to shoot me with adrenaline. She was alone. The cops had just finished their patrol. But her family would be back soon. This would be the only chance I'd get. It was now or never.

Lucky I'd brought that rifle.

And if I got caught, so what?

I lifted the weapon and balanced it in my hands. I was getting used to the gun, but it was still heavy and difficult to hold. I looked down the barrel and got her right in my sights.

Was I really going to do this?

Boom.

I guess so.

The end of the gun jumped. The sound almost deafened me. A little puff of smoke drifted out of the muzzle, blocking my view. When it cleared, there was Ava, still standing there, watering can in her hand.

I didn't know what the hell happened.

She reached down and touched her leg. Her hand came away red.

Pissed that she was still standing, I reloaded and aimed again. Fired.

Boom.

This time she went down.

It was quite the killer shot.

Her head landed in the flowerbed, as the watering can bounced with a splash, saturating the grass. A deep red stain spread across that halter top of hers.

Won't be bluebirds landing on your wrist now, bitch. It'll be vultures feasting on your flesh.

That was how I left her, sprawled in her perfect little garden.

Dead.

Right?

Then why wasn't it on TV?

As I watched, the local news show ended. An ad kicked in, announcing a sale at a furniture store. If I wanted to buy a new sofa set, there was no time like now.

I gripped the remote control hard in my fist. I wanted to hurl it at the screen.

How come the news wasn't talking about Ava Williamson's death? Why was there no reporter at the scene, pointing out the buzzards circling over that nice yard of hers?

A chill passed through me.

What if she wasn't dead?

She'd looked like she was dead. There was plenty of blood. She'd gone down like a rag doll. But I hadn't checked. And I hadn't left my signature message because I feared the neighbors heard the shot. I'd just hightailed it back to the car before one of them came out or the cops came back.

Maybe she was just dead-*ish*. Or maybe her family hadn't returned, and she simply hadn't been found.

I needed to make sure. I had to go back there. And if she was still breathing, I needed to finish her off. I tossed the remote control onto the sofa and strode down the hall to my room.

I was in there, gathering my thoughts, when Paxton burst through my door.

"Mom said to tell you lunch is ready."

"Ever heard of knocking? Get out!"

Paxton winced and slammed the door.

31

The last time Hagen saw Susie Mostrom, she had been more focused on polishing her porcelain dogs and blaming other parents than on tackling her grief. But her pain had been close to the surface. Hagen had seen her tears when he and Dani left.

He wondered how much difference a couple of days would make.

Beyond the Mostroms' stately home, the midmorning sun sparked off a bend in the river just visible from the house.

Stella pointed down the hill toward the end of the street. "That's the Cumberland River down that way, isn't it? Must be nice to live here."

"Sure. Add it to your list of spots for retirement. I can see you paddleboarding down the river when you're in your seventies. I'll even come up and see you. Bring my swimming trunks."

Stella shaded her eyes against the late morning sun. "You think we'll make it that far?"

"From here to the Cumberland River? We might need one of those golf buggies, but I think we'll manage."

"No, I mean to retirement." Her expression was serious, her forehead creased. She gazed toward the river as though the water carried an answer.

He had never seen her so doubtful, so unsure. "You thinking about what happened with the Curator Killer? The one who took your gun and—"

"No." She took a deep breath. "I was thinking about...we'll meet Joel. Confront him as soon as we get a chance. And then what? What do I do when I find the people responsible for my father's murder? I joined the FBI to find his killer. What happens after that?"

Hagen let her words sink in. The breadth of her determination hit him. She was strategic, playing a long game. "You joined the FBI to find your father's killer?"

Stella shrugged off his question, sending her brown ponytail bouncing. "Not *only*. I wanted to tackle serious crimes too. But I figured that maybe being in the FBI would help." She paused again. "I think sometimes we forget there's a whole world out there beyond murderers and psychopaths."

Stella was so focused. He was going to have to sharpen up. "Why join the Nashville team then? Why not go straight to Memphis?"

She shrugged. "I thought being in Memphis might attract too much attention. Being in Nashville let me use our federal resources without putting a target on my back."

Smart girl. It was exactly why he'd chosen the Nashville office too. Not that he was going to tell her that.

"Stella, let's find *this* killer. When we've done that, we can find who took down your dad. When we've done that...well, you can jump off that bridge when you get to it. Let's go."

He walked up to the house and rang the doorbell.

What would he do when he found his father's killer?

He didn't have an answer. Beyond that wall was blackness. Nothing. Like the view from the top of a bridge at night.

The door opened just as Stella joined him. Susie Mostrom wasn't as well-groomed as she had appeared just two days before. Her eyes were red, and her face pale. Her short hair was tousled as though it hadn't seen a comb in a week. Even the mauve t-shirt she wore was crumpled and loose. It had probably hidden out at the back of the closet just waiting to match the saddest moment in its owner's life.

Susie stared through Hagen before recognizing him. "You're that agent from the FBI. I'm sorry. I've forgotten your name."

"Hagen Yates. And this is my colleague, Stella Knox."

Stella showed Susie Mostrom her ID. Whatever doubts Stella had expressed in the car had vanished entirely. She was back on the job, her face serious, her back straight.

Susie pulled the door open. "Do you have any news?"

"Not yet. We're still following leads. We just wanted to ask you a few questions about the girls on the cheer team. And maybe some neighboring teams too."

He followed her into the house. Newspapers were piled on the coffee table. In the kitchen, crumbs littered the counter and dirty dishes filled the sink. The porcelain dogs looked down on the mess without complaint.

Susie waved an arm toward the sofa. "Please take a seat. I'm afraid my husband is out." She sighed as she collapsed into one of the armchairs by the window. "He walks all day now. He says it helps. I just nap."

Hagen sat at one end of the sofa. A deep dent ran the length of the cushions, evidence of Susie Mostrom's napping, a physical impression of the family's loss.

Stella took the other end. "Does sleeping help?"

Susie shrugged. "Until I wake up."

Hagen swallowed. Move on. The best thing to do for her is to find her daughter's killer.

"We're trying to understand the connections between the girls on the cheer team. We know who's on the teams now, but we want to understand who was on the teams in the past. Who were close friends? Was there any tension between any of the girls? Who else did they hang out with? That kind of thing."

Susie nodded enthusiastically as though the idea had brought with it an entirely different world. "And their parents. You should look into their parents too."

Stella met his gaze. The vindictiveness was clear in Susie's change in demeanor. "Yes. That would be helpful."

"I've got just the thing." Susie waved a finger. "You wait there. I'll be back in a moment."

She left the room and climbed the stairs. From above the ceiling came the sound of a drawer sliding open and banging closed. Then came the sound of footsteps, descending the stairs with purpose and fury.

She sat between Hagen and Stella, caught her breath, and emptied an armful of folders over the newspapers scattered on the table. Each folder was labeled a different schoolyear, and the covers were adorned with a photo of Olivia Mostrom in that year's cheer uniform. On one folder, Olivia grinned through gappy teeth, her head sandwiched between two blue-and-white pom-poms. On another, she wore braces. She grinned with straight teeth, held in place by a retainer in another.

Susie opened the first folder. "I collect everything. Each year, I open a new folder, and I keep a record. I have all her uniforms too." She sniffed. "It meant so much to her."

Hagen rested his elbows on his knees, preparing for a long dig through cheerleader world. He doubted that cheerleading meant as much to Olivia as it had to her mother. He pulled a photo closer. "This is this year's team?"

Susie nodded. She pointed to the blond-haired girl in the middle of the group. "There's my Livvie. She worked so hard to be cheer team captain. No one deserved it more than she did."

Stella indicated the two girls on either side of Olivia. "Taylor Sinn and Reese Wilder. They must have been—"

"Yes." Susie pushed the photo to one side of the table. She opened the next folder, removed another team photo, and pointed again. "And this was last year's. Here's Livvie. She looked so beautiful. Coach Burbank should have made her team captain sophomore year, too, as far as I'm concerned. Of course, it would have been very early, but she so deserved it. But, no, Coach Burbank decided that Alex Brockhurst should have the position. Ridiculous. Then she got caught with that weed..."

Hagen gave Stella his *I'm getting antsy* look.

Stella leaned closer. "Taylor and Reese are in this picture too. Who else was Livvie close to on the team?"

"Oh, she was close to all the girls. They all loved Livvie. She was so friendly, so kind. If one of the girls wasn't getting her jumps right—and believe me, none of the girls came close to Livvie's talent—she'd work with them and help them. Always so giving."

Stella ran a finger over the picture. "What about Sophie Powers? Did Olivia know her?"

Susie shook her head. "That's that other girl out in Petra, their varsity captain, yes? That's just awful. No, I...I don't think Livvie knew her. I'm sure she knew Livvie, though. All the cheerleaders did. They were all jealous of her. Look. Why wouldn't they be?"

She stared at the photo again, her head tilted to one side.

Hagen leaned back again and side-eyed Stella. This really

wasn't getting them anywhere. But going through the pictures did seem to help Susie Mostrom. The color had returned to her face, and the lethargy she had when they'd entered had given way to a new liveliness. Just looking at her daughter's team photos was taking her back, allowing her to spend time again in the world she'd lost.

Susie pulled out a third photo.

Hagen folded his hands in his lap and let her continue.

Stella shifted closer. She clearly had more patience than he did for this sort of thing.

Stella pointed to a girl at the end of the line. "There's your Livvie. Oh, look. There's Taylor and Reese again. What happened to these other girls? Graduated? I can see a few here who aren't in the later photos."

They'd examined all the team photos during the previous days, so Stella already knew the answer to her questions. She just wanted Susie's answer. So did he.

"Well, as you know, the seniors last year got booted for smoking marijuana. The seniors before them graduated, of course." Susie lowered her voice. "And the others weren't good enough for varsity. Those are the parents you should check. I'll give you their names. I've got them all here."

She reached into one of the sleeves in the binder and pulled out a list. "Here. You should talk to all of them. The parents of any one of those girls who got dropped from the team could have done it. I wouldn't be in the least surprised. They can be so mean."

They'd already cleared Coach Burbank with her DNA sample. And the seniors who got booted as suspects—they all had solid alibis. Susie's list of cheerleaders who'd gotten cut might be helpful.

Hagen took it and glanced it over to see if this was different from the one they already had. There were twenty-odd names printed in capital letters. In addition to that, each year had a list of its own, ten or so more names long. There were dozens of cuts, just at Chapel Island alone. They were already collecting similar lists for each school in the county. Those kids would have kids of their own before the cops were done interviewing everyone.

Susie ran her thumb over the photo with all the girls. "Oh, look. There's that Desiree Swedway. She and Livvie were quite good friends. The poor thing."

Hagen followed the line of her thumb to a blond-haired waif standing close to the middle of the photo, one leg raised straight above her head. "Why is she a poor thing?"

"Terrible story. She was very good. Not as good as Livvie, of course, but she was very talented. I blame that Alex Brock-hurst for what happened to her. Livvie said the girls weren't ready, but Alex wouldn't listen. No, no. She knew best. Always did."

Stella tilted the photo toward her. "What happened?"

"It was a pyramid stunt. Desiree was on top. She'd just climbed up when the whole thing wobbled and…" Susie took a deep breath. "Well, down she came. Broke her right leg horribly. Completely shattered. And then she got an infection, and it just got worse. She almost died. In the end, the doctors had to amputate. Can you imagine?"

Hagen shifted forward in his seat. He reached across the table and angled the picture toward him. Though thinner than most of the girls, Desiree looked fit and nimble. She balanced perfectly on her left leg. "Do you know what happened to her after that?"

Susie shrugged. "She took it very hard. She couldn't do competitive cheering anymore. She dropped out of school last fall. Her mother even quit her job to homeschool her. Cheri, Desiree's mom, had a good job at a law firm, and poof. It was all gone. It was quite the tragedy. I hope they're doing okay now. I haven't heard."

Stella lifted the photo with one hand. Her free hand spun the small gold stud earring. Hagen recognized the gesture. She had an instinct. "Do they still live around here?"

"Oh, yes. They're still here in Chapel Island."

"Do you ever check in on them?"

Susie put the picture back in the folder and closed the cover. "No, I…well, it was just too sad to be around the Swedways after Desiree's accident. They were always so down. And that poor girl, she really didn't want to be friends with the squad members anymore. I think it probably reminded her of what she had lost, you know?"

Motive.

Stella's expression hadn't changed. But she had to be thinking the same thing he was. They needed to talk to Desiree.

He picked up the folders. "Do you mind if we keep these?"

"Not at all. That was why I brought them down." Susie waved a hand. "Those are copies. I keep backups of everything."

Hagen held off from raising his eyebrows. As if keeping and storing all this information wasn't enough. Susie also kept copies?

"Thank you. We'll take a look through it all and see if there's anything useful here."

"I'm sure there will be." She poked a finger into Hagen's arm. "You talk to those parents. I'm telling you that's where you should be looking. Some of those mothers are just terrible. It wouldn't surprise me at all if one of them hadn't done this to give their own loser daughter a chance."

Hagen blinked.

Loser daughter.

Even now, Susie Mostrom could talk that way about other people's kids.

He would give her the benefit of the doubt. It was the grief talking. It had to be.

As he stood, Stella also pushed to her feet. "Thank you for your help. And, again, we're very sorry for your loss."

Susie showed them out, stopping when she reached the door. "You know, now that you've brought me down memory lane, I do wish I'd been a better friend to the Swedways. I wonder how Desiree is getting on. I think everyone just lost touch with her after the accident, what with cheer keeping them so busy and all." She shook her head and continued, more to herself than to Hagen and Stella. "Lost her leg. Just her leg. Lucky girl."

They left Susie standing in the doorway and climbed back into the car.

Hagen passed Stella the latest list and gunned the engine. "Let's go talk to Desiree."

32

Ava Williamson blinked twice. She was lying on her side. The damp soil was rough on her cheek and rubbed against her temple. Her entire body ached.

Worst sleep ever.

She slid a hand across the…grass? Where was she?

"Aaagh!"

An explosion of pain burst from her shoulder as she attempted to push herself up. It tore across her chest and ended in a sharp stab on the top of her thigh.

Ava groaned. She stopped trying to move. Her fingertips remained buried in the dirt.

"What…happened…?"

Her voice was weak. Just whispering aloud made her breathless.

She had been watering the plants. She remembered that much. There had been a bang, like a car backfiring. Pain in her leg. She thought she'd been stung, that she'd have to rush for her EpiPen, but there was blood on her leg. It ran from under her pocket. Too much blood.

A second bang, and she had spun around like someone

had smacked her in the shoulder with a sledgehammer. That was when the world turned black.

She panted. Breathing was hard and took more effort than normal. She barely had the energy to keep her eyes open, let alone talk or call for help. But hearing her own voice eased the strain in her chest. As long as she could hear herself, she was alive.

"How long...?" She coughed. There was a coppery taste at the back of her throat.

That can't be good.

She tried again. "How...how long have I been out?"

No one answered her.

Ava turned her wrist to look at her watch. Pain again. It rolled up her arm like a tsunami and crashed deep inside her shoulder.

She gasped and looked down.

Now, she understood. One side of her body was covered in blood. A red stain spread across the top of her chest, ran under her neck, and onto the ground. The dark patch beneath her cheek had the same thick, coppery smell she could taste.

A tremble grew from somewhere deep in her chest and made her entire body shake. Tears filled her eyes. *What happened?*

The answer came with the question. She'd been shot. Just like those other girls.

Panic attacked her, shortening her breath. The shooter might still be out there. Maybe they were watching, waiting for her move before shooting again.

"Oh, god. No."

She twisted her neck, ignoring the pain that blasted through her from even that miniscule movement. The tree line behind the house was empty. The road was clear. If someone was hiding out there, somewhere, they were well hidden. And her watch said it was nearly noon. She must have been outside all night and all morning. Surely, the killer was long gone.

Relief pacified her like a warm bath. She was going to be okay. She had to be.

Help, that was what she needed now.

Ava swallowed. She tried to push herself up. Again, pain tore down her body, slapping her to the ground.

"Okay, calm down." Her breath came in pants again. "I just need to call for help. An ambulance. It'll just take a few minutes. I can make it 'til then. Just need my phone."

She moved her arm again. The pain roared. She closed her eyes and ignored it. Her hand dragged across the sticky earth. More pain. She took a deep breath.

Keep going!

Inch by inch, she hauled her hand toward the pocket of her shorts. Each movement made the agonizing pain burning in her shoulder worse. Her breath came in shorter and shorter gasps.

She had to get there. She had to call for help. It was her only chance.

She rolled her hip, anything to bring her phone closer. The flame in her shoulder burned hotter as did the pain in her leg.

"Aaagh!"

Ava groaned. But she had no choice. She gritted her teeth and squinted through the pain as she shoved her hand in her pocket.

She was there. The back of the phone was solid against her fingers through the thin cloth of her shorts.

Ava breathed out in relief.

Just a little more now. Pull it out. Call. Help will be here soon. You're almost there.

She took a deep breath and lifted her shoulder. The pain

was unbearable—like a red-hot brand rammed onto her chest. Her arm was almost numb, but she could do this. Her fingertips landed on the top of her phone. Her middle and index fingers grasped the device.

Easy now. Easy.

She pulled. The pain burned down her arm.

Keep going. Pull!

She gripped tighter. She tugged. The phone wouldn't come. Why wouldn't it come?

Pull harder!

"Aaaagh."

With a scream, she tightened her grip and yanked hard. The phone slipped out of her pocket, slid down the front of her shorts, and landed on the grass.

Ava froze as reality hit.

Smashed.

The glass was shattered. One side of the phone was bent and twisted where the bullet had struck before grazing across Ava's thigh. The screen was black and would stay black forever.

Ava let her head fall back onto the blood-soaked earth. She sobbed.

"I'm going to die here. I'm going to die."

Her tears fell heavier. Drop by drop, they watered a rage that grew in her gut.

Enough. You're not going to die. I won't let you.

The house had a landline. She could call from there. She just had to get to the kitchen. That was all. She could do it. She *would* do it.

She rolled onto her stomach and pushed herself to her knees with her left arm. The pain was almost blinding, and, for a moment, it felt as if the football punter heaved his boot into her chest before stomping on her leg.

She took a deep breath, steadying herself. The flowerbed

with the zinnias was just two yards away. It may as well have been two miles. Leaving the remains of her phone in the grass, she crawled. Each movement tore at her shoulder. Her leg tingled as though she were crawling over frayed electrical wires lined with broken glass. Ava pulled herself forward until the petals were parallel with her cheek.

"Keep going. Go!"

Ava crawled on. She reached the circle of flowers and collapsed onto her chest. Sweat ran down her neck and turned the dried blood on her shoulder into a sticky river. The fire in her arm scorched.

Forward. One inch at a time. Let's go.

From the flowers, it was just five yards in the shade to the trunk of the apple tree. She crawled on. She could get there. She could. The tree was just three yards away now. Two. She was there. Almost home.

She reached the roots. Again, she collapsed onto her chest. One side of her body was almost numb. But she was more than halfway across the garden. Not much farther now. She wouldn't close her eyes again. Not 'til help came.

"Rest. Deep breaths now. Collect your strength."

Her eyes closed, anyway, as if they had a mind of their own. Her head swam like she'd fallen into a rolling sea and could sink forever. So warm. So welcoming.

She snapped her eyes open. Fear washed through her. That place was too good. She wasn't sure she would ever come back from it.

Ava pushed herself back up. Her right arm bent and collapsed.

More agony. As if her body had been dipped in burning tar.

Move!

She dug into the ground with her elbow.

"There. Now, move!"

She pushed again. The door was two yards away. Now one. She was almost there. The back door must have blown closed, but it didn't lock automatically.

She reached for the handle. The door clicked open.

Yes!

But the pain had become her entire universe. It filled her body and left her floating in a burning ball of agony. With one last heave, she pushed herself inside and fell onto the kitchen floor.

"I did—"

The world turned black.

33

To Stella, the Swedways' house on Lynwood Drive looked like it had sat there, abandoned, for a good fifty years. Some of the wooden siding was crooked. The gable under the eave was missing a couple of small, decorative pillars, and the window frames had old-fashioned cornices. The only visible renovation to the house was a pair of steel rails lining the stairs to the front porch.

Stella couldn't help but lay a hand on one of those rails as she approached the door. She wondered if Desiree was bitter about the need for that assistance. Someone who had prided herself on her athletic ability now needed help to climb the steps to her own front door. Stella strummed the galvanized steel with her nails.

She waited for Hagen to join her before she knocked. The door opened almost immediately, revealing a man who was likely in his late forties but looked almost a decade older. Dark half-moons weighed down the tops of his pale cheeks. His brown hair had turned mostly gray, and his polo shirt and slacks suggested that he'd taken on the role of a middle-aged father early.

Stella pulled out her ID. "Harlan Swedway? I'm FBI Special Agent Knox."

"Yes, that's right." The man stared at Stella's ID. His face paled. One hand flew to his chest. "Oh my god. Is it...? Are you here to tell me...? No, please. No. She's not dead. She can't be."

Stella jammed her ID back into her pocket as if she'd accidentally smacked him in the face with it. Of course, he would be concerned his former cheerleader daughter would be hurt and assume the worst at the FBI's presence. With all the news coverage, none of these cheerleading families could rest easy.

"Everything's fine, sir." She reached for his arm to steady him. "Do you have reason to be concerned about your daughter? About Desiree?"

He leaned against the edge of the door. "Yes, my daughter. Desiree went out about half an hour ago. She skipped out on lunch and she's not answering her phone. When I saw you were from the FBI, I just...I'm sorry. The news has us all on edge."

Hagen stepped forward. "She probably just put her phone on silent. Or maybe she didn't want to answer while she was driving. I'm sure there's nothing to worry about."

Harlan gave them both an uneasy smile. "I hope you're right. I tried to tell my son that. But ever since she left, he's been in tears."

He stepped to one side, allowing them to enter. At the other end of the living room, a boy stood in the doorway of the kitchen. His face was half hidden as he gripped the doorjamb. Tears streaked his cheeks, and his bottom lip stuck out, trembling.

Stella frowned. That was a big reaction from a kid whose sister went out midday. And this kid wasn't a toddler. He must have been about nine or ten years old, much too big to be this worried.

Unless he knew something.

"We did come to talk to Desiree. Do you know when she might be back?"

Harlan shook his head. "I didn't even know she'd left until a few minutes ago."

The young boy's eyes remained fixed on Stella. A weight grew heavier in her stomach.

Hagen had seen it too. His gaze was fixed on the boy, his expression serious.

Something was wrong. Very wrong.

Stella placed a casual hand on the doorframe and turned to Harlan. "We need to ask her a few questions about her time on the cheer team. But as she's not here, I wonder if we could chat with you and your son? Do you think that would be okay?"

Harlan shoved a hand through his hair. "Sure. If it's about the cheerleaders, anything."

He opened the door wider and stepped aside.

The living room had seen better days. A box of tissues balanced on the worn arm of a floral-patterned sofa. Another box sat empty on the floor next to an armchair. Someone had pushed an old card table into a corner of the room to serve as a desk. The surface was covered with textbooks, a pad of paper, and an overstuffed stationery cup with more pencils than even an art student would need. Stella supposed this was where Desiree was homeschooled.

On the wall, a television broadcasted the local news. A kid from Chapel Island had won some Lego building contest. His castle had four square towers, a multicolored wall, and a bunch of happy looking archers.

Stella watched until the news switched to the weather report. There was nothing about their case. That reporters had no information about more victims was a welcome relief, but there were also no reports on the arrest of the perp. Because the killer was still out there.

She sat on the sofa and waved for the boy to come join her.

He rubbed an eye and looked at his dad, who nodded. The boy pushed himself away from the door and took the cushion next to Stella.

His spot in the kitchen doorway was immediately filled by his mother, who leaned against the jamb and wiped her hands on a dishcloth.

Harlan joined her. "This is Cheri, my wife." He stroked her arm. "They're from the FBI, honey, but there's nothing to worry about. They wanted to talk to Desiree about the cheerleaders, but since she's not here, they're just going to ask us some questions."

Cheri Swedway's face darkened as though an expectant horror had arrived at last. Stella waved both parents over. Harlan took the armchair, and Cheri sat next to her son at the other end of the sofa.

Hagen squatted in front of the boy. "What's your name, son?"

The boy wiped his nose on the back of his hand. "Paxton."

"How old are you, Paxton?"

"Nine."

"Nine, huh? Big lad. Bet you're brave too."

Paxton didn't react.

Stella moved the box of tissues onto the table and rested her hand on the sofa's armrest. She hadn't seen Hagen talk to a kid before. The way he was talking down to him suggested he hadn't done it very often.

Hagen tried again. "Are you brave like Superman?"

Paxton scowled. "Superman sucks. And if you like Superman, you suck too."

"Paxton!" The boy's mother glared.

He lowered his head but didn't apologize.

Hagen glanced at Stella. He wasn't getting anywhere, and he knew it.

Stella turned in her seat and leaned closer to the boy. "I like Spiderman better."

The boy brightened. "Yeah? Iron Man's my favorite."

She smiled. "He's really cool. Does your sister like Iron Man too?"

Paxton's chin fell to his chest. "Yeah." The word was barely audible.

Stella licked her lips, giving herself a moment to structure her line of questions. "Are you worried about your sister?"

Paxton hesitated before nodding. The movement was shallow and brief. If Stella hadn't been watching so closely, she might not have noticed it at all.

Stella replied with a quiet, nonconfrontational, "Hm," and folded her hands in her lap. "Can you tell me *why* you're worried about your sister?"

Paxton didn't answer. He lifted his head just enough to stare at the table, as if he wished that somewhere beneath the piles of paper was a hole deep enough to crawl into.

Stella pushed on. "Is it because of the things you've seen on the news?"

Paxton's narrow shoulders lifted.

Stella took a deep breath. The kid was nine, too soon for him to be acting so much like a teenager. The kid was *nine…* too soon to be questioned by FBI agents too. But her gut twisted, telling her to forge on.

From the other end of the sofa came a quiet, "Oh, god." Paxton's mother wrung her hands on the dishcloth. "I'm sorry, this is all my fault. I've had the news on all day since the…you know. I didn't think what it might do to Paxton."

She clicked off the TV, came closer, and pulled the child into her chest. "It's okay, Pax. Desi's not a cheerleader anymore. No one's going to hurt her."

That was it. That was what Stella should have said.

But his mother's words didn't have the effect Stella expected.

"I know." The soft words trembled past Paxton's pale lips. He squeezed one hand with the other and stared at the floor.

Stella's pulse sped up, but she forced herself to stay calm. "How do you know your sister's okay?"

Paxton pushed himself out of his mother's grip. He swallowed hard. "She said...she's always saying how she's not a cheerleader anymore. And she hates them all anyway."

"Who? Who does she hate?" Stella needed him to be very clear.

"The other cheerleaders."

Stella breathed out slowly. She rested her elbows on her knees and leaned closer. "But how do you know that the person who hurt those cheerleaders won't hurt your sister, Paxton? You can tell me. Agent Yates and I are here to help."

Paxton shook his head. He squeezed his hand again, harder this time. His fingernails dug into his palm hard enough to draw blood, as though his betrayal demanded a punishment. "Maybe...maybe *she's* the one that hurt someone."

Paxton's mother shoved the dishcloth she was holding into his hand. "Paxton, what are you saying? Why would you think that?"

Stella's stomach wrenched. She eyed Hagen briefly. He was right there with her.

There it was.

She lowered her voice. "Go on, Paxton. Why do you think your sister might have hurt someone?"

Paxton swallowed. "Because…because when I went to tell her about lunch, she screamed at me when I barged into her room."

"That's what siblings do, Pax. It's normal." Cheri's logic wasn't backed up with a shred of confidence.

Stella glanced at Harlan. He'd seemed to age ten more years since they'd come in. "And…?" she asked the boy.

Paxton ran from the living room and down the hall.

Cheri got up and followed him.

Just as she was out of sight, the boy ran back in with a small, leatherbound book. He shoved it, opened-faced, at Stella. "She was writing in this when she screamed at me. Her pictures are really scary."

Stella saw what appeared to be a sketch of…a dead cheerleader, with angry writing all around it.

"I slammed her door and started to cry." Paxton was on a roll now, talking loud and fast, his adrenaline getting the best of him. "Then she opened her door and said 'sorry, bro' and, and…she said it wasn't me she was mad at."

Stella, remembering that Cheri worked for a law firm and fearing the inevitable, leafed through the book as fast as she could.

Hagen, still crouched down, must have remembered about Cheri too. He jumped right in where Stella left off. "Who was she mad at, buddy?"

"Paxton," his mother cried, beelining for the leatherbound journal. She snatched it out of Stella's hands.

"Cheri." Harlan stood.

"What name did she say, Paxton?" Hagen prodded but gently.

"Paxton, look at Mommy. You don't have to answer that."

"Cheri," Paxton's dad had tapped into some kind of energy source. "Lives are at stake, honey," he scolded.

"I know the law. I know our rights." She hugged the journal tight to her chest and started crying.

Harlan turned his focus on his son. "Pax, go ahead. It's okay. Talk to the agents. They can't help your sister if they don't have all the facts."

"Ava. She said it was all Ava's fault."

34

Ava's eyes opened. They drifted closed again.

No. Wake up. You've got to wake up.

She forced herself to look around. The kitchen floor was cold against her cheek, almost refreshing in the midday heat. But it was wet against her chest. Her shoulder was bleeding again. A dark red puddle covered several floor tiles that she could see, and trails of blood ran through the grout toward the kitchen door. One side of her body ached so much it felt like her skin and muscles and bones were made of pain.

And she was tired. So tired. All Ava wanted to do was close her eyes and drift to sleep. That peaceful rest was just there, almost within touching distance. She just had to relax. In a second, everything would be over. The pain would be gone. She could rest forever. She'd see her mom. They'd be together again. People always said they were so alike, so—

No!

Her eyes shot open again. She wasn't going to give up. She came in here to find the phone, to call for an ambulance. The phone was right there, hanging on the kitchen wall next to the door. She'd come this far. She could push herself a little farther. Three yards. Not even that. It was all that separated her from being rescued to ending up dead on the kitchen floor.

"Move!"

She laid one hand flat on the tiles and pulled. Her right leg was so stiff. She couldn't bend it at all. But she felt for grip with her left foot and pushed hard. Her chest slid through the wet blood.

An inch. She'd managed to move forward an inch. Her head seemed to rise up the wall, as light as smoke. The tiles rolled and spun on a wave of nausea. Ava blinked.

"Come on. You've lost too much blood. That's what… that's what's making you dizzy. Just a little more. You can do it."

Her voice faded, and she tried to think of something else to say to cheer herself on.

That was it. She needed to cheer.

"We've…got…spirit, yes we…do."

We've got spirit, how about you?

The chant bounced through her head. She could do it. She could win.

Go, go, go.

A rustle came from the garden, and Ava dropped back to the floor. The wind. The wind must be moving the dry leaves.

No. Footsteps on the lawn.

Ava's heart jumped. Tears came to her eyes. Her father and her sister. They must have come home early, decided to use the back door. She would be okay.

Thank you, God.

"Dad." Her voice was so weak, barely a croak. "Daddy, help."

The footsteps grew closer. A strange run. Slow and uneven, one foot landing harder than the other.

"Dad?"

"Aaaagggh!"

The unfamiliar scream was loud and piercing. It rattled through the kitchen, the tone sharpening as the noise bounced off the tiles.

"You're alive!"

That wasn't her dad. It wasn't anyone she knew.

Ava lifted her chin from the floor. Her cheek was sticky from where blood had smeared across the side of her face. A young woman stood just within her line of sight.

From what Ava could tell, the newcomer was about her age. She wore a pink t-shirt and long blue jeans despite the summer heat. Her face was familiar, but Ava couldn't place it. Had they been at the same school? Hung out in the same places?

Ava wasn't sure, and she didn't care. The pain in her shoulder was all she cared about. The pain...and the rifle the young woman cradled in her arms.

The nausea that had settled permanently in Ava's stomach expanded.

No. Please, no.

The girl walked into the kitchen until she stood directly above Ava, her shoulders framed by the doorway. "You're supposed to be dead, dammit. Christ, how perfect can you be? Even bullets won't kill you."

Ava tried to understand. "Who...who are you?"

The rifle dangled at the girl's side, the stock gripped in one hand. "Don't recognize me, huh? Of course, you don't. Why should you? Here. Maybe this will jog your memory."

She bent over and lifted the bottom of her jeans. The cuff rose over her sneaker and above her short socks to reveal not her ankle and a calf but a stretch of titanium.

Ava's head fell back to the kitchen floor. More wetness on her chin. A deeper smell of coppery blood.

A prosthetic leg. A teenage girl.

A connection began to form.

Sleep now, Ava. Just sleep. Maybe your mind will clear.

The woman dropped her pant cuff, but it stopped halfway down her calf. "Desiree Swedway. That's the name you're looking for. Recipient of a transfemoral prosthetic leg after her irresponsible squad dropped her, breaking her leg so badly it had to be removed. I made the front page for a little while."

"Desiree."

The girl's name fell out of Ava's mouth in a rush of breath. She'd heard about Desiree from Chapel Island. An accident in practice. A nasty one. A broken leg. It had been the talk of the team for a while. A rumor followed that she'd almost died, and doctors had cut the leg off, but Ava hadn't paid attention.

"I'm...sorry."

"Sorry, huh? But not sorry enough to ask after me. Not sorry enough to send me a message, to ask how I was doing, to invite me to your parties. No, not that sorry."

Ava closed her eyes. The tiles felt so cool on her cheek, so comfortable. "Have we...have we ever met?"

Cer-lick.

Ava didn't need to open her eyes to know what that sound meant. Desiree had flicked off the rifle's safety. Every synapse in Ava's brain told her to run, to fight with Desiree for the weapon, to punch her out of the way, and call for help. But every nerve and muscle in her body told her she wasn't going anywhere. She had no choice but to lie on the kitchen floor and either die slowly or die quickly. All she could do was open her eyes and gaze up at her attacker.

Desiree stood over her, the weapon gripped in both hands, but she didn't aim it. Not yet.

"Have we met?" Desiree gave a humorless bark of laughter. "Why, yes. Yes, we have. I cheered at every match between Chapel Island and Harnsey High sophomore year. Just like you. I saw you there, chanting, jumping. Waving your arms and your pom-poms about like you were the center of the world."

Desiree stamped her foot, but her prosthetic leg landed softly as though it had been drained of all strength.

"I'm the center of nothing. No one loves me!" Desiree screamed. A sob accompanied each word. "Oh, no. As soon as I fell, that was it. No one wanted to know me anymore. No one wanted to know about a damaged former cheerleader and her depressing story. My presence made people feel *bad*. A *cheerleader* can't make people feel bad. Oh, no."

Ava released a breath, knowing it could be her last one. Desiree was talking, screaming, crying. But she might as well have been a mile away. Ava had other things on her mind.

Just go to sleep now. Rest. When you're asleep, she won't be able to hurt you anymore.

Ava slid a hand over the cold, blood-stained tiles.

No.

This was her kitchen. Her house. Her life. She wasn't leaving it. Not now. Not while she still had a chance. She had to keep Desiree talking, build a bond.

Desiree bent down and smeared her hand on the bloody tile too.

She stood, turned, and scribbled *SPIRIT!* on the wall in angry capital letters. "Didn't get around to that the first time I killed you."

"I'm…sorry about your leg." It was all she had, all the feeling she could spare.

Desiree threw her head back and laughed. "Sorry? You have no idea what it's like. To be ignored. To be mocked. 'Dead-leg Desi' they called me. 'Titanium Barbie.' I heard them at the lunch tables laughing then falling silent as I limped past."

A heat grew in the back of Ava's throat. It wasn't like the fire burning in her shoulder or the fever flaming in her leg. This was an angry heat made of rage and indignation.

She pushed herself up. Pain spread across her chest, but she ignored it. She dragged her legs around until her back rested against the kitchen cabinet. The air was cooler on her face, and the flame in her shoulder turned down a notch.

"Yeah, I do. I understand exactly what that's like."

Desiree released one hand from the rifle. It hung from her right hand, the muzzle pointing at the floor. She cocked her head, incredulous. "And how do you know that, huh? Little Miss Perfect."

Ava waited for her breathing to slow. One breath, two. "My mom...she killed herself. Afterward, the kids at school? They were kind. Most of them. But there were some who called me 'Suicide Kid.' They'd call the teacher if I got too close to a window or...or swap my knife for a...for a spoon at lunch, like I wasn't allowed sharp instruments. Some of the kids told me to go kill myself. Just like my mom."

Desiree stared at her.

Ava's head dropped. The fatigue was pushing back. "I know, Desiree. I know what loss is and how awful people can be."

Desiree's breathing increased, but she didn't say a word.

With all the effort she had left in her body, Ava reached out a hand. "If...if I'd known when your accident happened, I'd have been there for you. I'll be here for you now. If you'll let me."

35

S tella gently grasped Paxton by his shoulders. "Ava who? Did she mention Ava's full name?"

Paxton shook his head. He burst into tears until his body shook, and the only noise that came out of his mouth was an unending wail. He ran into his mother's arms.

Her face was stunned, but she pulled him in close. She could only manage a soft *shh, shh*.

Harlan walked over and blanketed them both in a big embrace.

Hagen jumped to his feet. "The captain at Winter Creek."

Stella stood and looked directly at Cheri. "Do not alter or destroy any evidence or you'll be—"

"Understood, Agent," Harlan said with the strength of a man in charge.

They ran out of the house, leaving Desiree's stunned family behind.

The six folders Olivia Mostrom's mother had given them were sprawled all over the passenger's seat. Stella scooped them up and hopped in, as Hagen started the car, slammed the gas, and sped away.

Stella tore through the folders until she got to the original list from Coach Burbank.

Hagen called Slade as Stella plugged the cheer captain's address into the car's GPS.

Slade's number rang once, twice. "C'mon, answer already."

A third ring. Still no reply. Stella's knee bounced against the passenger seat like a drummer beating out a rhythm. Halfway through the fourth ring, Slade's deep voice sounded through the car's speakers. "What have you got?"

Stella relaxed. Just hearing Slade's voice was reassuring, a calm reminder that they weren't alone in this madness. "We've got a suspect and a potential victim. Looks like our suspect is Desiree Swedway, a former cheerleader from Chapel Island. She's angry at being abandoned after an—"

"Where is she?"

"About to kill Ava Breckin, the cheer captain at Winter Creek. Police have been patrolling the house, but if Desiree sees an opportunity—"

"We'll meet you there." Slade hung up.

Stella stared out the window. The Corvette would get them there faster than any other mode of transportation. It was up to fate now. But her leg wouldn't stop shaking.

"Your cheerleader angle was right. Nice work."

Stella heard him but was someplace else.

"What's going on?"

"Something's not right."

"Yeah, a teenage girl is about to murder another teenage girl for the fifth time in a matter of days."

Stella turned and looked at Hagen, searching for the answer in his eyes.

"What is it, Stella, I can practically hear the wheels in your brain spinning."

"Call Mac. Now."

Stella ran a finger down every page of Coach Burbank's list until she saw… "There are two Avas on this list."

"Hey, Hagen, what's up?" Mac's voice rang over the speakers.

Hagen stared at her. "Shit. What are you saying?"

"One of the entries next to the sketch of the bloody cheerleader in Desiree's diary said '*Get ready to see your mommy, bitch.*'"

"Holy shit, Stella, a diary? You called that on day one." Mac's excitement was palpable. "What do you need from me?"

"Ava Williamson of Harnsey. Mac, are both her parents alive?"

"Gimme two seconds."

"'*Get ready to meet your mommy.*'" Hagen nodded on hearing it out loud again. "If this Ava's mom is deceased, this is probably the one Desiree is after."

Mac confirmed it. "Her mother died a few years back. Suicide."

Stella plugged Ava Williamson's address into Hagen's GPS. "Tell the others we're going to Ava Williamson's in Harnsey. And tell Slade to tell Sheriff Day to put out a BOLO for the suspect's car. And get a search warrant for the Swedways. We need that diary."

Hagen flipped a U-turn and pushed his foot to the floor. The Corvette growled like a bear and roared into the fast lane. "She's not a captain."

"Because this murder spree is more personal. It's personal, I can feel it."

"Personal, we're going back to a crime of passion? A teenage girl? Have they lived long enough to develop that kind of rage?"

Stella looked at him nearly crossed-eyed. "Didn't you help raise two sisters?"

"…Shit."

Soon, they were pulling off the highway and down the small road that led to Ava's address.

Stella craned her neck over the dashboard, searching for the property. "Easy. If Desiree's there, we don't want to spook her."

Hagen slowed the car until they were moving at little more than walking speed.

Stella pointed. "There. Just one car in the driveway. Some sort of subcompact SUV."

Hagen craned his neck toward the house. "That's the only car I can see. Dammit!"

Hagen pulled the Corvette onto the side of the road.

Stella dropped back into her seat, pulling out her vest. She strapped it on as Hagen reached for his. "Desiree could have parked somewhere out of sight. There's a lot of woods back there. Could be a dirt road. Closest house is 500 feet back. Let's make sure this is it before we call it in."

Stella climbed out of the car. Hagen followed. Frustration rattled in her stomach like she'd swallowed a bag of rocks.

Stella approached the door and lifted her hand to the bell. That's when she heard a voice, then another. She pushed an arm across Hagen.

Ava wasn't alone.

"'Dead-leg Desi' they called me. 'Titanium Barbie.'"

That was it.

They were in exactly the right place. And they were alone against the killer. And her hostage.

Stella took a deep breath. As Hagen called it in and requested backup, she drew her weapon. Stella pointed right and, trusting Hagen to follow, made her way around the house.

From the side garden, the first voice—it had to be Ava's—continued to plead. Stella could hear her clearly now.

"Some of the kids told me to go kill myself."

Jeez. Stella stepped faster across the grass as she remained in her crouch. *That's it, Ava. Keep going. Build a relationship. Make it harder for Desiree to pull the trigger.*

"If…if I'd known you when your accident happened, I'd have been there for you. I'll be there for you now. If you'll let me."

Good, Ava. Keep going.

There was the garden. The lawn was thick and well maintained. An apple tree reached almost to the roof, throwing shade onto the back windows. A wide, red stain ran from the rose bushes across the grass to the back door as though a hunter had dragged his kill into the house for butchering.

And there in the doorway, her back to Stella, her feet standing in the middle of the bloody trail, was Desiree. One pant leg was high on her ankle, revealing a prosthetic calf. In her arm, she held a hunting rifle.

Ava's pleading had failed to move her.

Desiree shouted. "You don't understand. You should have been dead. You should all be *dead*!"

Stella slipped past Desiree, taking cover behind the trunk of the apple tree.

From her new vantage point, on the floor of the kitchen, at Desiree's feet, sat Ava Williamson. The back of her head rested against the kitchen cabinet. One arm was draped over her stomach, and her bare shoulder was covered with blood. More blood had drawn an untidy line from her knee across her calf to her bare feet and had formed a large puddle over the kitchen tiles.

Stella swallowed. That looked like a lot of blood. If they didn't get help soon, regardless of what Desiree did next, Ava wouldn't make it.

Crouching, Hagen ran across the grass.

Crack.

As a twig broke under Hagen's foot, the entire universe slowed. Ava turned her head. Her eyes met Stella's. Desiree spun around. Stella lifted her gun.

"FBI. Put down your weapon, Desiree. Do it now!"

"Noo!" Desiree's scream was the loneliest sound Stella had ever heard.

Quick as lightning, the teen darted out of sight. Two seconds later, she was crouching behind Ava, the muzzle resting against the back of the wounded girl's head.

Stella spread her feet and balanced her weight. Her arms were outstretched, the handle of her Glock resting in her palm. The sights targeted Desiree's face. Half her face. It was all Stella could see without hitting the hostage.

Her hands were steady. She could take her. She could shoot Desiree, she was sure—but the blast of the weapon, the shock, the fall, any one of them could cause Desiree to squeeze the trigger and blow off the top of Ava's head. Stella needed to be careful. She had to trust Hagen to be careful too.

"Put down the gun, Desiree." Stella's voice was slow and calm. "No one needs to get hurt anymore. You've been hurt enough. I know that."

Desiree crouched lower. The barrel of her rifle still rested behind Ava's ear. Only a third of Desiree's face was visible through Stella's sights. "You're too late. You're too late for me, and you're too late for this bitch."

Hagen passed over the lawn, one foot crossing over the other. "Don't do it, Desiree." His command betrayed no emotion. "Think of your parents. Think of your brother, Paxton. If you kill Ava, we *will* kill you. Do you really want to do that to your family?"

Desiree lifted her head. Tears streamed down her face. But she ignored Hagen and addressed Stella. "I don't care. I don't care about anything anymore. I died the day I fell from that pyramid. I lost my leg. I lost cheerleading, my friends. I lost my—" She cut herself off.

What is she trying to say? Stella's heart squeezed in her chest. Dealing with cold killers was easier. They couldn't feel so they couldn't suffer. But Desiree had suffered and was suffering still. She lost her dream and lost her friends. Wounded animals lashed out.

"Desiree, you can get over this. We can help you get through this." Hagen was strong and steady.

"No, you can't!" she screamed.

"Just put down the rifle."

"No!" Desiree shook her head, screaming at Hagen with rage in her eyes.

That's when it hit Stella like a thirty-foot wave.

Desiree's finger was still on the trigger. Just a little more pressure and Ava would be gone. "The doctors should have let me die. I want to go! And now this bitch will join me."

"Desiree, look at me." Stella knew what she had to do but didn't know if she could pull it off. "Look at me, Desiree. You don't have to do this." She coaxed the girl to meet her eyes. "He's not worth it."

A tiny smile parted the grief on the young woman's face. "Tate."

"Yes, Tate. You'll find love again. He's not worth it, Desiree. Please, don't do it. We can get through this. I'll help you."

Desiree stared at Stella. And, for a moment, Stella thought she had her convinced.

That's when the rumble of cars came into earshot.

Stella's stomach flipped. She knew what would happen next. And nothing she said would matter.

Though their sirens weren't blaring yet, the faint thunder of police cars barreling toward the house registered on Desiree's face.

Stella lifted her gun, finger on the trigger, decision made. Desiree was faster.

Click.

The hollow snapping sound froze the air. Desiree yanked back the bolt. The gun was empty. Her scream was even louder this time. "Nooo!"

In a fit of hysteria, Desiree swung the stock toward Ava's head hard enough to crush bone. She missed. Ava slid closer to the floor as the rifle rebounded off the counter and skidded under the table.

Taking advantage of the moment of distraction, Stella darted toward Desiree, knocking her down with the handle of her weapon.

Desiree's screams turned into wails of anguish. "Noo. You can't do this. It's not fair. She has to die. They all have to die. They took everything."

Stella dragged Desiree onto her stomach and pulled her hands behind her back. It was over.

But not for Ava.

Hagen raced into the kitchen, took a dishcloth from the handle of the oven, and applied pressure to the young woman's shoulder.

"You're going to be fine, Ava." His tone was more reassuring than his expression. "We've got you."

Stella applied the handcuffs. "You have the right to remain silent." The words came naturally, as though they'd been sitting in her mouth since the start of the case, waiting to be spoken. "Anything you say can and will be used against you in a court of law. You have the right to an attorney. If you cannot afford an attorney, one will be appointed for you."

Sirens blaring, cars screeched to a halt, doors slammed, and feet hit the asphalt of the driveway.

Desiree continued to sob with her cheek pressed into the

blood-stained tiles. "It's not fair. They all have to die. They've stolen everything from me…"

The girl's words came out as a chant.

A cheer.

Stella would never think of someone having killer spirit the same way again.

36

The ambulance seemed to take forever to reach Ava's house. Hagen sat on the kitchen floor, blood soaking into the back of his pants. With both hands, he continued to apply pressure to Ava's shoulder. The dishcloth was already crimson. He had to keep her awake, keep her talking until the ambulance arrived.

"Talk to me, Ava. Where are your folks?"

"My dad..." She coughed and tears sprang to her eyes. "My dad and my sister...they went to see my aunt. They'll be back today."

Stella crouched next to him, one hand on Desiree's cuffed wrists, keeping the girl still. Stella had pushed the rifle out of reach so that it rested against the wall.

Hagen caught Stella's glance. Ava's face was the color of ash. If the ambulance didn't get there soon, it would be too late, and Desiree will have managed to take one more victim.

He pushed harder on Ava's shoulder. He had to stop the bleeding. Ava had already lost too much blood. She had to stay conscious.

"Who else went to your aunt's? Any other siblings?"

Silence. Ava's eyes had drifted closed.

"Ava!" Hagen didn't like the sound of panic in his voice.

Ava blinked and blinked again. On the third attempt, her eyes opened. "Sorry," she mumbled. "I'm just so tired."

Stella spoke, her fingers still securing Desiree's wrists. "Stay with us, Ava. You're doing great. Not much longer now. So, it's just you, your sister, and your dad here?"

Ava attempted to lick her lips, but even that simple movement seemed to be too much. "My mom...my mom's dead. She died...couple years ago."

Desiree squirmed under Stella's grip. Stella held her wrists tighter. "I'm sorry. It's not easy to lose a parent."

Ava gave a shallow nod, little more than a light incline of her head. "No." She managed a small smile. "Getting shot hurts less."

Hagen chuckled. He wanted to tell her that getting shot also left fewer scars, but he said nothing.

The wail of an ambulance sounded in the distance, drawing nearer.

He leaned closer to Ava. "Help's here. Just hold on a little longer."

Ava gave him a weak smile.

Police entered through the back. Within a minute, paramedics were inside and took over, working hard to stabilize the girl.

The police escorted Desiree out of the kitchen and bagged the rifle from the kitchen floor.

Hagen stood and stretched out his back. He looked toward Stella. She was still sitting on the floor, her back against the oven and her feet just short of the bloodstain. He stuck out a hand to help her up.

"Let's get out of this room."

Avoiding the bloody smear on the kitchen floor, he stepped

outside, strode toward the end of the yard, and dropped onto the grass in the garden. The midday sun was hot enough to make him sweat, but the shade cast by an apple tree helped. He had no desire at all to go back into the house where police radios rasped, and late-coming law enforcement demanded answers.

Stella, trailing about a minute behind, sat next to him, and pulled her knees up to her chest.

"You did good work in there. One for the cells, one for the surgeon."

"We were lucky." Stella took a deep, shuddering breath. "She pulled the trigger, Hagen. Ava should be dead. We weren't fast enough."

"Stella, you had her. How the hell you put it together about Tate, I'll never know. But you had her until she got distracted by backup."

"Her broken heart felt bigger than just a lost leg. I could see it in her eyes. And then my brain landed on an entry I'd flipped past in her diary. About a tall boy with brown hair and brown eyes, and something about a dance. It had to be before the accident. They were going to a dance. And it hit me. Tate. He was the connection."

"You think if Ava recovers—"

"She'll tell us she was seeing Tate. Or at least texting or snapping with him or whatever teens do nowadays."

"That explains Taylor Sinn, Reese Wilder, Sophie Powers because of his relationship with Marisa Powers, and Ava Williamson, if it tracks." Hagen felt this theory was solid. "But Olivia Molstrom—"

"Wasn't the center of attention at the very end, after all."

"Just a girl who was in the wrong place at the wrong time. Her mother's not going to be happy about that." He pulled out his cell phone. "Meanwhile, the Romeo who helped create this chaos is riding off into the sunset."

"Like you said, you can't arrest someone for being a womanizer."

"A *Rico Suave*." He smiled and dialed.

She gave him an uneasy smile. "Who are you calling?"

Hagen put the phone to his ear. "Gotta deliver the news."

"Slade knows. I texted him on the way out. He's almost here with the rest of the team. And the cops have contacted Ava's dad. He and her sister will meet her at the hospital."

"There's still a couple more people who need to know."

Hagen made the call.

The phone rang just once before Harlan Swedway answered with a soft and shaky, "Yes?"

"Sir, this is Agent Yates of the FBI. I just wanted to let you know that the police have Desiree in custody. She'll be taken to Chapel Island Sheriff's Department."

"Oh, thank God." Harlan Swedway breathed more than spoke his relief.

Hagen frowned. Parents didn't usually thank God when they learned their kid had been arrested, especially if their kid was wanted for murder.

Harlan continued. "I was just about to call you. Paxton... he...he just told me my rifle looked like it'd been moved, so he took out the bullets this morning. Worried that his sister might..."

Hagen was silent for a long moment, letting that information sink in. He hadn't managed to stop Desiree. Stella hadn't managed to stop Desiree.

Nine-year-old Paxton was the hero in this story.

"You got a good kid there."

Harlan stifled a sob. "Two. Two good kids. Desi, she's not a bad girl, you know. She's just... she's been through a lot."

Hagen looked at Stella as he listened to Harlan break down. She gazed at the roses, admiring their bloom. Trauma affected everyone differently.

"I'm sure." He moved the phone to his other ear, noticing for the first time that Ava's dried blood was still caked around the edges of his nails. He wiped his hand on the grass.

Sure, trauma affects everyone differently. But trauma is no excuse for cold-blooded murder.

Hagen spoke between Harlan's sobs. "Desiree will get the help she needs. And you should be proud of your son. He saved a girl's life today."

The life your daughter almost ended. That part didn't need to be said.

Harlan couldn't reply. And from somewhere behind him came the more forceful sound of his wife's sobs. Their journey was just beginning.

Hagen disconnected the call. He tossed the phone onto the grass and sprawled on his back. This case was done.

Stella's case still waited.

Now, there was nothing between them and Joel Ramirez. He closed his eyes and took a deep breath.

Stella's phone beeped.

37

A notification ding interrupted the moment of silence. With a groan, Stella lifted her phone from the apple tree roots and checked the screen.

"They're here."

Hagen opened his eyes and sighed. "I was just getting comfortable. It's nice in this garden."

"Apart from that trail of blood from the rose bushes, you mean."

"Yeah, I could do without that. But I can't see it if I just lie here and look at the clouds."

Stella smiled and patted his shoulder. "Then you stay here and watch the clouds. I'll go and deal with them."

She pushed to her feet and made her way to the kitchen. A deputy was already applying tape around the perimeter, ready for forensics to photograph the scene and lift the bloody tiles from the floor.

Ava's family would be in for an unpleasant welcome when they came back from the hospital. Their home was a crime scene. Days would pass before they could live here again. Years would pass before they stopped seeing the red stain on the floor and the blood under the roses.

Events like these always made a splash. The ripples spread, producing big waves at first but still rocking the surface long after everyone else had forgotten and moved on.

Stella ignored the kitchen and passed around the side of the house. A deputy stood near the open front door, his radio squawking as the law enforcement teams coordinated. Three cars were parked at strange angles in the driveway, their red and blue lights still flashing.

Desiree sat next to a uniformed deputy in the back of one of those cars. Her hands were cuffed, and her seat belt was on. She'd soon be taken to the station for booking. Her eyes were vacant as though she had long ago left this world and built herself a new one, a place where all the people she had once known and loved were evil and deserved to die.

"It's not fair."

That's what Desiree had screamed when Stella knocked her to the ground. And she was right. Life had been unfair to her. But life wasn't fair to anyone.

It's how you reacted to that unfairness that made the difference.

Desiree had chosen revenge. She'd killed four people and wounded a fifth not because killing would make a wrong right or prevent another act of unfairness in the future. She'd killed to balance one act of unfairness with another. She'd wronged others to make herself *feel* right.

And what would justice have looked like for Desiree?

Stella really didn't know the answer to that question. For Desiree, there was no crime to uncover or criminals to arrest. There could be none of the satisfaction that justice promised. She had suffered from bad luck, unrequited love, and then really bad manners.

"Stella!"

Behind the police car, Mac waved through the window of

a black SUV pulling up outside the house. A weight dropped from Stella's shoulders. She pushed Desiree out of her mind, strolled to the end of the driveway, and rested an arm against the SUV's hood just as Ander climbed out from behind the driver's seat.

"How'd it go? You or Hagen hurt?"

Stella shook her head. "Not for lack of trying, though."

Ander grabbed a handful of blond curls on the top of his head. "I can't believe we were halfway on the other side of town while you two were here tackling her by yourself."

Stella looked back toward the squad car. Desiree hadn't moved. She still stared straight ahead as if peering into the endless, unfeeling blank space of her future.

"Just a kid with an empty rifle and a broken heart in the end. You didn't miss anything."

Chloe and Mac stepped out of the car.

Mac prodded Stella in the shoulder. "A kid who's killed four people with that rifle. The boss is livid with you for going in and not waiting for backup."

"We didn't really have a choice. You know we'd have waited if we could."

Ander looked at Stella. His blue eyes bored into her for a moment, giving her a short burst of discomfort. He turned away and nodded at the door. "Hagen still inside?"

"Round the back. Lying on the grass like a puppy."

Ander raised his eyebrows, amused. "I'll go and throw him a stick."

He headed around the house with Chloe.

Mac watched them go as she eased her own door closed. She took Stella's arm. "Come with me."

Stella let her friend lead her away from everything. The farther she moved from the scene, the lighter she felt. She really did need a day off, just binge-watching her favorite shows and working through a gallon tub of ice cream.

She'd heard that people did that kind of thing. And even enjoyed it.

Mac's fingers wrapped tighter around her upper arm, bringing her back to reality.

Stella turned to her friend. "What's going on?"

Mac pulled Stella away from three deputies standing in the shade of an elm tree at the corner of the property. The cops rocked on their heels, thumbs in their belts, and ignored them. "Remember you said you thought you were being followed?"

A twinge of worry shot through Stella. "I was probably just being para—"

"You are. Being followed, that is."

Stella took half a step back. She glanced around, keeping her movements casual. Apart from the police cars and the clump of cops in uniform on a quiet suburban street, there was nothing unusual there. No old car was parked up the road that she could see. No creepy guy with binoculars.

"Are you sure?"

Mac dragged her phone out of her pocket and opened the photo app. "I pulled the camera footage from some of the traffic lights you passed through over the last couple of days. I looked for the times I knew you would have passed through them and watched the cars that came next. Here, look."

She flipped through her images to a screenshot of a beat-up Toyota Camry passing through a junction. "This was coming out of Atlanta." She flipped to the next picture. It showed a different junction but the same car with the same dents in the passenger door. "And here it is again. This was at the Harris Hotel."

"Jeez." A ripple of nausea passed through Stella. Again, she looked around her. No old car. She looked back at the footage. The guy in the car was the same guy she'd seen in the café in Atlanta. He was creepy as hell. "I knew Atlanta would lead to trouble. But I just had to know, you know."

Mac nodded and slipped her phone back into her pocket. "I ran the plates. They're cloned, of course."

"Of course."

The back of Stella's neck tingled. Maybe she should do now what Desiree should have done. Let the past be. Move on. Leave the injustice she had suffered behind her and get on with her life.

Wasn't that the healthy thing to do?

Her nausea escalated. But the sour taste at the back of her throat didn't come from the thought of being watched. It was the idea of giving up that made her feel ill. She would push on. And if someone wanted to stop her, she'd go right through them.

"Earth to Stella!"

Mac was clicking her fingers under her nose.

Stella shook the thoughts out of her head. "Sorry, I was just—"

"Miles away. I know. Listen, you're not alone. We'll find out who's following you and what they want. Together. Whether it's related to Joel Ramirez, a case you've worked on, or some creep in the grocery store who just likes the cut of your jeans, we'll find out who it is, and we'll deal with it. Okay?"

Stella forced a smile. "Yeah. Thanks."

Mac gripped Stella's arm. "Hey, you've got friends. Whether you like it or not."

In place of the nausea came a wave of joy, warm and happy. Stella hugged her friend.

She did like it.

A lot.

38

Junior crouched behind a bush two dozen yards from the back of a house at the end of a cul-de-sac in an upscale neighborhood in Harnsey. His knees ached, and the sun burned his cheek, but he didn't dare move.

The place was crawling with bugs. And cops. When he'd followed Stella and her partner as they rushed out here, he thought they'd do what they usually did...talk to people. He'd sit outside and keep watching his targets, making sure they didn't do anything that would interest Boss. And when they were done here, he'd follow them somewhere else and watch while they talked to some other witness or spoke to some other suspect. Lather, rinse, repeat.

That was the problem with the FBI. They were too procedural.

You could get the same information with a hammer as you could with a question. And a hammer was faster.

But that process hadn't happened this time. The road had been too empty for Junior to stop without being obvious, so he'd continued past the parked Corvette until he came to a road that turned into the woods behind the girl's house. He'd parked by the side of the road and sprinted through the undergrowth until he reached the end of the garden.

The moment he'd found his hiding spot, he knew he was going to be stuck in the woods for a while.

A long red trail stretched from the rose bushes to the back of the house, looking like someone had dragged a corpse. He had to hold himself back from tramping across the lawn to see what was going on.

Boy, that would have been a stupid thing to do!

Just the thought made him knock his knuckle twice on his forehead.

He'd barely settled in before Stella and the other Fed crept around the back, guns out, ballistic vests over their clothes. That's what had taken them so long, he knew. They'd probably also been told to wait for backup.

They hadn't.

And he'd had a grandstand view of the whole thing— right up to the moment they both ran into the house. There'd been a whole lot of screaming and talking, then there'd been a whole host of sirens wailing down the road. One deputy car after another screeched to a halt outside the house. Now a bunch of other FBI agents were here too. And more cops.

Junior massaged the backs of his thighs. Every time he moved, the bushes creaked, and the dry leaves under his feet crunched and cracked.

He should have left as soon as he saw that bloody trail. He should have hightailed it back to Stella's apartment and planted the bugs when he had the chance. If she was going to be out here for a while, it had been the perfect opportunity.

But he couldn't move now. The police were on high alert, prepared to note any car passing through. They'd want to know what he was doing out here. They'd track his movements and figure out where he'd been.

He scratched the back of his neck. Three mosquito bites were already swelling, causing a torrent of itching.

How would he explain being pulled over to Boss? A chill ran down his spine, despite the heat. No way was he going to put himself in that position. He'd stay out here all day if he had to, until all the cops had gone, and all the FBI agents were safely tucked in their beds. His cheeks could turn as red as the inside of a watermelon, but there was no way he was going to risk getting caught.

He knew what Boss did to people who got themselves caught.

But, lord, his legs were aching, and his bladder was fair fit to burst. How much longer could he stay hidden? How long did it take to clean up a bit of blood?

Heck, he'd carved up a whole convenience store clerk and washed down the mess in less time than it took law enforcement to deal with one bloody room.

"Should never have taken this damn job," he muttered to himself. "Whole thing's been stupid. Traipsing around the city, then the suburbs, and the countryside just to keep an eye on one woman. If Boss wants to know what she knows so much, then maybe *he* should come out here and follow her."

The thought made him snigger. Boss doing his own dirty work. That would be the day.

Crack.

Junior spun around. Dry leaves crunched under his feet. He looked at the house from the corner of his eye, not daring to move again.

That agent who had been lying on the grass, the one who had been in Atlanta, was gone. A cop stood by the back door, but he hadn't heard Junior's movement.

Lucky.

Crack.

That same noise came from somewhere behind him. Maybe the cops were trawling through the woods, looking for evidence.

Junior's brain scrambled for excuses. If they found him, he could say he was out here walking in the woods and just wanted to know what the commotion was about. Or maybe his dog had run off, and he was trying to find it. Or perhaps he lived out here in the woods by himself, and it was none of the cops' damn business what he did.

That'd teach them.

Crack.

Another footstep, louder this time. Someone dragged back a low-hanging branch not three yards away. The leaves shuffled.

Junior's heart thumped in triple time like a punching bag getting hit by a heavyweight. He was going to have a heart attack. He could feel it. Well...that would solve the problem. He'd have plenty of time to think of what to tell the cops on the way to the hospital.

The voice came next, that no-good hissing sound that always filled him with dread. How he hated it.

"Hey, bro, I hear you're really screwing this mission up."

He should have known it would be her. Come to check on him. Like he needed his sister to look at his work.

Sis stepped out from the woods, her mousy brown hair the exact same shade as the tree bark. She blended in, her lightly tanned skin the same tone as the earth. Her eyes were blue like the sky. They shared the same coloring, but she was on the skinny side, all bone and bossiness. It figured. She'd once been a cheerleader—she and that little psycho the FBI just arrested could probably bond if ever given the chance.

He glanced at the house. The cop he was worried about had gone. Still, he kept his voice low. "Where the hell did you come from?"

She hooked a thumb over her shoulder. "There's another road back there. If you weren't such an idiot, you'd have found it."

Junior stared past her. Did she mean he'd stood in these woods for hours for nothing?

Naw, she couldn't mean that.

"Like hell there is."

"I didn't drop out of the sky, Junior." She jammed her thumbs into the pockets of her jeans. "Hey, don't feel bad about screwing up this job so much. You've been trying to follow an FBI agent. That requires brains. And you, brother, have always been a bit short in that department, haven't you?"

Junior's hatred for his sibling grew. Here they were, standing in the woods on the edge of a crime scene filled with cops and federal agents, and she was still giving him a hard time. Who the hell did she think she was?

"What are you doing here, Sis? Did Boss send you out to bring me some coffee? And how did you find me anyway?"

She glared at him. "Very funny. You see me holding any coffee?"

The glare transformed into a grin, the horrible, self-satisfied smile she always made when she was about to do something very bad and was proud of it.

Junior's mouth went dry. "What are you—"

"Y'see, Bro. Boss has had enough. He's had enough of your screwups, your laziness, and your complete inability to get even the simplest job done. You're a moron, Junior. And you're being replaced. By me."

Junior took a step forward. The dry leaves crunched under his feet, but he no longer cared. "What do you mean 'replaced'? You can't do that."

"Can. Am. Have done. Orders is orders."

"And what the hell am I supposed to do?"

"You? You stay right here."

"Why would I—"

The pistol appeared out of nowhere. The barrel was longer than Junior expected, the silencer almost doubling the size of the weapon.

Junior's breath caught in his throat. "Now, just a—"

"Sorry, brother."

With a *pfft* and *click*, Junior's brains were sprayed all over the hedge, all his worries laid to rest.

39

Stella flipped the cap off the container and sprinkled fish food into the tank. The goldfish flicked his tail and rose gently to the surface, gathering the pieces in his open mouth like a kid catching snowflakes.

"Go easy, Scoot. You don't want to give yourself a tummy ache."

Stella replaced the cap and watched her fish vacuum up the falling particles. "What am I telling you that for? Like you ever do anything that's not easy. You just swim around all day, eating your food and checking out the kitchen. The most exciting thing you ever do is swim under your bridge. You can't even fall off it."

The goldfish flicked his tail again and drifted toward the front of the tank, his mouth opening and closing as he moved.

"Yeah, yeah. I know. You've got food, and I don't. You don't have to rub it in."

Stella glanced at her watch. It was almost nine. She'd been home less than an hour, long enough to shower and change into a t-shirt and shorts. She'd just been about to order some Thai food, find a show to watch, and enjoy an early night when her phone pinged.

She'd assumed it was Mac, inviting her out for a drink and a chat. She was wrong. The message was from Hagen.

He'd ordered Korean, enough for three. Did she want him to bring it over and see if the two of them could finish it all while they figured out what to do about Joel Ramirez?

Stella hesitated a second before agreeing. Already, she wondered if she'd made the right decision—and not just because Thai food would have arrived in twenty minutes while Hagen wouldn't arrive for another forty.

Stella wanted nothing more than to put this case behind her and try to forget all about it. The image of Desiree pulling the trigger on an empty gun haunted her.

During her time at the Nashville PD, she'd been called to a domestic—the most volatile of all situations. Two armed male subjects, brothers-in-law, were fighting over money. The fight escalated, both subjects turning their weapons on Stella and her partner at one point. Right when it seemed like the moment had de-escalated, one man shot the other, pulling the trigger the same way Desiree had tonight. Like the decision had been made long before she and her partner had arrived at the scene.

Only his gun had been loaded.

Today, Stella had been lucky.

Ava had been lucky.

She knew her hesitation made sense, logically. Ava's head had been so close to Desiree's. If Stella had fired, *she* might've killed Ava.

Luck, she supposed, was something to be grateful for.

But, with the FBI's Violent Crimes Unit, Stella was getting one brutal killing case after another with barely a break between them to process the details of each event. She needed to find a way to box up the murders as soon as they were done and move on. She didn't know if Hagen's visit tonight would help.

And maybe she needed a bit of distance from him.

She dropped an elbow onto the kitchen counter and rested her chin in her hand. "What do you think, Scoot? One minute he's jumping to help and wants to spend the weekend with me in Atlanta. The next, he's just a colleague, the guy at the next desk with a badge and a gun. What do you think I should do?"

Scoot drifted down the tank before turning and diving under his stone bridge.

"Turn and run, huh? That could be wise. But you're just a fish, Scoot. And you probably want me all to yourself." She sighed. "Let's see what he does next. Maybe he'll open up and tell me how he really feels. Maybe he'll show me that he trusts me as much as he wants me to trust him."

Ring.

Scoot stayed under the bridge, his tail waving gently in the direction of Stella's face.

"Yeah, yeah. Don't rush to the door. I'll get it."

She buzzed Hagen up. A couple of minutes later, a knock was followed by light scratching. Stella stopped.

That scraping sound was too strange for Hagen.

But when she checked through the spyhole, the fish-eye lens stretched Hagen's cheeks and lengthened his already prominent jawline.

She unlocked the door, which was immediately pushed open by a dog's strong paw.

Hagen reached for the dog's collar, but his hands were full of takeout bags. "Bubs, easy there."

Stella crouched. Hagen's dog looked like a cross between a pit bull and a boxer, the kind of animal she'd often come across while arresting low-level drug dealers and their even lower-level customers. But Hagen's dog didn't snarl at her or cower at the sound of a raised voice. He placed one heavy paw on her knee and lifted a nose to sniff her face.

Stella scratched under the dog's chin. "Bubbles! Well, this is a surprise."

Hagen kicked the door shut with his heel. "It's Bubs. He doesn't like his full name."

Stella stroked the dog's head. "You do like Bubbles, don't you? Totally suits you."

"Hm." Hagen placed the bags on the counter next to the fish tank. "I've hardly been home the last few days, and I didn't want to leave him by himself again. You don't mind, do you?"

Stella stood. She didn't mind. "I'm okay, just keep him off the—" Bubbles jumped onto her mattress and settled down with a quiet groan against her pillows. "Bed."

On the kitchen counter, Scoot opened and closed his mouth as if shocked and offended by this large mammal.

Hagen stopped taking the boxes out of the bags. "Do you want me to…?"

"No, leave him. He looks comfortable. What have you got there? I'm starving."

Hagen grinned and lifted another carton out of the bag. "Okay, I might have overdone it. We've got two kinds of *bibimbap*, beef barbeque, chicken wings, and a couple of noodles. And *kimchi*, of course."

"Of course." Stella reached for a pair of chopsticks and settled onto one of the barstools. "When you said you had enough for three, I didn't think you meant enough for three weeks."

"Eh. I'd knock this stuff off in a couple of days. As long as I get to stay at home for two whole days in a row. Fat chance of that lately. Whoa, what are you doing?"

Stella's chopsticks were halfway inside the box of beef. She stopped. "Helping myself?"

"Plates and bowls, girl. Show the food some respect."

Stella rolled her eyes. *Girl?* She pointed to the mini dishwasher next to the sink. "There's clean stuff in there. You want it, help yourself."

He pushed himself away from the counter, grabbed some bowls and plates, and took a couple of bottles of beer from the fridge. He emptied the cartons into the bowls before straddling the other stool.

"This is how you eat takeout. *Bon appetit.*"

Bon appetit?

When Stella had been a kid, the proverbial "dinner bell" was followed by an order to chow down and pass the ketchup. They came from different worlds.

Stella helped herself to noodles and *kimchi*.

After a few minutes of pleasant chewing, Hagen broke the silence. "How is it?"

Stella nearly moaned in pleasure. "Good. Like Japanese but with extra cabbage."

Hagen shook his head and shoveled in a mouthful of *bibimbap*. "Blasphemy."

"This something you used to eat a lot of when you were a kid?"

Hagen took some *kimchi*. He ate it one piece at a time, savoring the chili heat. "There was a Korean place next to my dad's office. He used to take me there after school sometimes."

"Must give you plenty of good memories then. Food does that."

"Mm. Not all good. The place my dad took me to was a hole in the wall. Man, what a poster for uncleanliness. There were, like, six tables. All of them dirty Formica with wobbly legs. There'd be one guy in the kitchen with a big fire and the same sweat stain all the way up the back of his undershirt."

Hagen winced like he'd bitten down on something sharp and hard. "The cook's brother would take the orders. He never smiled. Never wrote anything down. He'd take the plates from the kitchen and pile them up on his arms like an octopus juggling at a circus. Both their wives worked there too. They'd take the money, load the dishwasher, shout at their husbands in Korean, and, maybe once a month, wipe down the tables."

Stella grinned. This was the kind of thing she wanted to hear. She seemed to be slipping into Hagen's life, seeing the world through his lens. "Those are always the best places. The ones only the locals know."

Hagen jammed his chopsticks into his bowl and took a swig of beer. "Locals? Yeah, they were there too. Every other table had some local criminal or other and his friends. You had one gang in one corner, a dealer and his partner in another. They'd come out of court and wash down their success with *kimchi* and Korean vodka."

"Your dad liked it?"

He dragged his bowl closer and slurped up some more noodles. "It was like my dad's second office."

The *kimchi* burned in her stomach, and Stella sipped her beer. She let Hagen continue. He slurped up another noodle, his head bent over his bowl. "Dad loved it. He'd go from table to table, slapping shoulders and shaking hands. Made me feel like I was the son of the most popular guy in the world."

"You were only a kid. You didn't—"

"Yeah, I didn't know a damn thing." The smile faded. "I thought those guys loved him, but they didn't give two shits. As long as he could find some loophole that would keep them out of prison and in their stinking business, they treated him like he was the messiah reborn."

"But he must have known. It wasn't like he was their friend. And he wasn't involved in their business. He was a lawyer, not a gang member."

"Nah, but he loved it." Hagen lifted his head. "He loved the attention and the adulation. Can you imagine what that's like? You see all these guys, men with face tattoos and bullet scars, guys you cross the road to avoid, whose ring other hardened men kiss, treating your dad like he's some damn hero? I didn't know why they liked him so much. I just knew they thought he was great."

Stella took another sip of beer. She was beginning to understand. "So, when one of those guys killed him, it must have—"

"Yeah." Hagen pushed the bowl across the counter and chugged down the rest of his beer. "So, what are we going to do about Joel?"

Boom. The gate had clanged shut again. Just like that.

Stella sighed and took a long, slow sip of her beer. She put the bottle back on the counter. "I'm not sure."

"I'll tell you what we should do. We should go back to Atlanta. Heck, I'd leave right now if you want. We knock on his front door, and we surprise the heck out of him. See how he reacts."

Stella nodded. Here they were again. Hagen full of action, and Stella with that nagging feeling. Why was he so eager to help her? Didn't he have enough criminals to lock up in his day job?

"Yeah, I know that's what you'd do. If we had done it your way, we'd have run Joel off the road and scared the living hell out of that little girl."

Hagen pushed himself off the barstool, crossed to the fridge, and helped himself to another bottle of beer. "You don't mind, right?"

Stella shook her head. Actually, seeing Hagen make himself at home in her apartment was surprisingly soothing.

He popped the lid using a bottle opener hanging from the fridge door and rejoined Stella at the counter. From the bed, Bubbles made a quiet *harumph*.

"We're not monsters. The kid would ask him who we were, and he'd come up with some suitable excuse or other. A guy who's been lying for all these years can always find a way to lie a little longer."

"Hm." Stella ran a finger over the top of her bottle. She pictured that little girl running to the car, waiting for Joel to lift her into the seat. She looked so happy, so trusting. "Who do you think she is? Daughter? Granddaughter?"

"My money's still on granddaughter. Not easy to start another family at that age. It's not impossible if you've got the looks. Or the money. But granddaughter is more likely. Does it matter?"

"Not really." Stella stacked one empty food box inside another. Some things just fit together so smoothly. It was hard to keep them apart. "It's just…it bothers me, you know? Seeing him with a family. When I thought he was dead, it hurt, but I wasn't angry at him. Getting murdered wasn't his choice. But while I was mourning, he was watching his kids grow up, taking vacations with his wife, playing with his grandchildren. Now, I just feel…"

"Abandoned?"

Stella took a deep swig of beer. "It's stupid, I know. What's he to me?"

Hagen patted her arm. The contact was friendly and warm, but in its brevity, distant and formal. "I get it. He was your dad's partner. It was natural you'd want someone like him around after your dad was killed."

"Is that what happened to you? Did you have—"

"Listen." His bottle clanked on the counter. "The answers

are in Atlanta, so that's where we need to be. We've got a few days of paperwork ahead of us, but assuming Tennessee's population of psychopaths and disgruntled ex-cheerleaders can take a break through the weekend, once we're done, we can head down there. This time we won't waste a second. We on?"

She couldn't think of a good reason to say no.

40

The day was just beginning. The time had been chosen carefully. Night would have seemed the obvious choice, fewer witnesses and the least chance of being seen. But it's what they would have expected. Today, and in the days to come, the hunter needed to ensure they wouldn't *and* couldn't expect anything.

When they seek a shadow, they look into the darkness.

The hunter chose the sun. The early morning, just before the first agents arrived for work. Commuters would be filing past the building to begin their day.

That was when the strike would occur.

Standing at a traffic light on the corner, the hunter was camouflaged by a small group of people waiting for the light to change. They numbered no more than half a dozen. Two men in suits. Lawyers probably. A couple of guys in jeans and t-shirts already showing signs of sweat. It was going to be a hot one. And two women in skirts that came just above the knee. One of them wore too much makeup for an office job.

Who is she trying to impress?

The sight of them made the hunter a little nervous. Had

the day's attire been chosen wisely? Never one to be mistaken for an office slacker getting ready to sit behind a desk, the hunter had dressed like a server ready to begin their shift. That was why this route had been chosen so carefully.

Nothing to see here, you federal pigs.

Cameras had been scouted as had the number of guards patrolling the area. Break times had been noted. Even the times when people were most likely to cross the road had been determined. Weeks of diligent reconnoitering would culminate today.

Later, the Feds would watch their cameras and spot a lone figure approaching their building. It would be too late by then. The hunter will have come and gone, just another person in the crowd, streaming away from the FBI's office.

The research hadn't been easy, but it had been necessary, and conducted professionally. Not rushed. Planned precisely. That was what made the difference between success and failure, between a special force and a regular force.

The hunter was a special force, no matter what the military said.

The light changed, as the next phase of the plan began. Pretending to be distracted by a message, the hunter waited. The others didn't even notice. They were so eager to make it to the other side of the road like they couldn't make their office chairs wait a minute longer to hold their asses.

That was part of the plan. Only when the light changed to yellow did the hunter stride across the street. Be last in line. Unseen. Unnoticed.

Security camera at twelve o'clock.

A lowered head took care of that little problem. There were so many of them around here. It was hard to keep track of which cameras were where and in which direction they pointed, but the hunter had memorized the area well.

This place was swimming in security. This was the damn FBI! They saw everyone coming a mile away and put them all through a dozen different checks just to get through the front door.

An Average Joe trying to accomplish this mission would be stopped the minute he reached for his bag.

The hunter wasn't an Average Joe. The hunter planned… stalked…took steady aim.

Only twenty yards from the entrance and, still, there was no sign of an alarm.

Take your time. Walk natural. That's the way.

One of the women, who had crossed the street, stopped. The hunter was forced to slow in response. The woman put one hand against the wall of a building, reached down, and adjusted the strap on a heel. Peach and shiny enough to be new.

That wasn't in the plan.

The phone came back out, a necessary accessory to stall for more time.

Come on, damn you.

Little Miss Peach Shoe needed to stay in front. She couldn't witness the next step of the plan.

Maybe she was one of the agents in that building, though the hunter didn't recognize the woman at all. Of course, the visit inside the FBI's hallowed halls had been brief. Other than the two interviewers, the hunter hadn't spotted more than five employees.

And what a dumbass pair those interviewers turned out to be. FBI hadn't been able to see what was in front of them.

Did they ever?

Guess we'll see.

Little Miss Peach Shoe lifted the other pump to adjust that strap. The hunter adjusted the backpack, growing heavier, and took a deep breath.

Easy now. Get a grip. You've come this far. Not much farther to go now. Just take it nice and slow.

After what seemed like hours, the woman put her foot down and walked on, just the slightest limp indicating things still weren't fine with her new purchase.

Strappy heel crisis adverted. The plan could now continue.

Following along, the hunter inspected the surroundings behind sunglasses dark enough to hide any eye movement. Another part of the plan. *Come early enough that the parking garage will be empty, but late enough that the morning sun will make dark glasses necessary.*

The timing had to be perfect.

And it was.

The parking garage, where the agents rocked up in the morning before taking on the bad guys, was empty. The hunter knew their schedule. Knew their building.

The garage entrance was five-and-a-half paces from this point. There was no one behind, and only Little Miss Peach Shoe ahead.

Cameras were directly above the hunter's head. One pointed north. Another aimed south.

Invisible in plain sight.

The hunter's watch vibrated. It was time.

As anticipated, the security guard came around the building, his head on a swivel as he took in the empty spaces of the garage. Forty-seven point six seconds later, he turned down the north side of the building. In exactly three minutes and twenty-three seconds, he'd be back.

That was more than enough time for what needed to be done.

As the sound of the guard's boots faded, a dark gray Toyota 4Runner entered the garage, waiting for the arm of the barrier gate to raise. It was Stella Knox's vehicle.

She's early.

The hunter had a decision to make. Follow through or abandon the plan?

It really wasn't a decision at all.

Pulling the knife from the backpack, the hunter smiled.

Go time!

The End

To be continued...

Thank you for reading.

All of the *Stella Knox Series* books can be found on Amazon.

ACKNOWLEDGMENTS

How does one properly thank everyone involved in taking a dream and making it a reality? Here goes.

In addition to our families, whose unending support provided the foundation for us to find the time and energy to put these thoughts on paper, we want to thank the editors who polished our words and made them shine.

Many thanks to our publisher for risking taking on two newbies and giving us the confidence to become bona fide authors.

More than anyone, we want to thank you, our readers, for sharing your most important asset, your time, with this book. We hope with all our hearts we made it worthwhile.

Much love,

Mary & Stacy

ABOUT THE AUTHOR

Mary Stone

Mary Stone lives among the majestic Blue Ridge Mountains of East Tennessee with her two dogs, four cats, a couple of energetic boys, and a very patient husband.

As a young girl, she would go to bed every night, wondering what type of creature might be lurking underneath. It wasn't until she was older that she learned that the creatures she needed to most fear were human.

Today, she creates vivid stories with courageous, strong heroines and dastardly villains. She invites you to enter her world of serial killers, FBI agents but never damsels in distress. Her female characters can handle themselves, going toe-to-toe with any male character, protagonist or antagonist.

Discover more about Mary Stone on her website.
www.authormarystone.com

Stacy O'Hare

Growing up in West Virginia, most of the women in Stacy O'Hare's family worked in the medical field. Stacy was no exception and followed in their footsteps, becoming a nurse's aid. It wasn't until she had a comatose patient she became attached to and made up a whole life story about—with a past as an FBI agent included—that she discovered her love of stories. She started jotting them down, and typing them out, and expanding them when she got off shift. Somehow, they turned into a book. Then another. Now, she's over the moon to be releasing her first series.

Connect with Mary Online

facebook.com/authormarystone

goodreads.com/AuthorMaryStone

bookbub.com/profile/3378576590

pinterest.com/MaryStoneAuthor